To alliso

love,
Pamela.

ON THE SWING
OF ONE STAR

By

Pamela Duncan

ON THE SWING OF ONE STAR

by Pamela Duncan

Published by Author Way Limited through CreateSpace
Copyright 2013 author

This book has been brought to you by -

Discover other Author Way Limited titles at -
http://www.authorway.net
Or to contact the author mailto:infp@authorway.net

ISBN: 1493669257
ISBN-13: 978-1493669257

Dedication

This Book is dedicated to all my family and friends who have supported and inspired me over many years

Acknowledgements

Thanks go to Google whose links proved a valuable source of research, to Sheila for her honest appraisal, to Andrew Skinner for his skill and patience in producing the cover and mainly to Gerry and Elaine Mann for making this publication possible..

CHAPTER 1

The tables at the V E Day party ran like a giant red, white and blue crocodile, down the middle of the avenue. A seagull swooped towards them, the afternoon sun flaming its wings.

Angie flinched, shrinking back on the bench seat, as she recalled another huge bird with rigid wings and swastika eyes that had dived tail-blazing from a September sky. Those pilots must have known they were doomed but they'd aimed their machine guns and fired at them; just kids climbing Brayne Hill on the way home from school. What had children to do with war? Angie closed her eyes. She could see Shirley sprawled on the pavement. The blood. Milk from her shattered flask turning deep pink as it trickled to the gutter. She could hear the screams and the shouts of the women as they opened their doors and dragged them inside. Yet the all clear had sounded. It should have been safe.

Angie looked at the scene around her. She was the last to remain seated at the table. The others gathered in animated groups waiting for the entertainment to begin. Faces that had been strained were relaxed. Mrs Crofthouse, a large woman, with greying hair and big feet, stood among those chatting to the Reverend Spicer. She was wearing her best dress. The same dress she wore almost five years ago when Angie first met her. The day she'd been plucked from the line of evacuees straddling the grass verge. Her life packed into a small carrying bag and a gas mask slung over her shoulder. She'd clasped the bundle of photographs her mum had given her.

"Now be a good girl," Mum's soft, sunlit voice had been clouded. "You'll like the countryside. London's no place for children what with the blitz."

Mrs Crofthouse was good to her. She only had sons and

3

they were in the army.

"It's nice having a girl around," she would say. "They're less work than boys."

But Mrs Crofthouse's cotton best hadn't compared with the warmth of her mum's green velvet as she crushed her tightly. Angie guessed her Mum had been right, but they'd both been upset. She had tried to be good and brave. She'd honestly tried. She hadn't cried since. Not once. Not even the day Dad had come to tell her about the bomb.

"A direct hit. They couldn't do anything to help her. Your mum didn't suffer." He'd held her close and she'd scuffed her face against his coarse naval uniform. "We'll go away when it's all over. America, Australia, New Zealand even," he promised. "I'll show you the mud pools, the volcanoes and golden beaches. Sand so hot you'll burn your toes. Maybe, we'll stay there. You'd like that, wouldn't you?"

Angie lived for that dream. Uncle Cyril had ruined it. She'd snatched the buff envelope from his fat, sausage fingers and torn it to shreds. Tomorrow, he was coming again to take her back to London. There was no-one else. Only Cyril, his pig eyes blinking behind thick round spectacles and those horribly slippery hands. He'd touched her once. He felt like a slug.

Angie fought back tears. She was a stray like the seagull strutting on the table, feasting on the remains of the victory party, clumsy as its claws tangled with red, white and blue streamers, and ripped the juice-soaked paper cloth .

Mr Pratt, the church organist, supervised a team of lads as they wheeled an old piano down his garden path.

"Easy does it. Don't scrape the wood on the gate. Been in the family for years, that piano."

Angie got up from the bench and the seagull, startled by the sudden movement, prised a half-eaten sandwich into its beak and swept into the sky. Angie followed its flight and was convinced it looped-the-loop in a victory roll before heading seawards. One day she'd fly like that seagull. See all the places they'd planned. "I'll do it, Dad. I promise."

The twin heads of Sue and Pat popped out from beneath the trestles.

"We've crawled from the top of the hill and we're going on right to the bottom. Come and join us. It's fun."

Angie managed a smile as she thought of her gangling limbs weaving through the table legs.

"Grow up," she said. "You were thirteen last week, not three."

"It's the lemonade. It's fizzed to my head." Sue ducked back under and Pat, ever her shadow, followed.

"I'll miss them," Angie thought. In a day or two the twins were returning home to their parents. She'd been like their big sister here in Updean. They'd soon forget. Angie put her hands to her face and let the tears flow. They had been dammed long enough.

The Reverend Spicer escaped from the ladies and strode towards her.

"What's all this, then? We can't have you crying. Not today. The war is over, Angela. It's all over."

He placed a comforting arm across her shoulder.

"I'm alright," Angie sniffed. "Honest I am. I was just thinking back....I'm leaving tomorrow."

"So Mrs Crofthouse was telling me. Dave and Micky are on their way home. She's so excited. I hear your uncle's offered to take care of you. You'll be looking forward to that, no doubt."

"Uncle Cyril is a pig. A big, fat, ugly, gluttonous pig."

Angie's words were lost as Mr Pratt thumped the piano into life and everyone paired up for a quickstep. The Reverend Spicer grabbed Angie's hand and whirled her into the middle of the dancers. A Paul Jones, with popular tunes led her from partner to partner - 'We'll Meet Again, 'You Are My Sunshine'."

"You are you know."

"Are what?" Angie asked of the vicar as he caught up with her again.

"My sunshine. Just look at you? Minutes ago we were mopping up tears and now you're wreathed in smiles."

"It's the music. And the people. And, well, everything. I'll come back often."

"I'm sure you will," and the Reverend Spicer patted her head as if she were a pet lamb.

The merriment went on long into the evening. Mr Pratt's piano was accompanied by three mouth organs, an accordion, several combs covered in tissue paper, a soprano, a baritone and a slap-stick comedian. No-one wanted the day to end. Exhausted infants, wrapped in blankets, settled to sleep on the party benches. Darkness fell streets illuminated, houses lit up. No more blackouts. No more shaded torches.

Angie noticed a solitary figure creeping up the hill in the shadow of garden hedges. A floppy hat shielded her features. A full blouse flounced over her skirt. She was wearing big shoes. Huge, big shoes. Who would wear such monstrosities? Surely...Angie peered at the person intently as she passed under a lamp. It wasn't a woman at all. It was Harry Cornshake, the postman. Lips reddened, cheeks rouged, but unmistakeably, Harry.

Angie nudged Pat who was gurgling the dregs of a bottle of orange.

"Hey, look? That's Harry dressed as a woman."

Angie, forgetting her fifteen years, urged the twins and the other children to join her and they set off in a giggling march behind Harry, who lifted his skirt and ran. His turned up trousers unrolled down his calves. His balloon breasts bounced.

"Who's a pretty girl, then?" - "Give us your number, sweetie?" - "Come on let's have a kiss?" The youngsters jeered as they thronged around him. Harry made a frantic effort to break free but ended up lying on the grass verge with a dozen children on top of him. The watching crowds roared with laughter.

"It's a bet," he confessed. "There's a fiver in it for the forces widows' fund. I'll stand you sixpence apiece if you let me go. I've to reach the bonfire before it's lit."

Harry straightened his hat, adjusted his skirt and, egged on by his new found fans, resumed his mission.

"Made it," he cried, panting up to the stack of rubbish at the top of the hill. "Now, where's that ruddy Max?"

Max was the son of the local butcher. His father had agreed to finance any number of stunts for his favourite good cause. Harry laid claim to his bet, then ripped off the blouse and skirt and hurled them on to a bundle of discarded rags. "Such a waste," an old lady with whiskers tutted.

Harry paused with the floppy straw hat in his hand. He turned to Angie and placed it on her head.

"Here you have it. Help you become a lady in the big city."

Become a lady, Angie thought. It frightened her a bit. She would have to change. To grow up. Tomorrow, she would cease to be a child. Tomorrow she would...

The village clock struck ten and the huge bonfire crackled into flame. On the surrounding hills another half dozen fires beaconed the downs in a simultaneous blaze. Fireworks shot into the air, spraying the sky with a thousand stars. Tomorrow, she'd swing on one.

CHAPTER 2

Angie was up early despite the events of the night before. Mrs Crofthouse's Micky had arrived as the fun drew to an end and seemed surprised she was still there. Angie wasn't sure if he were just tired after his travels or annoyed, because he'd had very little to say. Mrs Crofthouse made up for that. She was all over him asking incessant questions without waiting for answers. He was thinner than when Angie saw him on his last leave. Then Mrs Crofthouse had sent her to stay with her sister in the next village and the room had smelt of beer when she'd returned. Angie pictured Micky on the couch downstairs and was glad she was going. Tonight, he could sleep in his own bed.

Angie finished packing and began to polish everything as if trying to wipe out her years there. It wasn't difficult Once she cleared her clutter from the dressing table the room looked impersonal. In a week or two they'd forget she'd ever lived there. She had to leave her mark in some way.

Angie looked around. She could scribble her initials on a corner of the wallpaper, but Mr Crofthouse was sure to redecorate and they'd be covered up. She needed to think of something that would be there for ever.

Angie felt in her pocket and touched the hard shell of a prune stone. There were two prune stones. She'd taken the prunes at breakfast from a bowl as they lay soaking in the kitchen and eaten them. She couldn't explain why she'd stuffed the stones into her pocket. If she could find somewhere to hide them - somewhere they wouldn't be discovered, they could be a symbol of her life in Updean. Aware she was being stupid, she pressed the stones firmly into a small gap between the built in electric fire and the wall. No-one would find them there.

Angie studied herself in the mirror. She would be taller than her mother now if... She ran her hands through her short fair hair and decided to let it grow. Long hair might make her look older. Snapping her suitcase shut, she carried it down to the hall where Mrs Crofthouse was standing beside the open door.

"Now, dear, you did take everything? Micky wouldn't want to find a pair of stockings in his drawers." She turned to smile at her younger son, who looked more relaxed.

"Nor navy blue knickers." Micky grinned as he offered Angie his hand, "Take care."

There were no kisses, not even a brushed peck on the cheek. Mrs Crofthouse hugged her warmly but not intimately and Mr Crofthouse came in from the allotment and ruffled her hair.

"Keep in touch. Be sure to write."

"I will. I'll not forget how you looked after me. Thank you."

Cyril was waiting impatiently at the gate. He moaned at the size of her suitcase and carried it with reluctance, grasping the handle firmly in his fat fingers.

"I'll take it," Angie said. "I can manage easily."

He pushed her ahead, "Don't fuss, Angela."

It was he who was fussing, Angie thought, as they set off down the hill.

It wasn't far. Barely a ten minute walk, but Cyril stopped several times to switch the case from one hand to the other, complaining as he did so.

They caught the slow train with plenty of time to spare and it ambled for an hour and twenty minutes before reaching London.

Victoria Station was much as Angie remembered it. Perhaps not as big and definitely duller and dirtier. Cyril made straight for the buffet.

"Tea - milk and two sugars for me, if she'll give it to you," he demanded, placing the case beside a table. He produced a small round purse and shuffled a few coins into Angie's palm.

Angie passed the message on to the woman behind the counter, declining sugar herself to be sure her uncle would be satisfied. The woman wore a scarf twined like a turban round her hair and puffed at a rolled cigarette. She slopped two measures of well brewed tea into the cups and over the saucers. She could have been the role model for the cartoonists.

Angie carried the tray back to the table.

Cyril groaned, "Spilt it, I see." He soaked up the drips with the edge of his handkerchief. "Where's my change?"

Angie pointed to the pile of coppers she'd already placed beside his saucer, and muttering about the cost of things he carefully replaced them in his purse.

So he's mean as well as ugly, Angie concluded.

Cyril spoke. It was the first time he'd attempted to link sentences. "You've never been to Dryden Terrace, have you?"

Angie shook her head.

"I've put you on the second floor beside my housekeeper, Edwina Ferrie. My rooms are on the first. Edwina's a distant cousin, very distant. Your father fancied her before he knew your mother, but she wasn't interested. We understand each other, Edwina and I."

Angie didn't pursue the conversation mainly because she didn't feel at ease and they fell silent. That sense of unease continued when they left the buffet and boarded the tube. She sat upright and taut whilst the underground train took them through dark tunnels, past dimly lit stations, to Greenstead. Angie had the feeling Greenstead had been used as an air-raid shelter. The station was unwashed and smelt of sweat and urine. She pictured it swarming with people and wondered if her mother had ever slept on a station platform, and doubted it. She might have been alive if she had.

They followed a passage that brought them to steps emerging at street level. Angie's feelings were confirmed because its walls were covered in messages. She read some of them in passing - "Margaret, Tom was here 9/4/43" and "Love you always, Betty". Arrowed hearts were scratched beneath cartoons of Winston Churchill and his huge cigar against a background of Union Jacks.

They moved along unfamiliar streets, Angie turning when Cyril turned. It seemed further than the five minutes he had estimated. The sun highlighted dust settled on dulled yellow and red brick buildings. Gaps in the rows of houses indicated where bombs had fallen. A torn curtain fluttered at a shattered window. There was nothing inside it, just a huge void and a mantelshelf on what remained of a far wall.

Scaffolding signalled restoration work on some of the homes but most, Angie guessed, were beyond repair. At the end of several streets, huts with corrugated iron roofs served as houses. A single tree, looking ridiculously out of place, blossomed in one corner. Angie found herself yearning already for the fresh air and green fields of Updean.

They turned into a square lined with houses. Dryden Terrace it seemed had escaped direct hits but not the dust. At the far end, there were shops - Hubbard's Bakery, Gray's Shoe shop and Cyril Bolton, Bespoke Tailors. The window of her uncle's business displayed rolls of grey suiting, a hand printed price list and the opening hours on yellowing card.

Uncle Cyril led Angie to a side door of the end terrace building. The brass knocker and letter-box shone but its green paint peeled to reveal bare wood. So this was her new home. Angie noted the number - 35. She had a thing about numbers. Add the three to the five and, take away seven - and you were left with one. One for sorrow. She had an uncanny feeling the number game would prove right.

Cyril opened the door with his key and scuffed his feet on the mat. They walked into an unlit hallway, and moved right to a sitting room. Beyond it, Angie could see a figure beside the cooker in the kitchen. It had to be the housekeeper.

Tall, her greying hair knotted in a bun, Edwina Ferrie had thin straight lips and sharp eyes that took everything in, yet gave away little. There was something commanding about her as she moved towards them.

"I was expecting you sooner. Lunch is ready. If you sit up I'll serve it." Her voice had a clipped authority. A person not to argue with, Angie surmised.

Cyril replaced his shoes with felt slippers and trotted into an adjacent toilet. Angie waited awkwardly until he came out before going in herself.

Edwina had obviously taken some trouble over the meal. The table was set with a lace cloth centred by a vase of roses, gleaming cutlery and white linen napkins threaded through silver rings. Cyril was already seated when Angie came out of the toilet. She took the chair nearest the window.

"Edwina sits there."

She changed to the seat facing her uncle. He drummed his fingers on the table and, as if summoned, Edwina appeared carrying a casserole

"Liver and onions. Morgan had offal. I was first in the queue." She turned to Angie. "It's Angela, isn't it?."

Angie gave her a nervous smile. "This is really nice, Miss Ferrie. Do you always eat as much for lunch?" She was used to Mrs Crofthouse's scrap soup with bread.

"Call me Edwina. Lunch is our main meal. Cyril prefers it that way. We lead an orderly life. Breakfast around eight. Tea and toast with, perhaps, a fish paste. Lunch at one o'clock sharp and high tea about six, depending on the shop." Edwina paused to check Angie was paying attention. "Supper's just a drink. You can make it yourself, as you please."

Cyril picked up the Daily News and played no part in the conversation.

Edwina continued. "This house was once divided and let out. I use the second floor bathroom between six-forty five and seven. If you're in a hurry, to use it then there's the washroom down here. Cyril has private facilities. You'll be sleeping in what was once my sitting room."

"I'm sorry. It must be inconvenient."

"On the contrary. I seldom used it. My bedroom's always been a bed-sit. You'll be expected to clean your own quarters and help with the washing up."

"Of course, I'll help with anything."

The thin lips parted into a smile. "I think you will fit in very well, Angela."

Maybe I will, Angie thought, but she didn't feel as if she belonged. She carried her own suitcase up the two winding flights to the second floor where she was faced by three closed doors. The first opened on to a bathroom. The second she was sure was hers.

Faded rosebuds replaced the distempered walls of the ground floor and floral curtains clashed with a green and black chequered blanket on the single bed. Angie noted the rest of the furnishings - a wardrobe, a two drawer chest doubling as a bedside table, a straight backed chair and two rugs partially covering brown linoleum.

On the low window ledge a pot trailed ivy but there were no other ornaments and no pictures hung from the rail that ran round the walls. The room was smaller than Dave and Micky's, but larger than the one she'd had in her parents' home. Angie jumped as Edwina called from the doorway.

"Good, you've found your room. Bathroom's next door on the left. If you've a wireless don't play it loudly. I'm a light sleeper with acute hearing." Edwina moved as if to leave, turned and spoke again. "Any questions and I'll be in the kitchen Come and go as you please. Two spare keys are on the hook behind the house door. Keep one. Cyril locks up at about ten-thirty when he's at home. " She touched Angie's arm, "And relax, child. You look like a frightened rabbit. I'm not going to eat you."

Angie was aware of her slender fingers. Not the least bit like Cyril's sausages. Yet she disliked their touch, too. Despite the housekeeper's reassuring words, she felt wary. Perhaps it was those thin lips. Something about Edwina definitely made Angie feel uncomfortable.

Edwina disappeared down the stairs. Angie crossed to the window and peered into the courtyard bordered by rose bushes and tubs of geraniums. A line of towels and sheets billowed in the breeze. At the far end, a gate led into what she assumed to be a service lane between Dryden Terrace and the street backing it. A wrought iron fire escape laddered from beside her window to the courtyard. If needed, an alternative way in and out. Cyril's ten-thirty deadline could have no meaning but it was late enough.

Angie unpacked her case, spreading her belongings on the available ledges and filling the drawers. She would need new clothes. Micky was right about the navy blue knickers. She began to make a list of what could be bought with limited cash and limited coupons. At fifteen years and eleven months, Angela Bolton knew she was taking hold of her own future.

Next morning, Angie entered Uncle Cyril's room in response to his summons. He was again beating out a steady rhythm with his finger tips - this time on his desk. Heavy chairs in creased leather and solid dark furniture made the room shrink. She could smell beeswax. Mrs Crofthouse swore by it and had used it in the lounge at Updean - "Rub it in well with lots of elbow grease." Here it mingled with the smell of cigars.

Uncle Cyril was not alone. A man with a lean face, little hair and heavy eyebrows sat beside him. She had seen him before at her father's funeral.

"Angela, you may remember Dillard Thrift, your parents' lawyer. As your legal guardian, he wants to talk about your future."

Uncle Cyril sat back and the lawyer took over. His voice wavered like an un-tuned violin. His smile was sincere.

"Nice to see you again, Angela. Must be over a year since your father's funeral. You've shot up. No doubt you know he left some money in trust for you. Not a fortune, mind you, but a very tidy sum. He was a careful, sensible man." Mr Thrift lifted his spectacles from Uncle Cyril's desk and put them on. "Invested well. The lump sum will become yours when you're twenty-one, meantime, I'm looking after it. There's a fair amount of interest." He took his spectacles off again and twirled them in his fingers as he spoke. "I intend to give your uncle twenty five pounds a month for your keep. He will

14

provide for your personal needs. I've proposed pocket money of one pound ten shillings a month. That should give you a sense of independence, eh?"

Angie smiled back at him and Dillard Thrift continued. "I'm aware you are at an age when you could have left schooling. It was I who advised you should continue your education at Updean. The school term ends shortly, but I've arranged for you to go to the local Verity Academy, till then." He flicked through some notes on the table. "After that you can decide if you want to continue or leave and find work. Your uncle's offered to make room for you initially in his business, if that's what you'd like."

Angie said nothing.

"You're right to take time to think it over. Meanwhile, school starts on Monday. Have you any questions?"

"If I decide to leave school I'll need new clothes."

"For anything of that nature I'd make arrangements for a lump sum to be paid into your bank. You'll have to open an account in your own name."

"And if I leave here?"

"We'd work that out in the event. It would depend on lots of things. Your age. What you intended to do. But I'm sure you'll settle nicely with your uncle."

Uncle Cyril and Mr Thrift rose simultaneously, as if pulled by puppeteer's strings. Cyril prodded his podgy fingers into the lawyer's hand.

"Thank you for coming," he simpered as he fussed to open the door.

Mr Thrift winked and handed Angie his card. "Keep in touch, Angela." Angie found herself liking him, scratchy voice and all.

She located the house keys on the door as Edwina had indicated, pocketed one, and made her way back to her room.

So that's how Dad set it up. She'd known there was some money. Still didn't know how much. One pound ten shillings a month would be useful. Mrs Crofthouse had given her a

15

shilling a week. And Uncle Cyril wouldn't be keeping her for nothing. She needn't feel so obliged to him.

Angie returned to her room and spent the remainder of the morning re-arranging her belongings. After lunch she offered to wash up and Edwina left her to it. The kitchen had old fittings but was clinically clean. A large metal wash tub bubbled on the gas. Edwina was boiling the whites.

Angie peered into a utility room like a giant cupboard. It housed a mangle and for a second she saw her mother standing turning the handle, easing the clothes through the rollers. A stone floor led to the courtyard from which the housekeeper brought in one load of washing and pegged out another. It was that kind of day. The heat of the sun was softened by a strong cooling breeze. Angie stacked the dishes on the open shelves, hoping she had chosen the right order.

Edwina appeared at her shoulder, "Cups and saucers on the first shelf, dinner plates, side plates and bowls on the second. Pans go in below the cooker."

Angie sorted everything out.

"I thought I'd take a walk this afternoon. Just to have a look around and get my bearings."

"I've already told you, come and go as you please, Angela." Edwina seemed unconcerned and continued her chores. The need to help with anything, other than her own cleaning and the washing up had, Angie felt, vanished when Mr Thrift told her she was paying her way. Edwina disappeared into the backcourt again. Angie gazed after her, an odd character, she thought, one minute friendly, the next aloof.

Angie left the kitchen, went through the hall, and out of the front door. She paused, uncertain whether to walk back along the terrace or round the corner into the next street. She opted for the corner and turned into a line of shops with flats above them. A newsagent, grocer, and ironmonger, were followed by a jagged gap where the centre of the row had been blown out. Beyond it were a cafe and a store displaying baby wear and nursery equipment. The street was drab. Paint flaked from window frames and grime gathered on woodwork.

On the opposite side of the road was a narrow strip of scuffed grass. Iron stubs in the ground showed where railings had been sawn down and carried away presumably to help the war effort. A small dog crouched, fouling the earth beneath a tree. It scampered, yapping, towards Angie, who put out her hand to placate it.

The dog ran round her legs, its tail wagging. She bent down, fondled it and felt the warmth of its tongue against her hand. "You're a little beauty," she said.

The dog followed her despite her shouts of "Home, boy." Angie decided to ignore him.

She continued her walk down long terraces, where again the uniformity was shattered at intervals by gaping holes. Against one wall a buckled stairway laddered to the sky.

Angie reached a small parkland area, where flats gave way to larger houses, and passed a tennis club. Half an hour elapsed. Time to retrace her steps. She turned and nearly tripped over the dog. She bent down to him again.

"So you're still here? Come on, I'll take you back."

She set off and was struck by the lack of colour everywhere. Few green hedges and floral borders, and the people in the streets wore clothes so dull, as if the vigour had been sapped from them. She began to count. Two brown skirts, one grey, one dark blue. Three brown jackets over grey trousers, a navy suit. Angie looked down at her own dress and realised it, too, was a plain grey.

She was beginning to think the whole district had become so used to mourning it had forgotten summer was the time for cotton prints and shirt sleeves when she saw a girl of about her own age striding towards her. Her full skirt was deepest scarlet, her blouse incredibly white. A scarlet ribbon scooped her long dark hair into a pony-tail.

"Here, Taurus," she called, "where on earth have you been, you rascal?" The dog scampered to her feet and nosed against her legs.

"He followed me," Angie explained. "I was bringing him back."

"The horror escaped from our garden." The girl pointed up a side avenue to a large walled area with a sweeping drive. Angie could make out a couple of chimney pots among the trees. The girl added, "Cavaliers, and Taurus in particular, rarely go with anyone else. You're privileged. Do you live near here?"

"Dryden Terrace - 35 - the tailor's. He's my uncle."

"You poor thing. Oh, sorry, I shouldn't have said that but..."

"It's okay I know what you mean. I can't stand him."

" And Edwina? How do you get on with Edwina?"

"I only arrived yesterday. She's a bit queer."

The girl laughed, "You're right there. Take care. Keep her at arm's length. She's far more dangerous than that porky.. whoops. I've done it again."

"Honest, that's what I call him - a pig. But what's up with Edwina?"

"Nothing, I suppose, if you like her sort. She's dead pally with Alice Belthorpe, number 48. Too pally, some say. It's the local gossip." The girl glanced at her watch, "I'll have to get a move on. I've a dental appointment. I'd to get time off school. Are you going to the Academy?"

"For a few weeks, anyway. I'll probably leave at the end of term."

"What's your name?"

"Angie. Angela Bolton."

"I'm Lynn. With a Y and two N's but no E. Lynn Arnold." And Lynn with no E, dark hair bobbing, moved on, Taurus trotting behind her.

Angie didn't turn back into Dryden Terrace. She walked on to the main road and took the bus to Verity Academy.

The school stood on a street busy with cars, buses and lorries. There were no green playing fields surrounding it, only tarmac grounds, white-lined to accommodate football, hockey and netball.

The red stone building rose to three floors. Most of the long, narrow windows were still crossed with strips of brown tape to prevent them falling out if shattered by a blast. Counting them, Angie estimated there would be about twelve classrooms on the ground level and a similar number on the second.

The third floor was damaged as if by fire. Singed timbers framed the windows and scaffolding ran up a blackened corner where tarpaulins replaced the slates of a section of the roof. An incendiary bomb, Angie guessed. Apart from this damaged area, Verity's looked sound.

Angie slipped apparently unnoticed into the grounds and walked round to the rear of the school. Here the play area had been turned into a huge underground air raid shelter. The sound of a piano playing and children singing came from a nearby classroom.

She returned to the street and looked up again at the school building. Above the arched entrance the year 1908 was carved in the warm red sandstone, the same age as the village school in Updean but compared with it, Verity Academy was enormous. A shrill bell sounded. Doors flung open and streams of eleven to sixteen year olds tumbled into the playground. Afternoon break.

"I reckon I'll stand it for a few weeks," Angie observed.

CHAPTER 3

For Angie, Verity Academy proved more entertaining than educational. In a state of limbo, having completed her school certificate examinations at Updean, she awaited the results with some confidence.

Sports day, she watched from the sidelines and cheered Lynn's team to victory in the relay event.

"I can run a bit myself," she confided later.

"Pity you missed the heats. It was a close thing but we made it."

Lynn was again in a prominent role in the end of year concert as she sang in the chorus and took the lead in a comedy skit about the home war. After the show Angie met her parents.

Sylvie Arnold, black hair sleeked in a tight knot at the nape of her neck, was as chic as the model Angie learned she had once been. Her mustard suit screamed Hartnell.

"Superb, darling," she enthused to her only daughter, and "How sweet" when introduced to Angie.

Angie's first impressions were that Sylvie was a shallow person, who opened her mouth and allowed appropriate words to fall out and because she was beautiful, she could get away with anything. Gideon Arnold, tall and suave, patted Lynn on the back, nodded at Angie and looked at his watch, then his wife.

"We can't stay," Sylvia explained. "A late dinner party in the West End. It's diabolical but absolutely unavoidable. Olga's at home, of course. Don't stay up too late, Darling, or your eyes will wrinkle."

"At least they came. Uncle Cyril would never have shown his face," Angie said when Lynn moaned that there were always dinner parties.

"I expect she wanted to show off her new suit. She hates Verity's, but I was expelled from boarding school last term and none of the private schools were willing to take me for so short a period. I didn't want to go to them, in any case. I'm a socialist."

"Expelled? What on earth for?"

"Smoking in the Art Room. Not during lessons, of course. I'd stayed on to finish a papier-mâché clown and set fire to a waste bin when I threw away a match. It wasn't really serious but the head took a dim view."

They arrived at the drive of the Arnold's detached villa with its privacy hedging.

"You could lose yourself in here," Angie had observed the first time she'd wound her way through the reception hall, past several doors to a small morning room Lynn claimed as her sanctum. On this occasion, she got no further than the foot of the drive.

"I'll not ask you in. Nothing to do with my mother's warning, but I do need some sleep," Lynn explained.

Angie was happy to agree and once back at Uncle Cyril's, she went straight to bed, but not to sleep. She lay for a while thinking. She had never met anyone like Lynn before. She seemed so much older and at school, even though she hadn't been there for long, she was very popular. Knowing her, Angie decided, was a passport to acceptance.

The morning post brought the anticipated exam results - seven passes, four at credit level and a coveted distinction for maths and no failures.

"World, here I come," Angie cried. She'd no fixed idea what she wanted to do other than travel. She'd been through them all - nurse, hotel receptionist, secretary. She was considering applying for a position with the Post Office as a telephonist, when Cyril renewed the offer he had made earlier.

"You can assist Conway in the shop, deal with customers' orders and there's the accounts. The pay would be fair."

Fair to Uncle Cyril was thirty-five shillings a week; not great, but comparable with similar jobs and she hadn't expected Cyril to come up with so much. Reasoning that the job would give her experience, Angie accepted the offer.

"You must be crazy," Lynn chided. "You know you can't stand your uncle and now you'll be working with him as well as living in the same house."

"It won't be for long. Just until I see what else is on offer. And it's convenient. Do you know, he was rubbing his hands with glee when I accepted. Guess he reckons I'm going to be good for business."

Angie started in the shop at the end of August and was relieved Cyril spent most of his time in the work room, at his cutting table or using his old treadle sewing machine, whilst she helped Jed Conway, his young assistant.

She was content to team her school grey with a cream blouse for work, thus saving up her coupons and allowing the money Mr Thrift placed in her account for new clothes to remain there meantime. Custom was good as the shop bell rang, and Cyril ensured there was plenty for her to do long after closing time. Angie wondered how Jed had coped on his own.

"I've a wife to support and a child on the way. I don't mind working extra time when I'm paid double. Mind you, I'm glad you're here. I'll need to be home more, what with the baby due soon."

Paid double? So, by employing her, Cyril probably saved money. She certainly hadn't heard any mention of double pay.

The shop had a long counter down one wall and stacks of shelving stretched to the ceiling on another. A set of step ladders leant permanently against them. Inadequate lighting concealed the dust that accumulated in the corners and on the top shelves. It was apparent Edwina's duties didn't include looking after the shop. Angie made it her prime task for the first two days to clean the place up and make it inviting to customers and pleasant to work in.

A spider plant in the window and two small table lamps she

found in a cupboard under the counter had an instant effect. She begged a cushioned chair from Edwina and placed it in the corner nearest the counter. To this setting she added as much spit and polish as she could muster. Cyril, who had to be aware of her efforts, passed no comment and Edwina rarely came into the shop. Only Jed seemed pleased.

"My shirt cuffs aren't so dirty these days. You're doing a great job, Angie."

Angie was still beavering away on Wednesday evening when Cyril's cronies, as Jed called them, sauntered in to share a meal and a session at the card table. There were three of them. One aged about fifty, had greasy hair sleeked back from his forehead, and a surprising number of warts on his chin. His two companions were, perhaps, some ten years older. One was tall and had about as much flesh on him as a picked chicken bone.

The third, who was addressed as Grimsby, was as fat as the chicken bone was thin. He was twice as round as Cyril and bounced into the room like an overblown beach ball. He wore a grey cardigan with patched elbows, over a checked shirt and had difficulty keeping the tail of it tucked into trousers, which slipped down his backside every time he lifted his arms or bent over. From their manner, it would appear that Angie, too, was part of the evening's entertainment.

The greasy hair eyed her from head to foot, "Your niece, you say, Cyril?" Angie felt herself redden as he put an arm round her waist and squeezed it. "There's not much of her but I expect she'll develop."

"Let her be, Matt, she's nowt but a kid." The chicken bone had a northern accent.

Grimsby was a Londoner and probably born within earshot of Bow bells. He had a liking for rhyming slang and, Angie learned from Jed, a loaded wallet to compensate.

"Take yer mince pies away from that bit of skirt and shift yer plates of meat into the kitchen." Grimsby pushed the others ahead of him, having dragged Cyril from his treadle. As he passed Angie he added, "Don't worry, ducks. We're 'armless old

23

buggers."

Angie was glad when Edwina suggested she should eat in her room.

"Just Wednesdays. They've known each other for years. Your uncle's good at cards. If you hear them shouting when they leave, then one of them will have won. If it's quiet, then Cyril will have lifted the kitty. I'm seeing my friend Alice tonight. Leave the landing light on, please." And Edwina smiled her stiff smile and squeezed Angie's shoulder with her thin fingers.

Angie ate her meal and washed up, then, satisfied Edwina had gone out and the light was on, she slid the sash window up and slipped down the fire escape and through the back gate. It was like having her own private exit and entrance. She was free but where would she go. The cinema? The nearest was more than a mile away and the film would have started. The youth club she'd seen advertised at the church in the next street? Saturday dance, Wednesday games night. It sounded like the Girl Guides and she'd given that up when she was thirteen. If only she knew more people. Maybe Lynn was home. "Don't forget to come over when you're not too busy," Lynn had said. Well, tonight she certainly wasn't busy.

Angie felt strangely nervous, as if trespassing, when she turned into the Arnold's drive and walked its length to the front entrance. She rang the bell and waited in the covered porch. A young woman answered, her accent foreign, her hair and skin Scandinavian fair.

Olga showed Angie into the lounge, an impressive room with bold furnishings. The three-piece suite, she recognised as Chesterfield. Gran Diamond used to have one in her house at Westfield. It took up the whole room. Covered in green floral tapestry, it was stained with ink and its springs sagged to touch the floor. She'd bounced on it often.

This one was perfect in delicate shades of rose pink. She daren't sit on it. The lounge looked and felt as if it were for display only. The ceiling was high and ornately corniced and from the centre a chandelier lit small tables of dark mahogany. High backed chairs stood rigidly against the walls. The room held no welcome. Angie didn't like it much, but she envied it. Lynn's family had to be very rich.

In a few minutes Lynn came, her usual sunny expression dulled. Her eyes were red-rimmed and her lips quivered as she greeted Angie, "Glad you've come." The brightness of her words belied the obvious. "Let's go to the kitchen. There's some lemon barley and Olga was baking today."

They filled a tray and carried it through to Lynn's sanctum.

"So what is it? What's upset you?"

"What do you mean, upset me?" Lynn turned away angrily.

"Sorry, I shouldn't have asked."

There was a silence then Lynn said, "I might as well tell you. I had the most awful row with my parents. Nothing new about that. But this was the worst yet."

"What about?"

"Me. My future. Dad's arranged for me to go to Scotland. He said it would have been France but for the war. I've to attend a college for young ladies for the next *two years.* They didn't ask me. Didn't tell me a thing until it was all fixed." Lynn was on her feet, pacing up and down, flinging her arms about. Playing a star part.

"Scotland? I'd love to go to Scotland." Angie's voice was wistful. "I want to travel more than anything else in the world. Scotland's as good a place to start as any."

"There's nothing wrong about going to Scotland. I'm sure it's great. But a College for Young Ladies - two years? I couldn't stand that."

Angie felt herself getting angry. "Change places with me, then. Work for Cyril in his grubby little shop. Let his pig eyes watch you every day. And his friends. Old men who can't keep their hands to themselves. Change places with me. I'll do your stint in Scotland any day. At least you've got parents to plan for you."

Lynn fought back. "I'd probably be better off without them.

They don't really care. As long as what I do fits in with their lives, they're happy. I wish they were dead." She burst into tears and flung her arms around Angie's neck.

Angie pushed her away, "You can't mean that, Lynn. You don't know what you're saying. I'd do anything to have my mum and dad back. To get a cuddle and some reassurance. It may be easier as I get older but it still hurts. Don't ever wish anyone dead."

Lynn calmed down. "Angie, I didn't mean it. Not really. But I long for cuddles, too. I can't remember the last time I got one. Dad's better, at least he gives me the odd kiss. Goodbye, usually. They're always off somewhere. "You'll be fine with Olga." And I am. Olga's brilliant. But it's not right. It's not right."

Angie looked at her friend, "I see what you mean. God, life can be a mess can't it? And we've only just begun living. Tell you what, when I leave Cyril to fend for myself, you can come with me if you want."

"We'll shake on it." Lynn was bouncing back to her bright self, "Together we'll sail the world."

"One day, I'll do just that. I promised my dad. Hey, let's get out the atlas and plan a journey. Where would you like to go first?"

"America., California - Hollywood. It's in my blood. My mum's half American."

"You would. That starring role's gone to your head. I can just see you in the Movies."

Lynn took an atlas from a bookcase and they traced routes across the continents.

"That's where I'd like to go," Angie said, her finger pointing out the islands of New Zealand. "My dad's told me about the mud pools and the volcanoes and there's hot steam everywhere and caves with giant stalagmites and glow worms."

It had been dark for some hours when Angie slipped through the back yard gate, up the fire escape and through her open window. She'd learnt something that night. Money wasn't that great. It might make you more comfortable, though remembering the Arnolds' icy lounge, she doubted it. It certainly didn't buy you a ticket to euphoria.

CHAPTER 4

Angie spent her days working in the shop, familiarising herself with suit lengths, materials, prices and customers. Victory in Japan brought another spate of street parties, but they were different in London. Less personal as hoards of strangers got drunk together. American soldiers yankee doodling everywhere and explaining how they'd won the war. Angie made a point of avoiding most of the celebrations.

At least the city was livening up. Clement Attlee was injecting changes. Boys leaving the forces invaded the shop for their demob' suits. Business it seemed was better than for years.

"If it weren't for the coupons we'd be really booming," Cyril crowed, rubbing his hands at the thought of an increased bank balance.

"That young niece of yours does the trick," Grimsby said, having come for the card session. "You were on to a spinner when you took her in Cyril. She's a dish already. Destined to turn a few heads, I'd say. You'll have to keep your mince pies open."

In the shop, Angie cringed as she heard him, and Cyril's sniggered response made her shiver. "As long as I'm the one doing the watching."

Angie attempted to distance herself from Cyril by keeping as much as possible to the front shop.

"You don't like your uncle, do you?" Jed Conway observed one day.

"No," she replied simply, "I don't."

"But his given you a home," Jed said.

Angie shrugged. Maybe she did sound ungrateful, but she couldn't help how she felt. She saw little of Edwina, either. The three ate together sometimes. Cyril's face was normally buried in the daily news and what conversation there was concerned the state of the country, the price of a roll of Harris Tweed or the weather. Sometimes she caught Edwina looking at her and when their eyes met, the housekeeper would smile that weak, thin smile.

Any spare time she had Angie spent with Lynn - dances at the local hall, the latest films at the Toledo, window shopping in the city. Oxford Street, Regent Street, counting their coupons. And all the time she knew she was becoming more assured. Confident she could stand on her own feet, but despite the apparent comfort, Dryden Terrace was still merely a place to eat and sleep. She hated living there.

Angie didn't deliberately avoid Edwina, but she didn't seek out her company. She left that to Alice. She was surprised when she met Alice for the first time at Dryden Terrace. She'd imagined a small, middle-aged spinster with a fluffy personality. Alice matched Edwina for height and was slim to the point of being thin. She was much younger, perhaps in her early thirties and stunningly beautiful.

Most afternoons, Alice called for Edwina and Angie would see them leave together. They haunted Brannigan's tea rooms in Chancellor Street. Angie stumbled on them there, seated at the table furthest from the window, as she waited to enquire about a job as a waitress. Anything to get away from Cyril's shop. Their heads were close in conversation and their hands touched. Totally engrossed, their intimacy was undeniable. This, Angie understood, was what Lynn had hinted at and she had not dared to accept. She felt a wave of revulsion and flushed with embarrassment, slipped out of the tearoom. She couldn't work there, that was obvious.

Back at the Terrace, Angie thought about the relationship between the two women. How could Edwina arouse in Alice an affection that went beyond normal friendship? How could any woman for that matter? Alice could have a choice of men even in the war years. Angie confided in Lynn.

"Well, I did warn you. It's local gossip. Takes all kinds,

29

you know. And keep your wits about you. I've heard Edwina's not above looking elsewhere. Though heaven knows why."

The scene in the cafe led Angie to examine her own feelings towards love and sex. At sixteen, she'd had a few boyfriends. Flirtations at school. Holding hands in the park, a kiss. Her breasts fondled by inexperienced hands. But there'd been no-one serious. She wasn't even sure she liked being kissed. She remembered Ken Lawrence, his breath smelling of cigarettes. It would be nice to be loved by a boy, she guessed, if you in turn loved him. Perhaps you could even learn to be happy with someone you didn't truly love. She would like a real boyfriend. No doubt he'd come along some day.

But, for Angie, the word 'lesbian' had remained undiscovered in the Oxford Dictionary until then. It made her feel uncomfortable. The sight of Edwina and Alice locked together in such a tense relationship frightened her. She liked Lynn a lot but never in that way. Maybe she'd understand when she was older.

Edwina handed the mail out next morning at breakfast.

"Here's one for you, Angela."

Any fear Angie had of being seen leaving the tea-rooms was denied by Edwina's manner. The letter was from Mrs Crofthouse and it brought the countryside to London.

Mrs Crofthouse hoped she was well. Both boys were now home and demobbed, picking up the threads of their past lives. The village was holding a "Holiday at Home" week at the end of the month. Would it be possible for Angie to come for the week-end? They could offer a put-u-up in the lounge. Regards to her uncle. Remember to write.

Angie realised she missed Updean. Its countryside and the warmth of Mrs Crofthouse's kitchen and the stability of their home, but it was too soon for a visit. She would write. She did the dishes and went through to where Jed was already releasing the bolts of the shop door. Uncle Cyril, too, was working on a rush order.

"If Naismith comes in, Angela, before the turn-ups and

pressing are complete, keep him happy. I need another forty minutes, and I'm not to be interrupted"

Mr Naismith, a small man with a goatee beard and a poxed complexion, appeared within the half-hour, and was obviously in a hurry.

"What do you mean? Not quite ready. I've a train to catch. I must see Mr Bolton, immediately." His voice had a rich Scots burr. Angie showed him to the cushioned chair.

"Please take a seat, Mr Naismith, and I'll see if he is free."

She made a face at Jed as she went into the backroom. Angie daren't disturb her uncle, he would explode, and Naismith would almost certainly leave without his order. Peering through the frosted glass panel of the workroom door, she could make out the figure of Cyril at the ironing board.

She checked the kitchen clock. If his estimate was right, he needed another five or ten minutes. Angie put the kettle on and made tea. She covered a tray with an embroidered cloth and placed two digestive biscuits on a plate.

Naismith leapt to his feet as Angie re-entered the shop.

"Mr Bolton will be through in a minute or two. Your suit is ready." She placed the tray on the counter. "I've made you tea."

Mr Naismith sat down again and lifted the cup.

"We have a new range of ties for the business man. Let me show you a selection." Angie motioned to Jed and he handed her a rack of ties. "This one would, I believe, go beautifully with your new suit and compliment the colour of your eyes." She gave Naismith her most radiant smile.

"What does a young lass like you know about the colour of my eyes?" But he melted enough to choose not one, but two, ties.

Cyril came in from the back shop carrying the suit on a hanger.

"Angela, has Nais...Ah ...I hope I haven't kept you long." He stared at the tray with the empty cup and plate. "I see Angela has looked after you."

31

"You've a good girl there. I was none too pleased. I've a train to catch. And the lass managed to sell me a couple of ties. I'd never have believed it."

Mr Naismith tried the suit on in the fitting room and satisfied, paid Cyril and left.

"It's as well you sold those ties, Angela. We are not in the habit of turning the shop into a tearoom. Normally, I would deduct the cost from your wage, however, in this case it worked out well."

Angie stiffened as, in a rare show of affection, her uncle placed an arm round her shoulder.

"Conway," he called, "Take the tray into the kitchen and clean up." He smiled smugly at Angie. She squirmed.

"It's no good," she confessed to Lynn that evening in the sanctum. "I can't stand it much longer. Cyril trying to be pleasant is far worse than Cyril ignoring me. I'll just have to find another job."

"You'd have to find somewhere else to live. He'd make it intolerable for you."

"I expect you're right."

Lynn was sifting through snapshots. "Two more weeks and I'm away to Lochend House. I'm trying to sort things out. My mother's actually taking time off to go up with me. We're holidaying in Ayr for a week before the term starts. Now, which of these should I take?"

"That one of you with your dad and maybe this of your mum." Angie flicked through the photos. "You're quite photogenic."

She set aside a few then picked out a holiday shot of Lynn in a swimsuit and a snap taken at the school play. "I'd take both of these."

"I'll take the glamour one. You can have the rising star."

"Thanks," Angie said, "I've a thing about stars." She placed the photograph in her handbag. "We've had fun this summer, haven't we? I'll not forget you."

"Won't give you the chance. I'll write every week. Well,

every month, anyway," Lynn laughed, "And I'll be home in a few weeks for mid-term. And I'll see you at Christmas."

Angie returned to her room via the fire escape and wrote to Mrs Crofthouse. She was sorry she wouldn't manage to the Fair. Her best friend Lynn was leaving for Scotland that week-end and she wanted to be around.

Lynn left London. The casual summer cottons replaced by an elegant suit. Her hair smoothed into a chignon.

"Doesn't she look sophisticated? Like a young version of her mother," Angie said to Olga as they stood in the driveway of Beechwood beside Gideon Arnold to see Lynn off. Angie waved cheerfully and reserved a tear for the privacy of her own room later. She was certain to miss Lynn. Life would be so dull without her around.

Angie woke next morning with a sore throat and a headache, got up, but was chased back to bed.

"Don't want the germs affecting the customers and I can't afford to be ill." Cyril was adamant and shoo-ed her upstairs. "If you feel like breakfast Edwina will bring you something."

"Just a drink, please," Angie croaked.

Edwina came to her bedroom minutes later, carrying a pot of tea and a bottle of painkillers.

"Take two of these with your tea. They work wonders." She placed her hand on Angie's forehead. Angie jumped back. "I'm just checking your temperature. You're flushed. I won't eat you."

The look Edwina gave Angie was challenging. She'd said that before on Angie's first day, "I won't eat you."

"Don't worry," Angie said to herself when the housekeeper had left "You aren't going to get that pleasure."

The sore throat lingered for two days. Angie slept, read, and caught up with her letter writing. Time on her hands gave her the opportunity to think. If only she didn't have to stay here with Cyril and Edwina. She longed for someone to love. Wished she could feel her mother's arms and her dad's kiss.

Tears welled in her eyes. She bit her lip. Angie Bolton

didn't cry. Instead she penned a note to Lynn and tried to keep it light.

'Bet you didn't expect to hear so soon. Truth is, I've nothing better to do! I'm in bed nursing a rotten throat. I'm managing to keep the wolf at bay (she won't eat me, she says).

You looked fantastic in that suit. Your father was sad to see you go. Have a good holiday before the grind starts. Miss you already. Write soon.'

"Take another day or two to get over it completely." Cyril said when Angie appeared ready for work. He drew out his handkerchief and covered his nose and mouth, "Won't do Conway any harm to have to work harder."

He's scared, Angie decided. Scared of catching my sore throat. She could see it in his piggy eyes. Illness meant less money. Not that Cyril needed money. The profits were good. She knew that from the books and the quality of his own clothes. For all she hated his appearance, her uncle dressed impeccably.

Feeling better and with two whole days free, Angie knew what she would do. She had been putting it off, uncertain of her reactions. She took the bus to Montpelier Road, turned into the first side street and began to climb the hill. It was a narrow street. The paving cracked and broken away. Rain had fallen during the night and it puddled in the rutted gutters. At the top of the hill a railway bridge led to the station. Rubbish littered the area. Sodden remnants of yesterday's news rotted beside an apple core and a discarded box, trampled flat.

A woman had set up a hand-cart and was selling fruit and vegetables. A girl of about twelve, a boy some two or three years younger and another girl aged about five played on the pavement. The older girl was pulling the little one, who was wearing a near ankle length white dress, like the kind worn at a confirmation.

The five year old cried out and fell into the gutter. The

older child lifted her up and carried her dripping wet to the cart.

"Rosie's soaked, Mum," and Mum's voice shrieked in a tirade of remonstration.

Angie recalled falling in a puddle once at that same spot. It was on her way to school and her blazer was caked in mud so thick she'd raced home to change. "How could you, Angie? Your new blazer is ruined," Mother had scolded, and later she'd been made to clean it off herself. It had taken hours.

Angie passed under the bridge into a lane that ran to the right of the station and followed it to its end before again turning right. It wasn't there. The side of Albany Place where her home had stood no longer existed. Angie had been told what to expect, but the devastation came as a shock. The crumbled walls were flattened and most of the rubble cleared away. A few boulders remained and two boys rolled an old car tyre along the uneven surface. At the end of the street, where Mrs Fairweather had served sweets from big glass jars, a row of prefabs stood. Angie crossed the road and moved along until she reached the 'WHITE LADY'. Her parent's home had been directly opposite its entrance. She crossed back again and stopped at what she guessed would have been her front door. Her eyes scanned the bomb site, trying to picture everything as it had been.

The hall, narrow, with its mirrored coat-stand, the sitting room - first door on the right, then the dining room and beyond the square kitchen with the cupboards Dad had put in.

"It's the smartest kitchen in the street", Mum had boasted, and she'd kept it spotless.

Angie wiped a tear from her eye before it reached her cheek. She looked up to where her parents' bedroom would have been and to her own room adjoining it. Neat lace beneath floral print curtains and the matching heavy quilt spread on their bed. On hers, plump pillows and her own cream woolly blanket.

She wondered if anything had been salvaged. If it had she'd no idea where it would have been taken. She, herself, had received nothing. If only there was something tangible to keep.

35

She bent down and picked up a small piece of red brick, blew the dust from it and put it in her pocket. It could have come from anywhere but there was just a chance... it was the nearest she would get.

Angie went back over to the bench outside the public house, facing the ruins. She felt almost numb. A young man, standing a few yards from her, was also staring across at the rubble. He came and sat beside her. Hands on his knees, he leant forward, "Ghastly, isn't it? I lived there once. I come most weeks. Can't get it out of my mind. My parents died and my three brothers and baby sister. Pedro, my dog. They all went. Those bastards got the lot."

Angie turned to look at the lad. He was of average height and build, with intense dark eyes set in a pleasantly boyish face. She didn't recognise him, but she remembered Pedro, a golden Labrador. Davy's dog.

"That," she said, pointing, "was my house. Number 8." She'd never forget - one for sorrow.

The young man jumped up, "We were Number 12. Number 8 was the Bolton's." He peered into Angie's face, "You're not little Angie are you?"

"That's me. And you must be Davy Crossart."

"I'm Nick. Davy's big brother."

"Nick? I would never have known you."

She remembered Nick, always playing football. He was about three years older than Davy and had never given her a second glance.

"I can't believe it. Little Angie. You were all teeth and look at you now. I can see your dad in you. He was great when it happened. Came home on compassionate leave and helped us all. God knows how we'd have coped without him and Monty. Remember Monty? He still lives round here somewhere. Walks with a limp."

Angie didn't recall any limp, but she'd known Monty. He'd been her dad's best mate.

"So where's your old man now, then?"

"He died at sea. Two years after......"

"Oh God, I'm sorry. I didn't know." Nick placed an arm round her shoulder. "It's a bloody mess, isn't it? A bloody mess."

He sat down on the bench again.

"So where are you now, Angie?"

"With my uncle."

"That's not so bad then. I tried staying with an aunt, when I was demobbed a couple of months ago, but it didn't work."

"Doesn't work for me either. Where do you live?"

"Oh, round and about," he said lightly.

"Where's round and about?"

"If I tell you, it's secret. Right?"

Angie nodded.

"I'm staying with friends in this house, see. In Park Way."

"Park Way. That's where the toffs stay. Were you left a fortune?"

"Fortune? Not a bean. We're squatting. That's why it's secret."

"Who are 'we'?"

"No one from here. Just some mates, Corey and Joan. The owners'll be back soon, I suppose, with the war ending. But we're sitting tight."

"But you can't just walk into someone's house and stay there. Not without giving it back, anyway."

"It's all very hush hush. We can, and we did. All the abandoned offices had been taken over, so we risked private. The owners will get it back when we find somewhere else to live. You've got to fend for yourself, Angie. I lost everything. Surely I deserve somewhere to live?"

"I guess so," Angie said. "You could go to jail."

"Don't worry. We'll be okay. I'll have to go in a jiff. I work evenings in the Carlton Bar in Nixon Road. Do you know it? It's beside the Gaumont."

They both got up, staring again at the rubbled ground opposite. Nick had his arm across Angie's shoulder again. She could feel him trembling and realised she, too, was shaking. He turned her round to face him and kissed her lips lightly. Angie stared up at him.

"You look like a lost kitten," he said and his lips touched hers again. His arms held her close. She clung to him, kissing him as passionately as he kissed her. Suddenly he pushed her aside and, without a word, he walked off and rounded the corner.

Angie stood shaking. She hadn't resisted Nick. She'd wanted him to hold her, caress her. They'd both needed it. Someone, something to cling to. All the emotion of the past overwhelmed her. She ran crying through the once familiar streets to the bus stop. For once she was glad to reach Dryden Terrace. She hurried up the stairs, grateful no one was about, and left a message outside Edwina's door.

'I'm feeling tired. Am going to sleep. Sorry, but I don't want tea tonight. Angela.'

And sleep she did, for several hours, before waking at nine o'clock. Her room was in semi-darkness. The rain of the previous night had returned. She lay watching its steady stream down the window pane. Like tears, she thought. Her eyes were dry now and the ache in her body had subsided. She felt hungry.

Angie straightened her skirt, pulled on an extra jumper, and went downstairs to the kitchen where Edwina was making her nightly cup of tea.

"Are you feeling better? You must share my pot. I'll make you a sandwich. You would like a sandwich?"

"Thanks. I'd love one and yes, I'm much better."

"We'll have it in my room. I've an electric fire. This rain's keeping temperatures down. It felt quite chilly when I dashed outside to rescue the towels."

She carried the tray ahead of Angie up the two flights. Angie had never been in Edwina's room before. She was taken aback by its size and its décor; spotless white walls, black woodwork, black and white spread and curtains. Grey Wilton

38

swirled on the floor and red and yellow cushions splashed colour on black leather seats.

On the walls, etchings repeated the theme of black and white and a swivel bookcase stood in one corner. It was at least six feet high. Edwina seemed to sense Angie's surprise.

"It is different, isn't it? It's my own choice and mostly my own work. I painted the walls, made the curtains and bedcover. Alice gifted the etchings and the cushions were a present from her niece at art school."

"It's really impressive. I'd no idea your room was so large." Angie sat on one of the armchairs to drink her tea. Edwina perched on the double bed. Angie felt relaxed. Off duty, Edwina was friendly and charming.

"How did you enjoy your day? It must have been exhausting to wear you out."

"Not really. I took a bus ride and went for a walk."

"Where did you go?" Edwina was inquisitive.

Angie was in no mood to satisfy her curiosity.

"Nowhere in particular." She was still trying to come to terms with what she had seen and the need Nick had exposed. She turned to the bookcase. "I see you read a lot."

"One's never alone with a good book. I enjoy light things - historical romance or a good mystery. If you want to borrow any help yourself. They've all got my name on the flap so you'll not forget where they came from. And I've a spare wireless if you'd like it. Or do you have one already?"

"I was thinking of buying one."

"Well don't bother. Take this, but remember to keep the volume down." She indicated a set in the shape of a half moon.

Edwina's hand touched Angie's as she pushed the wireless towards her. It lingered a second or two before she withdrew it. Then, to Angie's horror Edwina stroked her cheek.

"You've lovely skin, Angela. Take care of it." She moved her hand to Angie's forehead. "You're not at all feverish, but your cheeks look flushed."

Angie backed away. "Thanks for the supper. I'd better get

39

back to bed. Goodnight."

She lifted the radio and walked with it to the door. With her arms full she couldn't open it. Edwina turned the handle for her.

"Come again, Angela. I'll be delighted. "She moved into the corridor and opened Angie's door. "Goodnight." She leant towards Angie and for one moment Angela thought she was going to kiss her, but Edwina straightened up.

Angie slid into her room, placed the wireless on the table, and turned to shut the door. Edwina was still standing there, her lips stretched in the thin smile.

"Goodnight." Angie closed the door and turned the key in the lock.

In bed, she puzzled over Edwina's manner and her reaction to it. Why was she so wary? Edwina had been very pleasant. Her hands were soft not like Cyril's podgy fingers. Yet she sensed danger.

How very different the day's experiences had been. Nick with his impulsive passion and Edwina's touch. Angie's sleep was disturbed by muddled dreams, but she couldn't relive their detail in the morning.

CHAPTER 5

The rain had subsided and a bright sun laced Angie's pillows. She had no plans for the day until she went to get clothes from her drawer. It was, she decided, time to go shopping.

Angie excused herself from lunch and took the tube to Oxford Street. She stopped at her bank, withdrew twenty five of the fifty pounds Dillard Thrift had lodged in her account when she'd left school and stowed it in her purse. Feeling like a millionaire and with coupons to spare, shopping would be a pleasure.

The multiple stores confused her with their style and colours. Underwear ranged from fleecy bloomers to saucy, satin French knickers. Angie opted for cotton trimmed with lace and held them out to the assistant, delighted with their femininity. With thoughts of the winter season ahead she bought two wool vests, laughing at her fluctuations in mood. The remainder of her purchases confirmed the swings of fancy.

She left the multiples for the small shops and discovered one selling second hand clothes. The garments seemed to be very good quality and the joy was no coupons were required. She picked out a duck-egg blue crepe dress. It was very plain but slid over her hips as if made for her. The colour echoed the blue of her eyes and flattered her fair skin. She saw herself dancing in it, the flared hemline swirling as she twirled. For work, she chose a straight black skirt, two white blouses and a black cardigan. Moving on to another shop, court shoes and some stockings completed her purchases. She had saved some coupons but the notes no longer bulged in her purse. Angie was happy. It was a long time since she'd indulged herself. If only Mum and Dad could see her in that dress.

Not knowing any quaint little eating houses, Angie took her place in the queue at Lyon's tea rooms, lunched on fish and drank from thick china. She was just one anonymous person in a city filled with anonymous people.

By 1.15 pm, Angie had finished eating. Too early, she felt, to return to Dryden Terrace and the city was there to be explored. She decided to start at Trafalgar Square and turned off Oxford Street, walked the length of Regent Street to Haymarket, and on to the Square.

Often as a child she had stood among the pigeons and looked up at Nelson's Column.

"He was a sailor, too. One of the greatest," her father would say. "Fell for a Josephine, just like I did."

"Don't be daft. That was Napoleon," her mother would laugh. The kind of laughter that tinkled with happiness.

Angie watched a family fling bread to the pigeons, which swooped to catch the crumbs in the air and then raced in front of their feet to forage among the crevices of the paving stones. She walked the short distance to St James's Park. The pleasant weather had tempted the nannies with their charges and they pushed prams round the lake. Angie took the route across the turf to Buckingham Palace, pausing briefly to sit on the grass before joining the crowd gathered at the gates. A little girl ran forward and was beyond the policeman on duty before he or her mother could stop her.

"I need a pee-pee. There'll be a lavvy down here."

The officer caught her and scooped her into his arms, "Sorry," he said to the child's embarrassed mother. "Try the park." And they went off in search of a bush.

Queen Elizabeth wouldn't have minded, Angie thought. She was a mother. She'd have understood. It couldn't be all fun living in a palace, being a queen or princess. Even living with Cyril might be preferable. At least she could choose her friends and go for fish and chips at Lyons. A group of airmen came noisily up Palace Road as Angie made her way towards Victoria Station. They had obviously been celebrating and she ignored their wolf whistles but they persisted and called after her.

"Doing anything tonight, darling?"

"'Fraid so," she smiled, blushing at the attention. Only as they moved on did she notice that one had a hook for a hand and another a severe limp.

The Tube was busy and, lucky to find a strap to hang on to, Angie swayed homeward. Edwina was serving high tea and the smell of freshly grilled haddock filled the kitchen. Angie said nothing and ate it for the second time that day. Putting aside her reservations, she showed Edwina the blue dress.

"You've good taste, Angela. It suits you. You'll have to find somewhere to go to wear it, and someone to go with."

Upstairs, Angie told herself she'd been wrong. Edwina was a pleasant, middle-aged woman and whatever her relationship with Alice, she had no designs on young girls. She unwrapped the remainder of her purchases and put them away. The evening disappeared as she stretched out on the bed and tuned in to Tommy Handley on the radio. She wondered if Lynn heard the same programmes. Scotland must be a very beautiful place with its Highlands. I'm missing you, Lynn but not in the way I miss my mum and dad. I wish I could hear you laugh - and moan.

Some weeks elapsed before Angie received a letter from Lynn. She read it as she ate her breakfast toast.

"I'm having a fabulous time. How could I have doubted it? If only you were here too. If I tell you all about it maybe you'll share the experience.

School isn't at all as I'd expected. The building is like a huge manor house set amid avenues of trees. From my bedroom window seat, I can smell the scent from the rose garden. It's fading now and the soil is covered with petals.

Looking east, west and north, I can see the hills but here the land is fairly flat. The school is only a few miles inland from Ayr, in seventeen acres of grounds enhanced with autumn colours. Can you believe it - seventeen acres!

43

Inside there are marble topped tables and tapestries on the walls above a curved oak staircase. We've a twin bedded room with its own wash hand basin in olive green. "We" being Henriette and I. Henry, as I call her, is my room mate. She's part French and madly eccentric with a passion for cream cakes born, she says, from deprivation. Like you she's an orphan (must be something about me that attracts lost souls). She lives just north of Glasgow with her doting grandmother who, she says, is as Scots as they come but has the title of Countess something or other.

The Count who died yonks ago was Henry's grandfather. It's really Compte and Comptess, in French, I think. Apparently, he owned half of Paris.

Henry runs an old Austin, or rather it runs her. I gather Grandmother would not approve. She's nearly nineteen (Henry, not her grandmother) and has just completed one year here.

Learning to drive is part of my curriculum for next term. At the moment, it's deportment, etiquette, dress sense and make-up. To be honest that's in the afternoons. Mornings I still wrestle with general subjects.

Now for the real news. I'll be home next Tuesday for a full week and I'm bringing Henry with me. You'll love her. We'll have such fun. I can't wait.

She's extremely good at chatting up young men, by the way, and is usually surrounded by them when we go out. Me? I've got Angus. I'll explain about him when I see you! Dying to hear what you've been up to,

Lynn, xxxxx '

"And how is Lynn?" Edwina asked, "I expect you miss her."

"Yes, I do. She loves it. She'll be home in ten days."

"You must invite her for high tea."

"Thanks, I will."

Angie awaited the arrival of Lynn at King's Cross Station. Sylvie and Gideon Arnold were in the West Country on one of their unavoidable trips. Olga had been instructed to take a taxi to meet Lynn, but a bad night with a sore tooth made her contact Angie.

"You can meet Lynn for me?" she'd asked Angie. "I must go to a dentist."

Angie requested the afternoon off and Cyril agreed, but not without his usual gripe.

"I've a rush job on, and Conway's wife's expecting any day. I've said he can leave early. I shall have to shut the shop at four-thirty. Most inconvenient."

Angie remained firm. Apart from being off with her sore throat, she'd had no free time since starting. The half day was justified.

A mid-October wind kept the rain clouds scuttling past but played with her hair, sweeping it over her eyes as she walked from the underground to the main-line station. She brushed it aside and picked Lynn out from the passengers leaving the train but could see no sign of Henriette. She waved furiously but Lynn bounded on, her eyes fixed on the platform. Angie dived inside the gates to meet her and the pair hugged in undisguised delight.

"It's fantastic to see you. It seems like ages. So much has happened. The school - well, it's more like a college - is fab'. Few rules exist that can't be got round and there's Henry."

"Where is Henry? "

"I'm dying of thirst. Let's get a drink and I'll tell you."

They left the station and found a cafe where the lemonade fizzed.

"Henry's gone to her grandmother's for a couple days, first. She'll be coming here on Thursday," Lynn explained. "I've met Grandmother. An absolute gem. She popped over to visit us. She's as thin as a rake with a sort of regal majesty. And no wonder being a Countess. You find yourself imagining the tiara. The diamonds are there, of course. Dripping from her ears, wrists and fingers. And did I tell you? She's pure Scots. She brought us exquisite little gifts like silk stockings and

45

neckerchiefs and despite her appearance she's completely huggable. Just have to watch you don't break her bones. She even kissed me on both cheeks."

"Sounds as if she's a character," Angie managed to get a word in at last.

"Oh, she is. She is" Lynn enthused. "My grandparents on mother's side are American. Dad's mother has hibernated in Spain since my grandfather died. But none of them are like the Countess."

"I never knew my grandparents on my dad's side." Angie confided. "They were dead before I was born. That's not quite true because Mum had a birthday card she kept among her souvenirs. It said from 'Martin, Josie and baby Angela'. I think it was to Granddad Bolton, but he died when I was six months old. Mum must have been given it back."

"That's sad," Lynn interrupted.

Angie continued, "My mum never spoke about her dad. Grandmother lived on her own. She died the day the war started. I've always wished I had a brother, or a sister, I suppose. How about you?"

"Good question. I'm not really an only child. I've a half-brother, Sebastian. I think he's a bastard, but I'm not sure. My mother's never told me the full story. Seems she had him in her teens, before she married Dad. He really lives with my grandmother in America, but he was at college over here when the war started, and he's not been back there since." Lynn stood up and walked towards the window.

"For years I thought he was my cousin. Then I was nosing in Mummy's wardrobe and at the bottom was this box of letters. They were from my grandmother and mentioned Seb. It was obvious who he was. I daren't tell my mother I know. She'd go all dramatic and my life wouldn't be worth anything. He's studying at university now. I've met him a few times"

"Does he know he's your brother?"

"I haven't a clue, perhaps, perhaps not."

"Don't you want to tell him?"

"In a way. I don't think about it much."

"I'd never have guessed your mother was American if you hadn't told me. She sounds so English."

"Cultivated. Like everything else about her. She wasn't always rich, you know. My grandfather was head of a Los Angeles school. She came over here, met Dad and never went back. They were on the verge of taking up a post over there when the war started. We were all set. Cases packed, then ...Ah, well, enough of the history lesson. It's you and me on our own-some for two whole days. I don't suppose Cyril would let you stay at my house?"

"Doubt it. He was all of a fluster because I was meeting you. Edwina says you've to come to tea. It will give Olga a rest."

"Where *is* Olga? Mum said she'd be here."

"At the dentist. She's got toothache. She called in this morning to ask if I'd come in her place. We've to get a taxi. Olga gave me the money." Angie handed Lynn an envelope with notes in it. "Olga's going to get a few things in town. I told her not to hurry."

"So it's home to an empty house. Just like Mum and Dad to be away when I haven't seen them for weeks. Guess I'll take up Edwina's invite."

"I have already. I said we'd be round once you'd dropped your suitcases. It works out well. Cyril's card sharks are coming tonight instead of Wednesday, so we can eat in my room. I always do when they're around. They've got minds like swill bins."

"Keep the change," Lynn said to the taxi driver as he dropped them at Beechwood.

"Ta very much, Miss." From the look on the cabby's face he'd have been content with half the tip.

Lynn struggled with the key to the main entrance.

"It's always like this if the snib's down. Olga should have locked the door with her key. Don't worry, it'll work in a second."

47

But it didn't.

"It never happens to anyone else. There's something wrong with this key." She turned the keys on the ring round until she came to a small flat one. "We'll go round the back. Come on."

Angie helped her carry the cases to the rear of the house. On the step leading to the patio doors lay a small bird, its speckled breast uppermost, like a trussed chicken. There was no sign of injury but it was, undoubtedly, dead.

Lynn put down the case she was carrying.

"The poor little thing. It must have flown into the glass, and with some force. Hope it's not a symbol."

She lifted it gently in her hands. "We'll give it a decent burial before some cat gets it or Taurus decides it's a toy."

Lynn opened the patio doors and, passing the bird to Angela, flung her luggage inside. She went in search of a spade in one of the outhouses and returned with a trowel.

"This should be okay," she said leading the way to a secluded corner of the garden. "I buried my hamsters here when they died."

Lynn dug a shallow grave, took a handkerchief from her pocket and wrapped the bird in it before burying it.

"Rest in Peace," she said softly. She brushed loose earth from her hands and set off across the lawn. "We've all got to go sometime. Life is for the living. Tomorrow, today is yesterday. Past."

They stepped into the lounge. "I wonder where Taurus is. I suppose Olga's taken him with her."

Angie thought that an unlikely supposition but Taurus was certainly not in the house. Lynn threw the cases on her bed, opened one, and rummaged to the bottom to bring out a parcel.

"It's not typically Scottish or anything but I thought you'd like it."

Angie removed the wrapping to reveal an ornate silver photograph frame.

"It's beautiful. Now where's the picture to go in it? I've already framed the rising star."

"I was hoping you'd ask. You can choose." Lynn handed over several portraits of herself taken from various angles. "It's part of our training. We have to study ourselves to make the most of our good points."

"Sounds like an ego trip to me. Can I really have one of them?"

Lynn nodded and after some deliberation Angie picked a photo of Lynn staring straight ahead. The sparkle in her eyes captured in a look of absolute frankness.

"That's one of my favourites," Lynn admitted, "And I just happen to have another identical frame. I'd like a picture of you, now."

"Haven't had any taken in ages, unless you want the school tunic."

"Wait, I'll get my camera."

"But we'll be late for tea." Angie protested.

"Won't take a sec', promise." Lynn got the camera. "Say cheese."

Angie obliged with a huge grin.

"You look like a magazine advert for Colgate," Lynn laughed, and Angie's big grin turned to a natural smile as the camera clicked. "Now we'll be able to sit and admire each other. I'll get it developed first chance. Let's lock up and get moving."

Edwina had prepared and served a mixed grill of bacon, mushroom and tomato with hot toast. She took the plates from the oven and set them on trays.

"Go ahead. Take the trays up. I'll follow with the tea and scones."

Angie paused, considering whether to ask Edwina to join them. The housekeeper seemed to read her thoughts.

"I've still to cook for your uncle and his friends. They're having a drink first in his room. Then I'm seeing Alice. Remember the light and, if you can manage, the dishes. Cyril usually puts theirs in the kitchen by eight. Enjoy your meal."

"Where will we begin?" Angie asked. "How about you

49

filling in what you've missed out in your letters while we eat and I'll give you my news after we've finished the dishes."

"It's like I said," Lynn began. "The last few weeks have been great and mainly due to Henry. I know you're going to like her."

"What's she look like?"

"She's smaller than us - about 5ft 4ins. Her hair's as dark as mine and she has a tiny waist and enough on top to get the heads turning. And she's always bubbly, like champagne. Mentally she's a bit of a nut case. Mind you, she's intelligent."

"Sounds a lot like you," Angie interrupted.

Lynn ignored her. "She's always having hare-brained ideas. For instance, we held a mid-term party before we left. She invited forty people. Can you imagine forty people in a room no bigger than this? The noise! The staff were a bit upset when they found out."

"Not surprised," Angie commented.

"Then there's Aussie, the Austin. She bought that from one of the boys in Ayr. It's serviceable - just. We wouldn't be able to do so much without it, that's for certain."

"I'm dying to meet her. And who's this Angus?"

"He's history. I'm with Fraser, now. Tall, blonde, muscular and protective. We're very good friends."

"Is that all?"

"Yes, that's all - for the moment."

"Wow! Look at the time. Let's clear up."

They reached the kitchen as Cyril and Matt were coming out.

"Two little darlings tonight. You do well for yourself, Cyril." Matt put an arm round each girl's waist and squeezed. Angie wriggled out of his grasp and set her dishes on the draining board. She turned to help Lynn, who was carrying a tray with the teapot, sugar and milk, but she needed no assistance.

Balancing the tray on one arm, she lifted the tea pot and poured the remains of the strong brown liquid over Matt. Angie stared fascinated as it ran down his face, over his collar, and on to his white shirt. Angie grabbed the tray as it was about to topple.

"Nobody," said Lynn, "takes liberties with me unless I want them to."

Cyril's pig eyes popped in his head. Matt looked sheepish. Angie was not sure whether to applaud or weep.

Cyril spoke first, "Really, you should not have done that. I must ask you to apologise." He wagged a sausage finger in Lynn's face.

Lynn was unrepentant. "Apologise, for what? This man tried to molest me. I was defending myself."

Matt, himself, saved the situation from escalating. "The girl's right, Cyril. I tried it once too often. I'm a silly old fool. No harm meant, Miss."

"Well said." Lynn placed a kiss on his wet forehead.

Angie thought Cyril would burst. He went up the stairs muttering about manners, or the lack of them.

"It's the last time that creep will try anything," Lynn said as she and Angie washed up.

Angie could see the funny side now it was all over and was having difficulty controlling a fit of the giggles.

"How did you dare? Did you see Cyril's face? He was the pinkest ever. Is that what you're taught at college?"

"More or less, when they're not training us to be young ladies." She placed the last plate on the shelf. "We're encouraged to look after ourselves. The teapot was there. Let's forget it. We've so much to talk about. Come on." She led the way back to Angie's room. "I want to hear everything you've been doing."

"I've worked and worked and ... okay, I've had some time off."

Angie described her visit to Albany Place and her meeting with Nick, omitting to mention the emotional embrace. She covered the shopping trip to the city centre, a couple of films, and a dance at the youth club.

51

"It was so funny. It started at seven-thirty. We girls stood down one side of the room and the boys lined the other and it stayed that way until about ten o'clock. Talk about boring. Then suddenly, we merged and after that things brightened up. Thirty minutes later the dance was over,"

Everything Angie had done sounded so dull compared to Lynn's packed weeks. To add spice, she expressed her fears about Edwina's attentions.

"I can't make my mind up if she's making a pass or just being kind."

"I told you to watch Edwina. You might as well know. There were rumours about her and a girl at school - Jean Swithers - she left before you came. Edwina is capable of complicating your life, if you let her. She does it so sweetly, you don't always see what's happening."

"She's harmless enough. If she starts anything, I could try the teapot."

Angie and Lynn convulsed in laughter, but quietened as they heard Edwina coming up the stairs. Her feet paused outside Angie's room before she went into her own.

"I'd keep the door locked, if I were you." Lynn glanced at Angie's alarm clock. "Is that right? Olga will be wondering where I've got to. I'll use the fire escape."

"I'll walk you to the end of the road."

They stepped lightly down the metal treads and through the back gate.

"'Night. See you tomorrow. I doubt if you'll be allowed to stay after tonight. I'll see if I can turn on the charm." Lynn waved and walked on.

Back in her room, Angie settled into bed. She heard Cyril's cronies leaving. From their cheerful banter, it was apparent her uncle was the loser.

The following morning, Cyril was more difficult than usual. Jed's wife had gone into labour during the night. He'd dropped a note in to say he was at the maternity hospital and would give them the news as soon as the baby arrived. A consignment of material was unloaded. Bales needed to be checked, quality verified, prices confirmed. The van driver was in a hurry.

"Can't hang around. I've to get to Newcastle," he said as Cyril insisted on going through every detail.

Angie was called away from the counter to help and, inevitably, the shop bell kept ringing. By eleven they were finished and the van driver left, moaning he'd have to miss lunch to make up time. An hour later the new materials were stocked. Cyril buried himself in the workroom and, between customers, Angie cleared drawers and shelves in readiness for Christmas displays. Jed burst through the door around four o'clock.

"It's a girl," he cried, leaping round the floor like a beheaded cockerel in reflex. I've a daughter - 7lb 2ozs - Wendy Elizabeth. The wife's jiggered but over the moon."

Angie was quick to congratulate Jed, making a mental note to buy something pink. Cyril came through to complain about the noise.

"How can I work against this bedlam? Oh - it's you Conway. A girl? Matt has five of them. More work than boys and more costly, he says. Your hand will never be out of your pocket. You'll be looking for a rise, no doubt. Times are still hard. Don't forget that. Times are still hard." He trotted back to his Singer. "Be back tomorrow, prompt." And he set the treadle in motion.

"His snort's worse than his gobble," Angie laughed. "Sit down and I'll see if Edwina's got any sherry or something."

"You're a doll, Angie. Brandy would suit me better. A good strong brandy."

Edwina wasn't sure Cyril would approve of drinking in the shop but she found a half bottle of good Cognac.

"Take this, he'll never miss it. He's stocked up since before the war. You can share a drop with the grandparents. Girls are so much quieter than boys."

It was as well, Angie thought, that Edwina hadn't witnessed the scene in the kitchen the night before, or she might have changed her views. They drunk to the health of Wendy Elizabeth and Conway rushed out again.

The shop bell rang almost immediately he left and Angie responded to it. This customer had no intention of buying anything. It was Lynn and her mood had changed from the confident buoyancy of the previous day to one of dejection.

"It's Taurus. They've sent him away. Olga's admitted it. He's gone to my uncle and aunt near Guildford. They've a poultry farm and market garden. Can you believe neither Mum nor Dad could find the time to take him for walks? I tell you, Angie, if I ever have to live with them again permanently, there'll be murder committed."

"Lynn, I'm sorry. Look, I can't talk now. Cyril's on the moan. I'll come round after tea. Say, about seven."

Angie ushered Lynn out and resumed clearing the drawers. Cyril ensured that she worked until six-thirty. Edwina took the late high tea in her stride. It was nearer eight o'clock when Angie reached Beechwood.

"It's another instance. Same old story. I wasn't consulted. He's my dog, Angie, not theirs. A Christmas present two years ago."

"Of course they're wrong, but it might be better for Taurus with you away and them not caring much. At least, in the country he's got fields to run in and he's not nosing around bomb sites."

"I suppose so. Taurus will love the farm. He probably has a ball chasing the hens. But I'm going to miss the little blighter and it doesn't make it right, does it?"

Lynn was doing her pacing act across the carpet like a demented bear. Angie knew how to handle her.

"Let's go and see Taurus this weekend. We could take the train and Henry could come with us. Go on. Ring your uncle now. You might even be able to have a chat with Taurus."

Lynn plucked a cushion from the chair and flung it at Angie. "You," she said, and after a pause, "I think I will. I'll ring to find out how he's doing and suggest a visit." She ran to the telephone and turned to Angie before dialling. "You don't think my visiting will upset him?"

"Upset him? He'll wag his tail in delight when he realises you haven't deserted him."

Ten minutes later it was all settled. On Saturday, providing Angie could get the time off, they'd travel to Guildford.

CHAPTER 6

Sylvie and Gideon returned from their business trip on Thursday morning and late afternoon Henriette hit London. It would be more accurate to say London hit Henriette. The wind blew and the rain lashed.

"There she is," Lynn cried as she swept past other people to greet her.

Henry was almost exactly as Angie pictured from Lynn's description. Dark brown hair and eyes, an olive skin and an expressive face which at that moment reflected true pleasure. Her raincoat hung loosely from slender shoulders over a plain wool dress in darkest green which outlined her figure. She was struggling with two large suitcases and a vanity bag.

"Are you staying for months?" Lynn asked.

"I couldn't decide what to bring, so I brought it all."

"Not the cat suit with the zebra stripes?"

Henry looked puzzled. "Cat suit? Zebra stripes...oh, my black and yellow tiger. Why, yes, of course. I never travel without my tiger." She turned to face Angela. "You must be Angie."

"Who else? I've been dying to meet you. Lynn's gone on about you something awful."

They moved across the concourse dragging the cases.

"Mummy has a headache. She's gone to bed. Daddy's coming to collect us when he's free. We've to eat here. He said he'd be about an hour." Lynn explained

"Edwina's expecting me back. I said I might be a bit late."

"In that case," Lynn said, "You'll be later."

Angie telephoned Edwina from the station and the girls climbed the stone steps to the restaurant, where steak pie was a crust above the sausage rolls of the cafeteria.

Gideon came looking for them within the hour and paid the bill. He dropped Angie at the corner of Dryden Terrace. Lynn tried to persuade her to go home with her and Henriette but she pleaded she'd to wash her hair and get on with some ironing. In truth, Angie felt Henry and Lynn would be more than enough for Sylvie's migraine. She made herself tea and was relieved Edwina was not around to join her. Henry, she thought, should make a lively addition to her list of friends.

Lynn and Henry called at the shop next day.

"Angie, we're going to invite you somewhere and you're not allowed to refuse."

"Somewhere nice, I hope?"

"The invite's from Mummy, really. She's taking us to the West End to dine. A club called 'Chartres'. She's going to ask Cyril if you can stay overnight at ours."

"I suppose there's a chance he might let me if your mother talks to him."

"That's what I thought. I warned her he might not like the club bit, so she agreed to say we're going out for a meal and travelling to Guildford early the next morning. If we're late to bed though, we probably won't go until nearer midday."

Cyril was flattered by Silvie's visit. Beautiful women made him simper. "Delighted. I'm sure Angela will be thrilled," he drooled, rubbing his fat hands together. "So good for her to have friends of her own age."

Angie watched him. He can't take his eyes off her, she thought. Lynn had her mother's charm when she cared to use it, and Henry? Henry seemed so like Lynn. Same zany ideas, same lively personality. All the things Lynn attributed to Henry applied to her. So where did Angie fit in? She reckoned she slotted into one side and guessed she was happy to be there.

Angie arrived at Beechwood early in the evening.

"You're in here with me," Lynn said, indicating a Z-bed that had been put up in her room. "Henry and I share all year at college, so she's got her own place. I've cleared space in the

57

wardrobe. If you need anything I'm not using, help yourself."

"Great," Angie said, "as long as you don't talk all night."

She unpacked her holdall - her blue dress for that night, heavy jumpers for the trip the next day. Lynn rummaged in a drawer.

"Daddy's booked for nine o'clock. That's quite early. They seldom eat before ten when they go out. Now what did I do with my new stockings? Ah, there they are. I'll get Olga to bring up tea and biscuits, or what have you, to tide us over."

Henry joined them to ask, "Can I bags first bath?"

"Sure. You after, Angie, and I'll settle for a cool plunge."

"I'm clean," Angie laughed. "A wash will do me."

They got ready, dashing around in various states of undress while nails were varnished, make-up perfected, hair brushed.

"Reminds me of back stage the night of the school play," Lynn said.

Sylvie came, wrapped in a silk dressing gown to check on their progress.

"We're leaving in thirty-minutes on the dot.   Gideon insists."

"No problem, we'll make it."

Henry disappeared into her room to get ready. Lynn flung open her wardrobe.

"Now for the big decision. The pink with the sequinned neckline, the black with the side slit, or the virginal white? Help, Angie, what do you think?"

"I'm glad I don't have a choice," Angie replied, slipping into her one and only blue. "Wear the white. It won't clash with your dad's Mercedes."

"Stop taking the Mickey. I've made up my mind. The lemon."

The lemon was a slinky mid-calf, with a dropped waist and deep V neckline.

"How on earth do you have so many dresses?"

"Adaptations mostly, from my mother's cast-offs. She rarely wore anything more than a couple of times before the war. Dear old Sybil - Mother's dressmaker does the business."

Henriette came through, gloved in a black dress. The olive skin of her bare shoulders complemented by a diamond necklet. A matching bracelet ringed her wrist.

"Fasten the top for me, Lynn, please?"

Angie stared. Henry looked so glamorous. She turned to see Lynn emerge from the other side of the bed. The lemon was perfect. She had caught her dark hair back in a matching bow and she, too, wore diamonds on her ears and at her wrist. Lynn seemed to sense what Angie was feeling and came across to reassure her.

"You're so lovely in that colour, Angie. I adore the flare."

Sylvie called, "Come through to me when you're ready, which should be now."

A few seconds titivating and they were happy. Sylvie stood back and examined them, flicking a pin head of fluff from Henry's black.

"I've rarely been faced with such competition," she exclaimed. "Gideon will be popping his shirt buttons with pride."

Sylvie could stand the competition, Angie thought. Lynn's mother's bisque silk dress flirted with her waist before falling to her ankles. Her hair glistened, sleek smooth.

"I've laid out three furs. Lynn, this for you." Lynn wrapped herself in honey mink. "And Henry, I think the black." It was trimmed with ermine. "Now, Angela." Sylvie went to her dressing table and brought out a sapphire pendant. "There. I knew it would be just right?"

Angie put her hand to the pendant, "It's very beautiful." She took the white fur bolero Sylvie handed her. It was soft as Angora.

Sylvie draped a dark mink stole over her own shoulders. "We'd better hurry. Gideon is locking up. The car's already at the door."

Gideon let out an exaggerated gasp when he saw them coming, but Sylvie spoke first.

"You're the model escort, Darling." And he was. Tall, in a black tuxedo, his strong features still handsome, his hair, streaked grey, was as thick as a boy's.

It was, Angie thought, as if the Fairy Godmother had waved her wand and Sylvie, Gideon, Lynn, Henriette, and yes, even herself, had stepped out of a picture book. She half expected them to turn into mice when the clock struck twelve.

"Chartres" was underground. Down a flight of steps, through gleaming glass doors, across thick piled carpets. Sipping sherry, they studied the menu, sitting on plush velvet chairs in a reception alcove.

Luigi, the club manager, ushered them into the dining area. Intimate tables, laid with delicate pink cloths and napkins and silver cutlery and curve-backed chairs with pink brocade seats. Candles set in rose coloured globes played against the grey stone walls and pillars, which arched to the ceiling. At intervals glass panels mirrored the settings.

They took their seats. Around them groups of diners chatted and laughed discreetly and a band played softly beside a circular dance floor, marked out by tiny footlights. A few couples moved gracefully across its sprung surface.

Angie spotted a group of elderly people talking in hushed tones. She was reminded of the Sunday worshippers in Updean Church, whose voices remained whispers until after the service, and rose as they neared the village pub. A dozen diners, some old, some young, encircled the table on their right. A family celebration, she guessed.

Gideon, too, was looking around. Angie saw him acknowledge someone several tables away and then turn his eyes to the large party beside them.

He jumped up, "Michael, how are you?" The man he addressed was possibly in his sixties. He rose to his feet.

"My dear boy. You know Rachel, I believe." He waved his arm round his other guests. "Ben has just returned from a Prisoner-of-War Camp. We're building him up." Ben half stood to take Gideon's hand.

"No, no. Get on with your meal. We'll share a bottle later," Gideon said.

"Delighted. I see you are well catered for tonight. Sylvie's as beautiful as ever."

Smiles were exchanged.

"My daughter, Lynn, and her friends - Henriette and Angela. Henriette has a French background. That should interest you, Michael, as a professor of modern languages."

"Ah, yes, indeed. Perfect, just perfect."

Angie glanced at Henry, who was lapping up the attention. Almost, she sighed, but not quite. The mouth was too wide. Perfection would be unbearable.

The wine waiter came for their order.

"We'll have a bottle of champagne. Your best."

"Thank you, sir."

Angie looked up at the young man. He was staring back. Her mouth opened in disbelief. It was Nick. She was about to say something when he shook his head to silence her and moved away. What was Nick doing in "Chartres"? He must have changed jobs. She wondered if she could manoeuvre a chance to speak to him.

Nick returned with the champagne in a bucket of ice and the cork popped like gun fire. He ignored Angie as he filled her glass.

She heard Gideon comment to Sylvie, "Haven't seen that boy before. Must have started recently."

Angie wanted to say that she knew him. That he was her link to the past, but Nick's signal kept her silent.

Pate-de-fois-gras on a bed of salad with wafers of toast. Medallions of beef in red wine sauce with wild mushrooms, green beans and baby roast potatoes. Fruit Fool in a delicate raspberry sauce. The meal was the best and most elaborate Angie had ever tasted. And the champagne, she had never tried it before, made her head sparkle with the first sip.

She listened as Lynn and Henry chatted wittily with Sylvie and Gideon. They were at home in this setting. They hadn't had to watch to see which cutlery to use. This was their world. Angie felt she didn't belong, but she was loving every minute of it. Soon surely the curtain would fall. The play would be over.

Between courses, Gideon danced with them - Sylvie first, followed by Lynn and Henry. Then it was her turn.

"Angela, will you give me this dance?" Gideon asked formally.

"I'm not very good," Angie confessed.

"Just follow my lead."

Under Gideon's guidance, Angie felt herself gliding over the floor in a slow foxtrot. Her feet slipped easily into the rhythm.

"You are too modest, Angela," Gideon said. "You dance like a feather."

When the music stopped, Angie excused herself and made for the powder room. In the mirror she could see her cheeks flushed - a mixture of excitement, exercise and champagne. As she left the ladies' room, she saw Nick standing near the entrance to the dining area.

"You've changed your job?"

"I would have dropped you a note, but you didn't give me a clear address and I wasn't sure you'd want to know me. I've been here two weeks."

"Are you still squatting?"

"Yes. Trouble's brewing. The owners are back, kicking up a stink. They've given us three weeks to clear up and get out. You've gone up in the world, coming here to dine."

"I'm a guest of the Arnolds."

"Lucky you. Look, I'll be in trouble if I'm seen fraternising with the patrons. We'll have to meet somewhere. I'll be at Albany Place Sunday afternoon. Can you make it?"

"Can't, I'm spending the week-end with them." Angie nodded towards the table.

"Week after, then?"

"Okay."

Nick moved off to refill glasses. Angie returned to the table which was empty but for Lynn. She picked out Sylvie and

Gideon on the dance floor, cheek to cheek, and spotted Henry, held as if porcelain, in the arms of Ben from the adjacent table. He towered over her, a jumble of limbs.

"So you fancy the waiter? I must admit he has something." Lynn said.

Angie blushed. "It's not like that. It's Nick. Remember I told you about him."

"Oh yes. From your previous life. Why didn't you say so earlier?"

"He warned me not to. He's not supposed to fraternise and please don't say anything."

"Fair enough. If that's what you want."

Gideon and Sylvie returned and the subject of Nick was dropped.

"More champagne, everyone?" Gideon asked. "I see we've lost Henriette."

Henry was still talking to Ben at the edge of the dance floor and swung into a Samba as the next tune started. Gideon snapped his fingers and Nick appeared at his elbow. Angie kept her gaze on Lynn as he filled the glasses from a new bottle and she saw her give Nick a huge wink. She's incorrigible, Angie concluded.

Midnight passed and the magic didn't disappear. When they left "Chartres" at a quarter-past-one, the stars shone in a clear sky and no glass slipper glinted on the steps. Angie pulled the white angora firmly round her and let the champagne bubble up inside.

Any fears she had of not getting a good night's sleep were unfounded. She and Lynn fell into their beds and snoozed solidly until Olga woke them after ten thirty with tea and toasted muffins, oozing honey.

An hour later, with Lynn and Henry, Angie was on the train to Guildford.

Uncle Morton met them at Guildford with the station wagon.

"My goodness, I was expecting to meet children not young

ladies. How you've grown up, Lynn," he said "I hardly knew you. What is it? Two years, anyway. You should have come sooner. Mind you, the war .. we did offer to have you, you know. Not that we were far enough away."

Lynn kissed her uncle, "I know you did. I wanted to stay in London. Danger's my middle name."

"Foolhardy, more like." Morton turned to Angie and Henry, "Now, introduce me to your friends."

"Angela and Henriette. A couple of strays I've picked up. Angela lives near us in London and Henriette's home is near Glasgow, but she was born in Paris."

"Mais oui, Mademoiselle, enchante." Morton kissed Henriette on both cheeks. "Can't leave you out now, can I?" he said to Angie and he repeated the process.

"Don't torture yourself over the French, Uncle Morton. Henry's English is as good as yours."

"What a pity."

"Where's Taurus? I thought he'd be with you." Lynn asked as they drove to the farm.

"Boys have taken him for a run with Muppet. Up Hay Lane. By the chalk pit."

Morton, Angie observed, wasn't at all like Gideon. The few strands of hair he had were spread in a pretence of covering his head. His thin form was drowned in a tweed jacket, which smelt of chickens. He puffed continuously at a pipe.

"Dolly's set up a buffet lunch in the conservatory. You can sit and watch the leaves falling," he told them. He parked the car in the drive and led them through the entrance hall to a rear room.

For all its acres of land, the house was quite small. Unlike the Arnolds' home it looked lived in; the cushions crushed, the carpets slightly worn. Dolinda came to greet them. She was a small, slightly plump woman, with wisps of brown hair curling against her round face, and soft grey eyes.

The buffet was a work of art. Beds of lettuce cushioned hard boiled eggs and quartered tomatoes and flower shaped radishes floated on a pool of sliced cucumber. Stalks of celery formed an arched bridge from which watercress hung. Cheese straws, sheafed like corn, lay beside ringed onions. Mushrooms sprouted in a field of green aspic. The centrepiece was a dish of home baked bread surrounded by cheeses.

"I'll fetch the soup and we'll start. You girls must be starving." Dolinda disappeared into the kitchen, returned with a tureen of broth and placed it on a tripod set up on a side table. She put a ladle in the dish and indicated a pile of bowls, plates and cutlery. "It's self-service. Kevin and Lorne should be home any minute, but we'll not wait."

Angie, Lynn and Henry, chatting noisily, queued up as if at school dinners. It was that kind of home. No need for restraint. No awkward silences.

The soup was winter hot, justifying the cold buffet. Angie noticed Lynn looked continuously through the full length windows as she ate. Her eyes and ears alert. She was rewarded as Taurus came bounding across the grass followed by another cavalier and two young boys, aged, Angie guessed, about eight and eleven years.

Lynn flung open the patio door. Taurus and a flurry of leaves gusted through. The conservatory filled with excited yaps. He hadn't forgotten her that was obvious. She lifted him into her arms and he nuzzled against her face, his tongue washing every inch of it. Lynn buried her head into his coat, then placed him back on the floor and examined him as he trotted in and out of her feet.

"You're fatter, Taurus. It's Dolinda's cooking."

"Doesn't work for me," Morton said.

"You were born to be a rake," Dolinda bent down to greet the dogs. "Taurus loves it here, Lynn. Settled like a duck to water, as they say. The boys adore him and so does Muppet. Don't you, girl?" She patted the other cavalier, who had done a tour of the hen coops before joining them.

"That's obvious," Lynn said. "Mummy and Daddy were right to send him to you. I had to see for myself he was happy."

65

She gave Taurus another hug, before he went out again to romp with Muppet.

"She'll not stand a chance when she's in heat." Dolinda observed. "She'll have a kennel full before long. Mark my words."

Angie, Lynn and Henry took the dogs for a walk in the afternoon. They climbed a hillock and looked out over the farmlands.

"Amazing, isn't it? So near the city," Angie enthused. "I could stay here for ever. Wide open fields, trees. I love them. Dad said New Zealand's like that."

"And when the wind's driving snow and blocking roads, and the trees bare their branches to steel-grey skies. Will you love it then?" Lynn asked.

"I doubt if they get that much snow here. And I don't think New Zealand has much, except on the mountain tops."

"I've seen the farm cut off. It can happen. What do you think, Henry? Would you like to stay here for ever?"

"It's too isolated for me. Lochend's bad enough but at least there are the other girls, and it's only fifteen minutes to Ayr and less than an hour to Glasgow. I need the night lights. The proximity of people. I think in the country I'd grow fat like Dolinda. I'd hate to be fat."

"Dolinda's not fat," Angie protested. "She's comfortable. Round and content. I think she's lovely."

Lynn agreed. "And Morton. They're so right for each other."

"But your parents are beautiful, too," Henry told Lynn. "Elegant and obviously happy."

"With each other, yes. But with life as a whole? I'm not so sure."

"I see them as fairy-tale people," Angie said, "Almost too good to be true. Appearance wise, anyway. To be honest, I wasn't sure I liked them at first. But they grow on you."

"One day," Lynn observed, "I love them. The next I hate them. They can be so stubborn and lacking in understanding.

So... so self absorbed."

"Well at least you don't want to throw up at the sight of them. Just seeing Uncle Cyril makes me feel ill. His piggy eyes peering disapprovingly through those round specs. His simper. When he's angry or excited, he slobbers saliva all over you. Have you ever touched him? His skin is cold and slimy. And he's as tight as a pulled noose. I reckon he only offered me a roof to get at my money. And as for Edwina .. Ugh." It was a damning outburst and Angie felt herself blush as she finished.

There was a pause before Lynn said, "That's a bit harsh. I've got to admit, Cyril's not got much to offer. He has to have a good point. Everyone has."

"God forgot Cyril when he was dishing them out."

"Talking of God. We might make the local church tomorrow. Dolinda wants us to stay over-night. She's phoned Daddy and he's in favour. He said he'd settle it with your uncle. Hope it's alright with you, Henry? Can you bear to lock yourself in the country for another day?"

"Of course, but not your church. Remember, I go to Mass."

"There's an R C in the town. Someone will see you get there. Where are those dogs?....Taurus ... Muppet."

The cavaliers flew out of the trees like a couple of aced tennis balls and bounced up to them. Lynn put their leads on.

"Come on. Time to go back."

Dolinda's stew was even thicker than her soup. The fresh air helped Angie fill her plate and empty it.

Dolinda had crammed three camp beds into a room the size of the silver cupboard at Beechwood. By ten o'clock, all three of them were tucked in bed like the bugs in a rug.

"It's so quiet," Henry wailed.

"Listen and you'll hear the night owl hooting in the woods," Lynn told her.

Angie curled up under a quilt and, shutting her ears to the giggles of her friends, fell asleep.

She woke, not to the night owl but the rooster as dawn broke. Rain lashed against the window and a strong wind howled. The country, she decided was testing her affections.

Lynn and Henry were still sleeping. Angie slid out of bed and was first in the bathroom. She pattered down the stairs in her nightdress. Sitting in front of the lounge fire, she began drying her hair with a towel.

A door clanged shut. Dolinda appeared at the entrance to the lounge.

"You're up early, dear. I hope you slept well?"

"Like a top, thank-you."

"I'll get rid of these wet clothes and make a pot of tea." She placed a basket of eggs on the sideboard. "What a morning. My guess is we'll be over the worst in an hour or two. There're some breaks in the sky to the west." Dolinda shook her raincoat before pegging it on the hallstand.

She returned to the lounge. "Morton's having a bit of a lie in. The boys won't be up for an hour yet, it being Sunday. Come through to the kitchen when you're ready. It's warm in there with the Aga."

Angie gave her hair a final rub, brushed it, and joined Dolinda in the kitchen.

"Help yourself to milk and sugar. Would you mind having breakfast with me before the others are down? Save me coping with you all at once. Is it the full grill with fried egg?"

"Just egg with a piece of tomato, please"

"No rashers?"

"No thanks. I'm not a morning eater. I usually have toast and a spread."

Over breakfast, Dolinda wormed the family history out of Angie. She placed a warm hand on Angie's.

"I was orphaned, too. When I was eight. A dreadful storm. The chimney crashed on my parent's bed. Mother died instantly. Dad lingered awhile, but he'd lost the will, I think. I'd my sister to look after me. She was an angel. Died a year ago. She was twelve years older than me, but still young." Dolinda lifted the teapot, "I'll make fresh. Can't stand it stewed or watered down, for that matter. Just fifty. I've a brother. He lives in Dunbar, on the coast not far from Edinburgh." Taurus and Muppet padded into the kitchen and sniffed at their empty bowls.

"All right, it's your turn." Dolinda transferred her mothering to the dogs.

As she ran upstairs to dress Angie thought, "She's a bit like my own mum."

Lynn woke while Angie was finding her clothes.

"Help," she said, "is it really that time?"

She put one leg out of bed and Henry grabbed it.

"Got you," she cried.

Lynn pulled herself free and dragged Henry to the floor and the pair raced each other to the bathroom. Henry won.

"Don't take all day," Lynn wailed. Taurus heard her voice and, his short legs awkward on the steep risers, came upstairs yapping a greeting.

"Here, boy." Lynn scooped the cavalier into her arms. "I'll hate leaving him again," she said, putting him down and taking over the bathroom.

Angie sat and read the papers in the conservatory, while the others breakfasted. Lynn came through when she'd finished in the bathroom.

"Church is at eleven, are you coming?"

Church hadn't figured in Angie's life since she'd left Updean, but she replied, "Why not?"

"Henry's going to Mass when we get back. She's going to stay with Taurus and Muppet while we're out. Pity about the weather, isn't it? Do you still love it here?"

"Yep, rain and all."

The weather didn't merit Sunday best, which was as well, Angie decided as she pulled on a heavy jumper. Dolinda found a couple of berets. Their heads would be covered.

At the foot of a winding avenue of tiny, low-roofed cottages was the sixteenth century village well, intact but no longer operating. At the top was Saint Peter's. They passed through a wicket gate and up a pebbled path to the church doors, in a

69

procession of squelching shoes and dripping umbrellas. The verger greeted them with hymn books.

Inside the aisles were flanked by rows of polished oak pews, each place having a padded velvet hassock. Standing in the chancel, the choir, in royal blue robes with white collars, were preparing to sing. All around were huge, stained glass windows depicting scenes from the Bible.

The congregation of about forty sang vigorously, prayed earnestly, listened intently to the sermon, and left gossiping. From the way they scrutinized her and Lynn, Angie suspected they were the fodder for much of the tongue-wagging.

The heavy rain had given way to a glint of sunshine as they walked back to the farm. Dolinda's idea of Sunday lunch was soup followed by a full roast - beef, Yorkshire pudding, potatoes, Brussels sprouts and carrots - with a sweet of fresh fruit.

"I'm going to starve myself when I get home," Lynn said indicating her waistline. "How on earth do you do it, with the rationing?"

"Most of what we eat is self-produced, or bargained for. For instance I couldn't eat our own hens or rabbits - so I eat my neighbours' and they, in turn, eat ours."

"We do quite well at home compared to some people," Lynn observed. "I put that down to Olga's ability to twist arms. She smiles, pleads ignorance of the language, and gets extra portions."

"I'm convinced Cyril dabbles in the black market," Angie piped in. "There're often slabs of butter, packets of tea and a dozen or so eggs in the kitchen, and once he brought in a box full of bags of sugar. Says it's from grateful customers."

"Show me a man who doesn't get a little on the side." Morton came into the room, chuckling.

Dolinda reprimanded him, "Now none of your innuendos. You don't mean it, anyway. You're as straight as the vicar."

"And who says he doesn't pick up the odd titbit?" Morton turned to the girls. "If you want to get home for the evening, you'll have to move. The wagon's out the front. Have you seen Kevin and Lorne anywhere?"

"They're playing shove half-penny on the table shelter. Did you see the column in the Messenger? The Council are collecting them soon," Dolinda said.

"What, the boys or the table shelter?"

"You know very well what I mean." Dolinda fussed about as the cases were packed in the station wagon. Lynn fondled Taurus, reluctant to leave him, but he struggled to get away and dashed off to romp with Muppet.

"I'll let you know how he's doing from time to time. Take care of yourselves. And Angie, you're not living in foreign parts like these two runaways. Promise you'll come again, soon. I've so enjoyed having you." Dolinda had a hug for all of them.

The drive to the station took them through a country lane. Huge conkers still swelled on the trees and covered the verges.

"There's something about conker collecting," Angie said. "Running through the woods in thick soled wellies and waterproofs, flinging sticks up into the trees and trying to catch the prickly shells as they fall. And then threading them with string and having fights. I had a tenner once."

"What," Henry asked, "is a tenner, other than money?"

Angie explained the rules of conkers. "A tenner," she said," is a conker which has defeated ten other conkers without breaking. It's a champion."

"I'm still not sure I understand," Henry moaned.

"Could we stop and collect a few," Angie begged.

"Right. You can have five minutes. I've some string in the boot. You can teach Henriette how to play when you get back to London. You girls are as bad as the boys sometimes."

They didn't wait till they got home. Finding an empty carriage on the train, they cut the string and dug holes through the centres of their collection with a nail file. The intricacies of conker bashing became clear to Henry. By the time the train drew into Victoria, she was the possessor of a fiver.

Angie felt like a child again. Something she hadn't

experienced since leaving Mrs Crofthouse. She was still inwardly laughing when she arrived at Dryden Terrace. Edwina was in the kitchen.

"Did you have a good time?"

"Yes. Even better than I expected."

"We missed you, Angela."

Edwina clasped Angie's hand, drew it towards her lips and kissed it. Angie stiffened and pulled it away, sharply.

Edwina laughed, "What a funny girl you are, Angela. Can't I show you a little affection? Have you eaten?"

"I've had plenty to eat, thank you." Angie was already climbing the stairs. She locked the door to her room. She wouldn't bother with tea. Dolinda's lunch would suffice.

CHAPTER 7

While Lynn took Henry into the City to tour Harrod's during the day and take in a film in the evening, Angie settled to work in the shop and later seized the chance to catch up with some letter writing.

She found the address of Pat and Sue. Odd how she hadn't written to them before. Somehow it seemed so long ago. They'd still be kids whilst she...

It was a brief letter. Angie discovered she had little to tell them that they'd understand. Lynn and Henry earned a mention but Taurus and the conkers starred.

To Mr Thrift she wrote –

'I am managing well on my earnings and can even save a little. I used some of the extra money you deposited in my bank on clothes as arranged.

To be honest, I don't like living here at Dryden Terrace. I find Cyril obnoxious and Edwina disturbing.

I feel guilty for feeling this way and will stick it out as long as I can because I don't know if I'd survive on my own yet. It's a bit daunting. I will keep in touch.'

Angie was pleased with her choice of words to describe Cyril and Edwina. Exactly right for a lawyer. Mrs Crofthouse was given a full account of the visit to Guildford, with a pictorial description of the food. Letters completed, Angie did some light washing in the bathroom and left it to drip from the towel rail, hoping her new frilly pants wouldn't offend, or excite Edwina, before going to the post box.

Lynn and Henry were first to call at the shop the following

morning. Cyril, who had left the cutting room to match accessories to a suit, scowled when he caught them chatting.

"Angela, you're getting paid to work, not gossip."

"Please, Mr Bolton, just a few minutes," Lynn addressed him in her most sensuous voice and he melted.

"Well..er.. of course, but not long." Cyril retreated and Lynn continued what she'd been saying.

"We're off in the morning. Back at college on Wednesday. Mummy and Daddy are going to Newcastle or somewhere for a conference today and staying a few nights. Olga's agreed we can have a party tonight. Just a few friends. I've asked my cousins Seb - yes, the one - and Owen, they're in London for a few days, Owen's girl friend, Marsha, and Ben Packard - remember Henry's fancy from Chartres's? Ben might bring a friend. I wondered if you'd like to ask your Nick?"

"He's not my Nick," Angie emphasised. "I'll not have a chance to ask him. I don't have his proper address."

"You could phone 'Chartres'." Lynn said. "They'll have it."

The shop bell rang and an elderly gentleman entered. Angie looked across to Jed but his back was turned and he was engaged in counting stock.

"I'll have to leave it to you," she said to Lynn. "I must go."

It was that kind of day. Angie sold two shirts, a pullover, four umbrellas, a dinner suit and a number of black ties. She wondered who had died.

Cyril locked up the shop at five-thirty, and Angie hurried round to Beechwood.

"So what's happening?"

"Drinks and snacks. They're coming at eight. That is, Seb, Jake - the friend - Owen, Ben and Owen's girl friend, Marsha. Nick couldn't make it. I'd to send Olga with a message. He said to remind you about Sunday afternoon. He stays in Park Way. How come he works as a waiter if he can afford a place like that?"

"He's only staying there temporarily. The owner's away."

"Lucky Nick. Ben said he might bring a friend. And you

don't need to dress up."

Angie returned to Dryden Terrace but was back at Beechwood by half-past-seven. She had persuaded Edwina to let her make up some anchovy paste sandwiches and had triangled them neatly. She placed the food on the dining table.

Lynn was cubing cheese and pineapple and Henry was piercing the cubes on to cocktail sticks. Lynn threw the empty pineapple tin into the bin.

"The last one," she said. "From the state of it it's been in the larder for years. The fruit's okay though. I've tried it."

"It was just a little rust," Henry said. "Nothing to worry about."

A car could be heard coming up the drive. Olga rushed through to warn them.

"Aprons off. They've arrived." She hurried out to answer the bell, then disappeared to her own quarters.

"We arranged to come together. One car between us." Ben introduced his army friend.

"This is 7473251, Corporal Jake Harris. He was in my platoon. Captured before he'd time to earn promotion."

"Unlike you, dear boy, I didn't enter through the silver spoon door. No strings to pull in my family."

"Quiet," Ben ordered, "or I'll charge you with insubordination."

Lynn completed the introductions. At around six foot, Jake was some four inches shorter than the willowy Ben, but, if it were possible, he looked even thinner. High cheek bones accentuated the hollows beneath his eyes. It must have been hard in those camps, Angie thought. She observed that when he sat, his left leg shook up and down in a jerky, involuntary movement. He steadied it with his hand.

"Damn nuisance, guess I'll grow out of it," he said as he became aware Angie had noticed.

Angie smiled. "It's of no consequence, my legs kept shaking after I was machine-gunned. I wasn't hit but it took days for it to stop. They're steady enough now."

"Certainly are," Jake eyed them approvingly.

Angie reddened. "I'll fetch you a drink. What would you like?"

"What's on offer?"

"There's a little whisky, two-thirds of a bottle of brandy and dozens of bottles of beer and cider..."

"That's enough for starters."

"I was going to add red and white wine and soft drinks. Now make your choice?"

"I'll settle for a beer. It's what my stomach knows best."

"I'll get that for you," Lynn said, and, having poured it, she made a beeline for the vacant seat beside Jake. She fancies him, Angie thought, which suited her fine. Seb, Angie reckoned, presented a better proposition. Average height, average build and a quiff of thick, dark hair dangling over a pair of engaging eyes. Lynn's eyes. There was no mistaking the likeness. He looked a year or so younger than the other men, and couldn't be much more than twenty two.

"Are you in the forces?" Angie asked, forgetting what Lynn had told her.

"No, I was deferred because of my studies. I'm taking an engineering degree at Manchester. I'll do my stint when I've finished, if they need me. What about you? What do you do with yourself?"

"I'm here under false pretences," Angie indicated the sumptuous lounge. "I'm a working girl." She told Seb about life as an assistant in Cyril Bolton's Tailor's. "We have a great range in spotted ties. I'd recommend the black on yellow."

"Sounds like a blemished banana," Seb quipped. "Talking of bananas...." he leant forward and helped himself to a cocktail stick of pineapple and cheese.

The radiogram was in full swing. Glenn Miller spun on a seventy-eight and Bing Crosby crooned his heart out.

They took partners, Henry resuming her friendship with Ben, Lynn taking on Jake. Marsha, attractive but too horsy to be considered beautiful, nuzzled up to Owen.

Seb danced with both arms round Angie's waist. The deep pile of the lounge carpet fluffed as it hindered their steps. The drink flowed. Angie started with soda water and lime and progressed to vintage cider. She felt happy, relaxed and more than a little tipsy as midnight cukoo-ed.

"I'll have to go. I forgot to leave the window. I'll need to use the main door."

"I'll see you home," Seb offered and Angie was pleased to accept his arm as the chill October air made her reel.

They turned into the entrance of Number 35. Seb put his arms around her and kissed her. A long lingering kiss. She felt a flutter of excitement and her breasts tingled as he caressed them.

"You're very sweet, Angie. Very young and very sweet."

The doors opened and Edwina stood there in her dressing gown, her thin lips taut.

"You're extremely late, Angela," she said pulling Angie's arm and dragging her from Seb. "Goodnight, young man."

"Goodnight." Seb squeezed Angie's hand. "I'll see you."

Angie stumbled into the house and pushing Edwina aside, ran up the stairs. She heard the key turn in the storm doors as she locked herself in her own room.

Angie listened to Edwina's feet climbing the stairs to the landing. They stopped and Edwina knocked on her door.

"Angela, Angela I'd like a word."

Angie said nothing.

"Angela, don't be absurd. I want to talk to you."

Angie remained silent. With the door locked Edwina was powerless to get in.

"You are a very stupid girl. I shall speak to your uncle in the morning."

Not surprisingly, Angie rose late, skipped breakfast and made straight for the shop.

She had expected to have a headache. Instead she felt elated. In this mood she knew she could face Cyril. He called her almost immediately, not into the work room, but to his apartments.

"Someone's in for a wigging," Jed said, as she went towards the door. He gave her the 'thumbs up' signal and she responded with a shrug. In a gesture that Angie now recognised as customary, Cyril's podgy fingers were again drumming the desk. He cleared his throat.

"..Er....Edwina has told me of your misconduct last night. Apparently you came home accompanied by a young man and .em...were ..em....it was well after midnight."

"Henry and Lynn return to Scotland today. There was a party. Seb's her cousin."

"I am aware of that. Lynn was here this morning to see you. I told her you weren't up. She left this note." Cyril handed an envelope to Angie. It was partially opened. "I was.. er.. about to read it as your guardian but changed my mind. I have no idea of its content."

Angie's face was scarlet.

"You had no right to even think of opening it. And you are not my guardian. Mr Thrift is. I'm a paying guest in this house and I hope to leave as soon as ... as soon as I possibly can."

Cyril, too, was deepest pink. "As my brother's child, Angela, I have a responsibility towards you. I hoped that when you came here, we ......"

"I am responsible for myself. There's no need for you to assume ... no need for you to control my life. I'm not a child."

"So it seems, Angela. But I warn you, any further misdemeanours and I shall have to consider speaking to Mr Thrift. I intend to impose a curfew of 10 15pm. You might think you are an adult, but in fact you are very young and vulnerable, and, from the ungrateful way you have just spoken, extremely immature."

"Don't worry. For the short time I hope to remain here, I'll behave, as you put it. But I won't accept your curfew. I must be able to decide for myself."

Angie left the room without giving Cyril the satisfaction of dismissing her.

"Who won?" Jed asked.

"I reckon I got the decision on points.   How's Wendy Elizabeth?"

"Wonderful. Gaining weight already. She's the image of the wife. She's not quite settled into a routine yet. Got us up at half-past-four with wind or some such.   But you don't mind.   Not when you're a father."

"I'd like a daughter, one day."

"Don't be in too big a hurry, I say.   Time enough."

Angie read Lynn's note and was relieved Cyril hadn't opened it.

'I'm writing this in case the pig is trotting about and I can't see you before we leave. We'll be on our way at 8.15 (it's 7.30 now).

We got to bed shortly after Seb came back. Olga let them all stay overnight. They   squeezed into the spare room with cushions and blankets. Marsha had the camp bed in my room. I like her. She's different from Owen's previous girl friends. He usually chooses dumb blondes.

You seemed to hit it off with Seb.   Be warned.   He's a philanderer. I've heard his broken a number of hearts. He's a rascal, but we love him, if you get what I mean.   Do you think we're alike?

Jake was interesting but not really my kind of man. Too thin, for one thing.

Now Fraser...! I think Henry feels the same way about Ben. He's dotty on her, though.   It was a fun night, wasn't it?

Olga was terrific. She's cleaning up and restocking the empties when we leave. I'll arrange to send her flowers. Better still, you do it. I've enclosed five shillings. Choose something nice. I'll write soon. Henry sends love. See you at Christmas. We'll paint the town.'

Angie felt deflated. Lynn, Henry gone. Trust Cyril not to

wake her. And what right had Lynn to criticise Seb? She wasn't exactly an angel. Seb was different. When Nick had held her that day it was a passion arising from fear and despair. Seb had held her because he liked her .'Dear sweet Angela'...his voice gentle, his touch subtle.

Nick was raw. Seb knew how to arouse her. Perhaps that's what Lynn meant. Seb certainly sent her heart racing, but she'd not let it get out of breath. She wouldn't fall head over heels, yet they could have fun. Surely she deserved some fun? To hang. Life was short. The war had taught her that much.

"Angela, the accounts have to be sent out. Check and mail them today."   Cyril's voice was still icy cool. Angie doubted if any one had ever loved him. To think he was her father's brother. How could God make one brother good-looking and loving and the other odious?

The accounts were tiresome and Angie welcomed the walk down the road to post them before tea. She double checked the addresses and stamps as she put them in the box. The last letter, written in her own hand and addressed to Beechwood was a note to Seb. She kissed it, then let it go. Maybe she'd see him again before he went back to Manchester.

High tea was a silent affair. Edwina was in no mood to chat and Cyril was preoccupied with some paper work. At nine-thirty Angie tucked herself into bed and ran over the events of the previous evening. She willed Seb to contact her. The sandman was a long time coming.

CHAPTER 8

For the end of October the weather was mild and clammy and Angie looked apprehensively at the black clouds gathering to the west. Her nerves jingled and she felt uneasy. She hated storms. Nick came to meet her as she turned into Albany Place and they walked to the bench and sat down. Across the road, parked lorries showed work had begun on the bomb site.

"I'm surprised it's taken so long to get started," Angie said.

"This is just one district, remember. It's repeated all over London. Few areas escaped."

"I wonder if they'll put up houses again."

"Flats, more likely. If they're council, I'm going for one."

"You've not been turned out yet?"

"No. They've given us a month to clean up and get out. We'll not fight. After all, it's their place."

"It'll be ages before they rebuild these places. Where will you go?"

"Luigi'll fix me up. He knows so many people. I'll probably get a room with a mama-mia. Did you enjoy your night on the town?"

"It was exciting. I'd never been to a night club before. I didn't really feel as if I belonged, though. I wasn't born into it like Lynn and Henriette."

"So you see yourself scrubbing the floors rather than dining at the tables?"

"No. Not that either. In the middle somewhere. Not rich, not poor. I wish the world was a more equal place."

"My. There speaks a new thinker. So you're a bit of a communist, are you? I'm all for wiping out class distinction. Not that I'm deeply into it."

"The last thing I'm going to do right now is get involved in politics. I'm too young. I'm just beginning to live and mixing with the rich is part of the learning process. And it's fun. I've got some money of my own, you know."

"I can see that from the way you dress. Gives you confidence to have a pound or two in the bank. I save when I can. I've had to start from scratch, but I'm getting there."

"If I need anything now, it's people," Angie said. "People to talk to. To confide in. People I can trust, love even. Everyone in my life at the moment is new."

"Even me, I suppose?"

"Well, yes, sort of. But you're my link with the past. You knew my parents, knew where I lived, although you were too old to be my friend then. You understand."

"Right, Angie. I'll be your ears." He took her hand. "We'll be close even if we're miles apart. I don't mean like that clinch the other week. That was for the moment. You felt that, too?"

Angie nodded, "I knew why you did it. Why I let you."

"Settled then. No romance for the time being. Just good pals, as they say. I can't replace your family, but I'll be around. I need someone, too. Let's meet here the last Friday of every month?"

"You're on."

A huge clap of thunder, followed seconds later by a flash of lightening. Angie buried her head in Nick's shoulder.

"No romance, remember," Nick said grabbing her hand and running towards the nearest shops. "Let's get something to eat." He looked in his wallet, "And browse round the library."

"We'll go Dutch. That way we can afford the cinema."

Edwina was nowhere in sight when Angie slipped into the house minutes before ten-thirty. Cyril nodded approval from the kitchen door.

"Goodnight, Angela," he squeaked.

"Goodnight, Uncle Cyril."

The brief exchange marked a truce. She closed her bedroom curtains. The storm had abated long ago, leaving a clear, cool night. Angie heard Edwina on the stairway an hour later and guessed she'd been visiting Alice. The gurgling of the water tank told her Edwina was having a late bath.

The promise of the previous night was fulfilled as a cool, clear, sky dawned.

A letter in an unfamiliar hand landed in the hall with the morning post. As Angie slit open the envelope, Seb's name crossed her mind to be instantly dismissed. It was too soon for a reply to her letter. But Angie was wrong.

"Sweet Angel," it began, *"I dropped in on Olga and she gave me your letter. It's the first time I've been thanked for having fun. It wasn't me that made the party work. It was you.*

You don't need to apologise for someone else's rudeness. If you can escape the ogress meet me tomorrow, Tuesday, outside the tennis courts. I've a game on in the afternoon and will eat in the clubhouse. If you don't turn up, I'll presume you have a prior commitment or something.

Do try to be there. I leave for Manchester in a few days.

Love Seb. xxxxx"

So the other night had meant something to him. He did want to see her again. She swallowed her tea and toast and almost danced into the shop.

"Someone's in a good mood," Jed observed, "You haven't stopped smiling since you came in. Look, that shirt's upside down. You must be in love."

Love, Angie thought, was not the word. Infatuated, yes. Love was for the future. A long time in the future.

"Wendy Elizabeth's got a sniffle. Nothing serious, but she's not sleeping well."

"Poor little thing. I'm sorry."

"She's lively enough, kicking her legs and splashing her arms about in the bath. I did 'This Little Piggy' on her toes last night."

"Jed, you're besotted," Angie laughed.

"Guess I am. Give us a hand with these bales. They've to go on the top shelf."

* * *

Angie walked to the tennis courts after tea. She arrived well before seven and there was no sign of Seb. She could see people moving about in the brightly lit clubhouse. The street was dark and a glaze of frost was forming on the pavement. By the time Seb came out at a quarter-past-seven she was frozen.

"Sorry I kept you. I got talking and the time vanished." He lifted her face and kissed her lips. Angie could smell drink.

"You're shivering," he said, "Let's not hang around. I'm staying at Beechwood tonight. We'll go there."

"Are Sylvie and Gideon back?"

"Not till tomorrow. Olga's gone to see a sick friend. I'm house sitting."

They walked, arms entwined, to Beechwood. The house was in darkness.

"Are you sure they'll not mind my being here when they're away?"

"I can't think of a better time. We'll have the place to ourselves."

They went in. Seb poked the lounge fire into life and added some coals. He closed the brocade curtains and took Angie in his arms. She felt herself warm as he held her in the light of the flames. His touch made her quiver. His voice reassured. He guided her towards the couch and they flopped on to it.

"We'll crush the cushions," Angie said, breaking free from his clasp and standing up.

"You are funny. You didn't worry about them at the party."

"Lynn was here."

"Come and sit at my feet."

Angie lowered herself to the carpet and let her head rest against Seb's knees. He stroked her hair.

"So what have you been doing since I saw you last?"

"Working."

"Nothing else?"

"Not really." She wasn't going to tell Seb about Nick. "And you?"

"Meeting up with old friends. Last night I hit the town with some mates, was a bit the worse, so kipped down on the floor of one of their flats. Tom's a great guy. Maybe you'll meet him one day. He keeps tropical fish. The tank filter system buzzed all night. Like sleeping in a beehive. Despite the drink, I couldn't sleep for ages, but once I fell over I didn't surface till lunch."

Seb leant forward to kiss Angie's forehead and let his hands slide down to the buttons of her blouse. He undid the top two before she stopped him.

"Let's put the radio on."

"What the blazes do we need with a radio?" Seb's hand slid inside the blouse and fondled her breast.

"Don't rush me." Angie begged.

Seb straightened up.

"I promise, Angie. Sweet sixteen and never been...."

He didn't finish. Angie wondered what he'd been going to say. Not kissed anyway.

"Let's put the kettle on." She jumped to her feet. Seb stood up and drew her close to him.

"Let's put the radio on....Let's put the kettle on," he mocked. "Is that why you came here with me?"

Angie knew it wasn't. She wanted to feel Seb's lips against hers, to sense the nearness of his body.

His hands caressed her breasts, ran up and down her thighs. She found herself responding. Her own hands skimming his hips, defining their bony structure.

"You're so very, very sweet, Angel," Seb repeated. He pulled her gently to the carpet. Her whole body tingled. She didn't want it to be like this, but she knew she didn't want it to stop. Knew she couldn't, wouldn't, resist what was happening. She felt a sharp pain as their bodies fused.

"It's alright, Angel. It's alright."

Seb was stroking her hair, kissing her lips, her neck, her

shoulders, whispering reassurance. And then it was over. He turned on to his back and laughed and she was laughing with him.

"That," he said, "was magic."

It had been magic for Angie, too. She started to cry.

"I'm fine. Honestly I am," she said between sobs. "I'm so happy." She clung to Seb.

"Hey, let's get washed up," he said and, picking up her discarded clothes, Angie followed Seb into the bathroom.

Seb was first back into the lounge.

"Bring a cleaning cloth with you, Angie. Your virginity's splattered the carpet."

Seb rubbed at the spots of blood until they were scarcely visible. Like murderers cleaning up after a crime, Angie thought.

She recalled the start of her periods. Blood had trickled down her legs and on to Mrs Crofthouse's rug. She had screamed in horror.

"Don't worry, dear. It's just growing up. I'd been meaning to have a chat." And Mrs Crofthouse had taken her upstairs and given her a talk on the functions of the body. "I'd have told you sooner, but I thought the school did all that."

It did in a way. Whisperings in the playground which she hadn't always understood. It was like a club. Once your periods had started you could join. The rest of her sex education was gleaned from the girls and the writings in the toilets. But it couldn't describe the pain and the ecstasy. Nor the wonderful sense of belonging together. With Seb no longer inside her, she felt strangely empty and cold.

Seb noticed when he got up from his knees. "You're shivering," he said. "We'll put that kettle on now, and the radio."

They sat resting against the untouchable cushions, drinking hot chocolate.

"See me home, Seb?" Angie said when the drinks were finished.

"Your wish is my command, sweet Angel."

They said goodnight before reaching the house. Angie slipped inside unnoticed and went straight to her room.

From her window, she searched for stars but they were hidden behind a mass of clouds. .

The following morning, if Angie had any regret about the events of the previous night, it was that her mother, in particular, would have been furious.

"If there's a heaven," she said to herself, "I hope she wasn't looking."

Given a chance, she decided her dad might have understood. It was hard to believe in heaven and hell. Angie guessed she believed in God. Why else did she turn to him with prayers when things were going wrong? But a heaven with angels and a hell with devils? She hoped she'd meet everyone again, but didn't bank on it.

She supposed she'd sinned with Seb. It hadn't seemed wrong. In fact it had been so right at the time. Warm and secure. Would she be condemned for it? Surely God would understand and forgive her? Didn't he say as much in the Bible? "Suffer the sinners"...or something? Angie couldn't promise not to sin again. She was sure she would, often. Life would be so dull if you had to be good all the time. What would Lynn say if she found out? Angie had a feeling she'd be far from delighted. She vowed not to tell her.

Edwina appeared particularly happy at breakfast. Her thin lips parted into a smile.

"It's Alice's birthday. I'm having a day off. We're going to the West End to the ballet, then on for a meal. Don't worry about the light. We'll be late back so I'm staying overnight at Alice's."

Angie added some of Edwina's duties to her work in the shop and was glad to be busy. She heard nothing from Seb in the next few days, but he was scarcely out of her thoughts. She guessed he'd be back in Manchester. Two hundred miles was a long way. He probably had a dozen girl friends there. She willed him to write.

The next letter to arrive for Angela, however, came from Lynn and contained an invitation.

"I'm going to spend Christmas and New Year with Henry and her grandmother in Glasgow. You're invited too. You've just got to come. Imagine it. Christmas together - the three of us - all that Beaujolais.

We're having a ball here at Lochend. The men in Scotland are something special Don't believe all you've heard Glasgow's an okay place if you know where to go - or where not to. Fraser has competition in the form of Curtis.

I've been studying quite hard as well and have taken up Art. You will be impressed with my figure drawings, but it's the landscapes that earn the most praise. The countryside's so beautiful here. Maybe I'll be Lynnette Arnold and make millions of pounds when I'm dead.

Let us know soon if you're joining us, so we can make plans."

"Scotland?" Cyril choked when Angie told him about the invitation.

"Scotland? " Edwina echoed.

"I've been invited by Henriette's grandmother, she's a Countess."

Cyril jumped to his feet at the mention of the title.

"A Countess? Well, well. I'll make enquiries for you this morning. Mr Thrift will fix everything. A Countess ..."

Cyril, Angie realised, was all of a dither. It was something to boast about at the card table. Little Angela was turning up trumps.

Angie herself was two-minded about the invitation. She would go, of course. Christmas without Lynn would be unbearable, but what if Seb were to be in London? How disappointed he'd be if she were away. Angie decided she would go but would return before New Year. If Seb were around she could see him then.

Cyril fussed about Angie at lunch time.

"Everything's moving. Thrift's a competent man. He's placing a further £50 into your bank account. That's in addition to settling your fares. It's a lot of money, Angela. I hope you use it wisely. You're a very fortunate girl."

Angie knew this to be true. She wondered what Nick would say if he knew. So much to spend as she pleased. She determined to take him out for a really slap up meal when they met again on Friday week.

Once Angie really believed she was going to Scotland, panic took over. What would she wear? What should she take as a present to Henriette's grandmother? She decided on a new day dress, and because it was the festive season, another party frock. She found both in the little second hand shop where she'd bought things previously. The simple wool dress in navy blue was sophisticated enough to make her feel elegant. The pink taffeta party gown was fun.

In a nearby drapers, she found Grandmother's present - a silver coloured box containing a single handkerchief, exquisitely laced and pinned to a satin cushion. For Lynn and Henry she chose identical tiny glass slippers.

"They're utterly useless," she said to the sales girl, "But I'm sure they'll love them."

"I know what you mean," the girl replied. "That's their charm."

She took them home in layers of tissue and wrapped them in paper strewn with holly and Christmas bells. In four weeks she'd be handing them over to Lynn and Henriette, or placing them under the tree. That was assuming they had Christmas trees in Scotland. She'd heard they celebrated New Year.

Angie met Nick again as arranged. Same time, same bench. Snow had fallen in the night to form a thin white cover on the grass. The pavements had turned to a dirty slush.

"I wondered if you'd show," Nick said.

"I'm a girl of my word." She looked across the road to

where the lorries were still parked. "It's almost clear. They'll begin building soon. I wonder how many of my toys are shattered among the foundations."

"Or human bones under the floorboards. The place will never be the same, will it? They can't bring it back from the dead. Now it's clear, it's like a final burial."

"But life has to go on. When the houses are up and new people move in it'll be like a resurrection."

They stood in silence for a while. Angie again pictured the bomb site as it had been. Heard the children in the street, their mothers calling to them. Heard Mrs Fairweather's sweets tumbling from the jars into the scales, scooshing into brown paper bags. She felt her lungs swell as she remembered blowing into the empty bags and bursting them in a clap of her hands. A big bang. A big bang and it was gone. Everything gone.

Nick broke the silence.

"What'll we do Angie? It's too cold to hang around."

"Let's go to Fern Hill. We often went there on days like this. Perhaps the snow was a bit thicker."

"I'd an old metal tray. Badly battered, it was, but it went faster than the rest. Overshot the ditch at the bottom and right on to the road. A bus screeched as it swerved to avoid hitting me. I got the fright of my life and scarpered home. I was as white as the snow. My mother put me to bed, thinking I was sick."

Fern Hill ran parallel to Brayne Hill. From the top Angie and Nick surveyed the area around them.

"It doesn't look so different," Angie observed. "You can still pick things out."

"You left after that machine gunning, didn't you? When the kid was killed? Mum wanted my younger brothers to go, too. They made such a fuss. Didn't want to be split up. They'd probably be around now if they hadn't created."

"Mm. Life's full of 'ifs'."

"Shall we go down via Brayne Hill?"

They walked within yards of the spot where Shirley had been killed and Angie pointed out the house where she'd sheltered. A crowd was gathered at the foot of the Hill.

"What's up?" Nick asked the nearest man.

"Found an unexploded bomb the other day. An incendiary. Defused now. Say it's the biggest to fall round 'ere. There was dozens 'it this bit. Huge craters everywhere. Thing is, they used to let you walk across the 'oles on planks. Charged a penny for the war effort. To think I walked over those craters and that bloody thing was waiting to blow us all up."

War was still there, Angie thought. Peace might be declared but that couldn't wipe it out.

"We'll go to the cafe and on to the Tivoli," Nick said," I've done well for tips this week."

"No, Nick. I'm taking you to Orlando's. I've something to celebrate."

"Hey. What's that, then?"

"No questions. I'll tell you later."

They sat at a corner table spooning minestrone soup and forking spaghetti Bolognese.

"I'll need to get used to this Italian food." Nick said. "I'm leaving the squat for a room at Mrs Larante's, in Daisy Street. Luigi's fixed it. I'll be glad to go. There's been a lot of muck flung between us and the owners. Corey and Joan are holding out a bit longer. There's a chance they'll get a prefab. Joan's pregnant. Here, write this down somewhere."

Nick searched his pockets for a piece of paper, found none, and handed Angie his napkin and a pencil. He dictated his new address and Angie copied it.

"It's a pretty name...Daisy Street."

"It's not so pretty a place. Grey, with worn stone steps and in need of some paint. Inside it's warm and comfortable. Mrs Larante's had a tough time lately. Treated as an alien even though born and bred here. She's a gem."

"Well, I'm glad you're settled. I worried about you in that squat. It didn't seem right."

"Right, wrong. Who's to judge? Forget that and tell me why we're celebrating."

"I'm going to Scotland for Christmas to stay with Lynn and Henriette. Henriette's grandmother lives near Glasgow. She's very rich."

"You do mix your worlds, Angie. Guess you'll have a fabulous time. While I'm slaving in Chartres."

"We'll meet up when I get back. Say the first Friday of the New Year?"

"Why not? It's a date. I'll treat you next time."

CHAPTER 9

Angie added a wool coat to her purchases for the Glasgow trip as the weather remained cold. A letter from Lynn confirmed the arrangements.

'I've so much to tell you. I'm having the best time of my life. See you next week.'

Mr Thrift called with the rail tickets and hoped she'd enjoy her stay. Angie took her case from under the bed. Just two more days.

She had heard nothing from Seb other than a scribbled card telling her he was *'bogged down'* with study and *'the degree year was the toughest.'* Surely, Angie thought, he had some free time. If he cared he'd have written.

Cyril and Edwina were both out when the doorbell rang at about eight o'clock that evening. Angie left her packing and hurried downstairs to answer it.

Sylvie Arnold stood on the doorstep. Her face ashen against the black of her dress, a green jacket slung carelessly over her shoulders.

"Mrs Arnold, what is it? Something's happened."

Sylvie struggled to find her voice. "Can I come in, Angela?"

She didn't look capable of climbing the stairs. Angie led her into the sitting room. She could see Sylvie was shaking, yet she refused a chair.

"I can't stay. I had to come to tell you myself." Her hands gripped the edge of the table. "It's Lynn. There's been an accident."

"Lynn? Is she hurt."

Sylvie said nothing. She was staring down at the lace cloth and swayed as if she might faint.

Angie grabbed hold of her. "What is it? What...?"

A torrent of tears streamed down Sylvie's cheeks. She slumped into a chair.

"I'm so sorry, Angie. I'm so sorry."

"Lynn? She's not ..?"

Sylvie nodded.

"But she can't be. We're going to Glasgow....We're going to Glasgow. It's not possible she's ..."

She was going to say she's so much alive. But she knew from Sylvie's face that she wasn't. Lynn dead. Angie felt numb. Almost as if she, too, were dead. She was aware of Sylvie sobbing uncontrollably. She sat on the arm of her chair. Angie would never have dreamed of comforting Sylvie Arnold, with the sleek hair and designer clothes, but this Sylvie was different. A mother who had lost her child. And that child was Lynn. Her Lynn. Angie drew Sylvie towards her and together they wept until there were no more tears to be shed.

"I'll make some tea," Angie said. "We both need it." She tried hard to sound composed. Sylvie, too, made an effort.

"She was with Henriette in the car. It went out of control and hit a tree."

"And Henry? Is she ..."

"Henriette's in hospital. It's bad. Her legs, I understand, and her back. The police came and Henriette's grandmother phoned. She's in Ayr. We're going to Lochend in the morning."

"Can I come?"

"No, Angela. There's no point. They wouldn't let you see her."

Angie took Sylvie's hand.

"I don't know what to say."

"You don't have to say anything. I know you care." Sylvie picked up the jacket that had slipped from her shoulders to the floor. "I'll have to go. Gideon will be home soon. He was at a meeting when the police told him. He'll be devastated. He'll need me."

"I'll walk back with you."

"I don't think so."

Angie could see Sylvie's legs were still shaking.

"I want to. I need some air." Angie grabbed her raincoat from the cloakroom.

She walked with Sylvie to the door of Beechwood. Olga was standing in the porch and helped Sylvie into the house.

"Will you be alright?" Sylvie asked Angie.

"Yes the air's doing me good."

Angie walked back to Dryden Terrace. She looked up into the clear sky. "I'm with you Lynn. I'll always be with you." The tears flowed again as she stumbled through the door and up the stairs. Edwina was on the landing and heard her coming.

"Angela is that you. Where have you been? You've left dirty cups in the sitting room and lights on all over the house. I suggest you go and....whatever's the matter?"

It poured out and Edwina was there moving the half packed suitcase, tucking her into bed.

"I'll make more tea," and despite Angie's protests, Edwina went down to the kitchen and was back minutes later with a steaming pot and the best china.

"Tea tastes so much better from fine bone," she said. She had brought a bottle of aspirin tablets. "Now, two of these will help you sleep. I'll stay with you."

Angie took the tea and the tablets, turned her head into the pillows, and wished the nightmare would end. She could see the blankets vibrating and realised she was shaking all over. The more she tried to stop, the more she shook.

Edwina returned from taking the dishes downstairs. Angie heard the rustle of pages as the housekeeper settled in a chair to read. She heard Cyril enter the house and the lock turn. She lay for what seemed like hours without sleeping, watching the shadow cast on the wall by the table lamp.

Angie sensed, rather than heard, Edwina get up from the chair and lean over her. Then she heard her shuffle into the bathroom. Angie fidgeted in the bed. She was no longer trembling. She had to sleep. Exhausted she closed her eyes and began to count sheep.

Angie had no idea when Edwina came back. It could have been minutes or hours. She felt the covers on her bed lift and Edwina slip in beside her. Angie jumped, curling hard to the wall.

"It's all right, Angela, all right." Edwina's arms were round her, drawing her close. "It's all right," she repeated.

Seb had said that over and over again, but she had wanted his touch. In Edwina's embrace she froze. She tried to shout. At first, there was no sound, then came a loud, persistent scream.

Cyril bounded up the stairs and flung open Angie's door. He was completely out of puff. He flicked on the light.

"Angela, what's all this noise?" he demanded. "Edwina...." Cyril's voice registered surprise as he took in the scene. Edwina's legs were half in, half out of Angie's bed.

 Angie was sitting bolt upright, her knees tucked under her chin.

"It's not what it seems, Cyril. Angela's had a terrible shock. You must have read my note. I was comforting her and she started screaming."

"She was holding me in her arms. Pressing her body against mine."

"Angela," Edwina sounded indignant, "Don't be so ridiculous."

Cyril listened to the whole story.

"Edwina you may have meant well, but ..."

"She didn't," Angie cried. "She saw a chance and took it. She's tried to get close to me before. I've sensed it. It was only a matter of time."

"Calm down, Angela." Cyril implored. "You're distraught. We must all get some sleep. Edwina go to your own room."

Edwina picked up her book and left, still muttering how absurd it all was. Cyril turned to Angie.

"I won't expect you in the shop first thing. You can rest until lunch."

He left the room switching out the light and closing the door. Not a word about Lynn. Not a sign of regret. The grieving could last till lunch time. Cyril had given her that much grace.

The time was one o'clock. By two, Angie knew she wouldn't be unpacking her suit-case. Knew she couldn't spend another night at Dryden Terrace. By three, she was, at last, asleep.

Angie awoke around nine. Sleep had done little to ease her physically or mentally. Her head throbbed, her mouth felt dry, but she knew if she could keep her emotion under control she could cope.

Angie was surprised how much she had accumulated in just six months. That's all the time it had been, yet she had changed a lot. Lost weight, gained height. Left school, started work. Met Lynn and Nick and Seb. Now Lynn had gone and, probably, Seb. So short a time. So much done, so much that would never be done.

Angie took an aspirin from Edwina's bottle and doubted if it would help. There was no time to buy another suitcase. She filled two carrier bags. She checked the wardrobe drawers and shelves. Nothing was left. This time she would leave no prune stones, no hidden signatures.

Angie placed the bags by the door and went down for breakfast. Once in the kitchen, she realised she couldn't eat. Later perhaps, she would have to. She walked through to the shop. Jed gave her a hug.

"I've heard about your friend. You're not fit to be in."

"I'm not here to work, Jed, I'm leaving. Came to say 'cheerio'. Don't let him work you too hard."

Jed didn't ask questions.

"I'll miss you. Take care," he said simply.

Cyril was in the workshop.

"I didn't expect you down, yet. Better to keep busy. There's a new order of Harris Tweed arriving at eleven. Would you log it?"

"I won't be here at eleven. I came to tell you I'm leaving."

"Leaving?"

"That's right. Thank you for letting me stay and for the job."

"But you can't. If it's because of Edwina, I promise to talk to her this evening. There'll be no repeat..."

"I've made up my mind. I'm going."

"But Mr Thrift..."

"I'll contact him."

"Where will you go?"

Angie hesitated. She had reached this stage with no clear idea.

"I'll let you know as soon as I'm settled." She conceded that Cyril was her only close relative.

"Angela, you've had a shock. You must give yourself time to get over it. Take a week off, if you need it."

"There's no point. I'm leaving and I'm going right now." Angie turned to face the door.

Cyril stepped forward. He grabbed her hand, and she had to fight back a shudder at the slug-like touch.

"But what will I do? The shop?"

Angie freed herself from his grasp.

"That," she said, "you will have to work out for yourself."

She carried her case and the bags from the house and walked down the terrace. She was relieved to have escaped without encountering Edwina. She paused at the corner of the road. Where now? She set off in the direction of Beechwood. Olga answered her ring and stared in surprise at her luggage.

"May I leave these here for a minute. I'd like to see Gideon and Sylvie, if that's possible?"

"I'll tell them." And having shown Angie into the lounge, Olga went in search of Lynn's parents. The room looked and felt stone cold.

Sylvie came through on Gideon's arm. Her hair was in place, her dress immaculate and her face bright with too much make-up, only her eyes told the truth. Gideon had aged. He looked very grey.

"How are you?" Sylvie kissed Angie lightly, and there was warmth in her welcome. Gideon said nothing.

"I'm sorry to intrude. I came to tell you I've left Dryden Terrace. It has nothing to do with Lynn."

"But where are you going? I would invite you to stay here but we ..."

"I'm staying with friends. I'll ring you later to find out what's happening."

"We're travelling north this morning and we'll return some time tomorrow with Lynn, if possible.

"I'll probably ring you tomorrow night then, if that's alright?"

Sylvie nodded. Angie turned to go.

"Look after each other."

She saw Gideon's arm tighten against Sylvie, but it was his wife who answered.

"We will."

Back in the street, Angie wondered what she should do. She thought of Nick. "I'll be around if you need me," he'd said. My God, she needed him now.

Nick wasn't in when Angie reached Daisy Street, Mrs Larante regretted.

"He'll be along in a minute. He has gone for the papers. " She spoke in a clear voice which, despite the careful diction, hinted strongly of her Italian background. "Come in, dear."

She took Angie's case and placed it in the narrow hallway. Angie rested the carriers beside it. There was just enough room to squeeze past. The Larantes' dining - kitchen offered little space. Amid a glitter of Christmas decorations, a baby with dark, curly hair gurgled in a high chair, his mouth clowned in a white paste. Two little girls stopped eating their cereal and peered through black lashes at Angie. An older boy stood at his mother's prompting and offered her a seat.

Mrs Larantes poured coffee from a large jug and pushed a cup into Angie's hand.

"Nick should be two minutes. That's all."

"I'm Angie Bolton. I'm a friend of Nick's - since childhood."

A rustle at the front door and Nick appeared with the papers and two bottles of milk.

"Angie," he exclaimed. "What brings you here?" Before Angie had time to tell him he added, "It's that story isn't it? The one in the papers. I wondered if it was your Lynn when I read it as I walked down the street. I daren't believe it."

"It's true, I'm afraid."

"Go upstairs, second floor, first right. Door's unlocked. I'll be with you in a sec."

Angie found Nick's room. There was a small bed, a chair, a wash-hand basin and boxes still unpacked on the floor. Nick came in.

"Felt I owed Gina an explanation. She's bringing more coffee and her favourite fruit loaf." He put his arms round Angela. "It must be hell for you, Angie."

"I'm okay. I ache all over. I came because of what we said - that we'd be there for each other. I needed someone."

"Thanks for coming to me." He kissed her gently. "Poor Angie. Life keeps dealing out the dud cards."

"I didn't come for sympathy. Understanding - yes. I came to tell you I've left Dryden Terrace."

"Left? Is that wise? Haven't you enough on your plate just now? Where are you going?" The questions came in quick succession. Angie was about to tackle them, when realisation hit Nick. "That suitcase in the hall. It's yours, isn't it? There's not much room here but maybe I could fix a night or two for you."

"Don't be daft, Nick. I don't want to stay. I wanted you to know, that's all."

The coffee arrived on a tray covered in Mrs Larente's best

lace. Nick explained Angie's visit.

"If I can help, dear..."   Her voice held genuine sympathy.

Angie said, "You're all so nice, but I'm working this out my way. I'm going to see my guardian."

"Would you like me to go with you?"

"No thanks, Nick. I'll let you know when I'm settled."

"And the Friday after New Year?"

"I'll be there, I promise."

"Have some of the loaf."

"I can't. I'm sorry. Don't feel like anything."

CHAPTER 10

Mr Thrift listened as Angie recounted the events of the past two days.

"I'm so sorry about Lynn. It can't be easy for you, Angie. As for Miss Ferrie, is it possible you could have misunderstood?"

"Absolutely not."

"Have you any plans for Christmas now that you won't be travelling to Glasgow?"

Angie had forgotten about Christmas.

"I'll find a hotel."

"Surely there's somewhere you can stay other than a hotel, Angela."

"I know so few people. I could go to Mrs Crofthouse, perhaps."

"Would you like me to find out?"

"I don't think so. I'd just feel a nuisance, and I'm a different person now. No, I'd rather you didn't."

"And there's no-one else? In that case, I'll ring Grace. We've a spare room."

"Please don't, Mr Thrift."

"Well, you're not spending Christmas alone. It's unthinkable, particularly in view of what's happened."

"There's Dolinda. She's Lynn's aunt by marriage. We stayed with her a few weeks ago and loved it. She said I was to come any time but it might not suit now."

"We'll soon find out. Do you have a number? Don't worry, I'll explain the circumstances, but I guess she'll know about the accident."

Dolinda was happy to have Angie. "Such a charming girl

and particularly welcome now."

Closing his office at lunch time, Dillard Thrift drove Angie to Guildford.

Dolinda welcomed them at the door and insisted on serving afternoon tea with home baked scones before the lawyer left on the return journey. In the comfort of Dolinda's home Angie discovered eating wasn't so difficult. Dolinda turned her attention solely to Angela.

"I'm so glad you asked to come here. Morton can't talk about the accident. He was very fond of Lynn. We all were. And seeing her so recently..." she dabbed at her eyes and Angie felt her own tears welling up. "There, I'm upsetting you." Dolinda began tidying the dishes. "It's best to keep busy and there's so much to do. We'd made plans, you know. A lunch party on Christmas Day. I don't know how I'll cope. Now you're here, Angie, if you're up to it, I could do with a hand."

"I can't think of anything I'd rather do," Angie said truthfully. She had felt better the minute she'd stepped into the house. She followed Dolinda to the kitchen. Mince pies lay cooling on wire trays. White bowls filled with Christmas pudding and covered in grease-proof paper sat beside them.

"We'll put the string round the pudding covers first. Put your finger here while I tie the knot."

"Where are the boys? And Taurus and Muppet?"

"They've been staying with the Oxenby's two farms away. Four children and innumerable pets. The dogs were invited, too. They were due back yesterday, but we'd had the news and with the shock and everything, they stayed on till tonight. They'll be late, I think. Martha's taking them to the Panto'. It will give us a chance. The stockings have to be filled tomorrow night. We still keep it up although they've known about Santa for years."

Angie closed her eyes as she listened to Dolinda. Lynn would have chosen a better time to die if there'd been a choice.

"And there's last minute shopping," Dolinda continued. "It's such fun normally. Well, we'll do our best, won't we? Life has

103

to go on."

* * *

Angie browsed round while Dolinda finished her Christmas shopping. She realised she had no presents to give Morton, Dolinda or the boys. Hurriedly she chose a tobacco pouch and a jig-saw but had found nothing for Dolinda by the time Lynn's aunt appeared laden with parcels. Angie took some of them from her.

"I'm absolutely hopeless," Dolinda sighed. "Every year I promise myself I'll shop early and avoid the rush. But somehow it's part of Christmas. Watch that brown box. It's breakable." She paused to glance round. "With a bit of luck, I've got everything. Let's go to Lacey's for a cup of tea. I'm dying of thirst."

Morton was pulling off his Wellington boots when they arrived home.

"So there you are. Thought you'd got lost. That's it for today. Reckon there's snow on the way. I've fixed up the lads to take over the essentials for the next couple of days. I'm on holiday."

"I'll believe that when I see it." Dolinda said. "You'll be up as usual in the morning to check they're coping. And you can't put your feet up until you've fixed the tree lights, and we'll need more logs from the shed."

Angie watched Morton and Dolinda potter about the room finalising the preparations, the way they looked at each other, their gentle banter. She hoped she'd find happiness like that. Security and love based on a firm friendship. She helped Dolinda in the kitchen, peeling and washing the vegetables for the Christmas lunch.

"There're the Westerton's, Rob, Nancy and their daughter Claire. She's ages with Lynn. Was that is. She's a bit of a madam. Used to getting her own way. My cousins, Jack and Edith, my friend Bernice, we call her Bungie, and her two, Andy and Marie. Fergus was in the Guards. He didn't make it." Dolinda clapped the lid on the potato pot. "We wanted to cancel everything when we heard about the accident, but we've the boys to consider and it was all so near. It's not that we don't care. You know that. I tell myself I'm doing all this for Lynn. She'd have wanted us to carry on. It's so awful. Such a waste." Dolinda sat on the kitchen chair and buried her head in her apron. It was Angie's turn to supply the comfort.

"You're right, Dolinda. Lynn wouldn't want us to be miserable. We talked sometimes about death. She always said life was for the living. Maybe Lynn's the lucky one. Henry's very badly hurt. Sylvie says she'll be in a wheel-chair for months - perhaps for ever"

"I know, I know. Lynn would have hated that."

"And don't worry about me. We're all here together."

"That's one of the things that does worry me. So many of us. If you find us too noisy, Angie, you can go upstairs. It won't be a quiet Christmas. You were meant to join Lynn, weren't you? You must feel dreadful?"

"I'll be fine," Angie reassured her. "I'll get an early night, though. I am tired."

She slept in the room she had shared with Lynn and Henry, cosseted in striped flannel sheets. Dryden Terrace seemed an age away.

Angie woke early, the promised snow of the night before had turned to rain. She heard it beating against the roof tiles. Appropriate as there were tears this Christmas Day. Angie wondered what it was like in Glasgow. She still felt tired but knew she wouldn't sleep any more. Downstairs she found Dolinda placing presents under the tree.

"Merry Christmas, Angela." Dolinda kissed her on the cheek. "Morton's till snoring. It's his first real sleep since...What would you like to eat?"

"I haven't much of an appetite."

"Toast and tea, then - at the fire. But you've to eat some lunch or I'll be offended."

Angie agreed. She'd manage something. Morton joined them before they'd started breakfast.

"It's nice to have a few minutes to ourselves prior to the invasion. What's happened to Kevin and Lorne?"

"They were up at five. I persuaded them to go back to sleep after about an hour."

"Have you organised the presents?"

"They're under the tree."

"We have a ritual, Angela. All the family gifts are placed beneath the Christmas tree. We don't open them until after lunch. Another dozen pairs of socks, I expect."

"Don't go on so. You know you love it, and the socks." Dolinda kissed the top of her husband's head.

Morton was sitting in his favourite chair close to the fire and turned the toast on the end of a long fork. Angie took a slice, buttered it and was surprised to find she wanted a second slice. The peace was shattered as the boys bounded into the lounge followed by Taurus and Muppet.

"Look what I got in my stocking?" Lorne held a large box in the air.

"That's nothing. I've got four racing cars."

"Take your toys through to the conservatory. Lay out the train set, if you like. I'll bring your breakfast through. Will toasted cheese do?"

Taurus sniffed round Angie's legs, wagging his tail.

"He knows you all right, Angie," Morton said.

He's looking for Lynn, Angie thought, as Taurus explored every nook of the lounge before coming back to nuzzle against her knee. How do you tell a dog his mistress has died?

"Bungie and her two will arrive first," Morton predicted. "I'm going to do magic tricks."

"He's a wizard in disguise," Dolinda added. "He's quite good at it. You're in for a treat."

"How about you, Angie? Are there any party pieces up your sleeve?" Morton asked.

"Sorry, I can't sing a note in tune or do anything the least bit entertaining."

"You can join in the band then - combs and tissue paper and

Rob Westerton's accordion. We can't escape that."

"Andy's bringing his drum kit. Bungie says he's been practising for weeks." Dolinda sighed.

"What with that and Nancy's rendering of Noel, we'll put on a better show than the Gaiety."

"Ah well, let's clear up and set the table. Time I was organised."

"I've a small present for you and the boys but nothing for the other children," Angie confided to Dolinda when the last cracker was in place.

"Don't let that worry you, dear. I've some packets of sweets I've managed to save in the kitchen. You can give them those."

Angie took the sweets to her room when she went up to get ready for the guests. Her tummy, which had been churning over and over since Lynn's death, had settled after she'd eaten the toast. She went to her case to take out wrapping paper and saw the two tiny parcels containing the crystal slippers at the top.

She considered for a second giving Lynn's to Dolinda, but she knew she could never part with it. Henry would get hers soon. The third parcel - the exquisite lace hankie intended for the Countess, she had already decided would be for Dolinda.

Angie wrote a tag and substituted it for the one she'd already written. She wrapped the tobacco pouch and the jigsaw and tied a red ribbon round the parcel of sweets. To wear, she chose her dark navy, adding sparkle with a silver belt and necklace.

"Could I make two phone calls?" she asked Morton as they came downstairs together. "I'll leave the money. One's to Scotland."

"There's no need for that, go ahead. Better hurry before the mob descends on us."

Angie's first call was to Beechwood and Sylvie Arnold answered. Yes, they were glad to be back. It had been a harrowing trip. There was only the one train and it was crowded even in the 1st Class. Lynn, she said, looked peaceful with no outward sign of injury to her face. The funeral had been arranged for Thursday, the day after Boxing Day. She would be speaking to Morton and Dolinda in the morning. Meanwhile, perhaps Angie could let them know...and try to have a nice Christmas. Lynn would want that. She was sure Henry's grandmother would appreciate a call. She was staying at the Craigie Hotel in Ayr.

Angie contacted the Countess as she was leaving for the hospital. She felt tongue-tied as she spoke to the older woman, but was soon put at ease.

"Henriette's doing as well as can be expected. The news isn't good. It's too soon to be positive, but the doctors think it unlikely she'll walk for a long time, perhaps never again. I am hoping she'll be fit enough to travel to Glasgow in a few days. There's a spinal injuries unit attached to the hospital there. The consultant's a friend."

Angie expressed her sorrow at the accident. "Give her my love, please."

"It 's most thoughtful of you to ring. Once we're home, you must come up to see Henriette."

The door bell rang. Andy clattered into the house beating his drums. Whether Angie could face it or not it was Christmas.

CHAPTER 11

Angie had to admit she'd enjoyed the festivities even though Lynn had rarely left her thoughts. She had eaten turkey and plum pudding, pulled crackers and exchanged gifts. She'd even joined in the impromptu entertainment, blowing vigorously when instructed on the penny whistle that popped from her cracker, and, yes, she had laughed. Dolinda and Morton had tried so hard. Boxing Day, they lunched in the Furlow Inn on cheese and pickle.

Today, she would face the finality of Lynn's death.

Lorne and Kevin stayed behind with their friends as Morton, Dolinda and Angela travelled to St Peter's. The roads were quiet and they were among the first to arrive and they waited in a sombre black knot for the rest of the mourners. The hearse brought the coffin, unseen under a mass of white lilies and red roses. Appropriate, Angie thought, recalling the girl coming towards her in scarlet skirt and white, white blouse. Could so much life lie inert in that wooden box? Angie gripped Morton's arm, glad he was there beside her, as her legs jellied.

She picked out Seb from among the pall bearers. Sylvie and Gideon led the file of relatives and friends that filtered down the aisles into the oak pews. Sylvie's face was hidden behind a fine veil but she stood erect. Gideon was ashen, his head bowed. He looked up and Angie could see his eyes filled with tears.

"Sylvie appears to be coping well," Morton whispered. Angie said nothing. She had witnessed Sylvie's emotions bared and knew how much she suffered. Oh, Lynn why did you have to die?

Throughout the service Angie found her mind wandering. She didn't want to hear what the vicar was saying. Inevitably her gaze settled on Seb.

109

His dark hair curled against the collar of his suit. In profile his nose had a tiny bump at the ridge. Odd how she hadn't noticed that before. She was struck again by his eyes. There was no doubting he was Lynn's brother.

They moved out in a tight procession through the churchyard, where giant tombstones guarded centuries old lairs. Lynn's grave had been dug in an adjacent ground taken over primarily to bury the blitz dead.

Morton had one arm round Dolinda, the other round Angie, but it was doubtful who supported whom. Tears flowed unashamedly.

The winter sun glinted against the brass handles as the coffin was lowered. "Ashes to ashes....." One day they would all die, Uncle Cyril, Edwina, Morton, Dolinda. "Dust to dust....." It would be as if they'd never existed.

Angie stared up at the sky but there were no stars, only a sun too weak to hold hope. In the lounge of the Cobalt Hotel, Angie nibbled triangled wholewheat and drank hot tea. She hadn't spoken to Seb, but now he came towards her. A young woman clung to his arm.

"Angie," he kissed her lightly. "What can I say?"

You could say a lot, Angie thought. Tell me why you haven't written, but she guessed it was Lynn he was thinking about.

"You haven't met Christine, have you? We've shared a flat in Manchester for almost a year. I've asked her to marry me." Seb's voice hadn't faltered and his gaze was direct.

Angie looked at him in disbelief. His words stabbed. She swayed under their impact, yet she felt no pain. It was as if Lynn's death had left her immune to anything even Seb could hurl at her. She spoke through dry lips in a tone as controlled as his.

"Pleased to meet you. I hope you'll be very happy." Empty phrases. Angie felt defiant. What she'd meant to say was, "Do your own thing, Seb. See if I care." Maybe tomorrow it would hurt, but not this day, there was no room for more pain.

Dolinda, profuse with congratulations, fussed around Seb and Christine.

"It's wonderful news, Seb. Just what the family needs. The next gathering will be a happy occasion. I'm so pleased for you."

As Seb moved away, Angie glared at his back. Lynn had warned her. She was well rid of him. Sylvie joined Angie, leaving Gideon slumped in his chair.

"Morton tells me you'll be staying with them for a while, Angela. Dolinda will help you through all this. She's an exceptional person."

"I know that. How are you?"

"To be honest, I'm not really here. I'm playing a part. Acting the hardest role in my life. But I have to be strong for Gideon. He needs me." She held Angie's hand, and the guise slipped for a moment. Angie read the strain in her eyes, saw the tremulous mouth beneath the mask. This was the real Sylvie. She'd seen the real Seb, too. Not at all like Lynn. Lynn was open and honest.

Did he truly believe Sylvie was his aunt? Angie realised she would have to tread warily. She would love to have told Christine what a cad he was, but now wasn't appropriate.

The funeral reception was winding up when Sylvie took Angie by the arm and moved towards the exit.

"I'd like you to come round, Angela, in a day or two. There's something I want to talk to you about. Could you manage the Friday after New Year?"

"I think so. No, I'm sorry, I've to see Nick that afternoon."

"Make it in the morning and we'll have an early lunch."

Angie agreed. She had no idea where she would be, but no matter what, that Friday was earmarked.

As it turned out, Angie remained at the farm with Morton and Dolinda, easing her ache on long walks with Taurus and Muppet and learning how to plait bread. New Year passed with the briefest of celebration. Outside the world, wildly inebriated, brought in the first year of peace.

111

Angie was surprised how little she thought of Seb. The expected hurt didn't come. In fact, she found herself dismissing his part in her life as a huge rocket that had fizzed and burst into a million stars. All too weak to swing on.

Deep down, however, there were times she knew she still yearned for Lynn's brother. He had flattered her, made her feel desirable, but no one would ever know that and there had been another aspect to her friendship with Seb. His main home was in America. He might have been her passport to travel.

* * *

On the Friday after New Year, Angie walked up the drive of Beechwood at about ten-thirty in the morning. Olga showed her into the lounge. The room had thawed. A log fire blazed and Angie noticed the cushions on the Chesterfield were not quite smooth, the curtains not symmetrically drawn.

Gideon, Sylvie told her, had returned to work the previous day. He was still a sick man but pressure of business was helping him climb out of the stupor Lynn's death had created in him.

"Angela, in case you think I'm acting impulsively, I must tell you I've given this a lot of thought. I know it's what Lynn would have wanted. You were very special to her. Upstairs, I've packed a trunk full of Lynn's clothes, and shoes and things; most are almost new. I couldn't bear to give them to someone I didn't know. I'd like you to have them. What with the coupons and shortages, I hope you'll make use of them."

Angie had not expected this. She wasn't sure how she felt. There was a saying, wasn't there, about dead men's shoes but she couldn't remember the exact words.

"It's very kind of you. I'm not sure...." Angie saw the pleading look in Sylvie's eyes, as if begging her to accept. "I'd love them and I'll be proud to have them" she said, but she wasn't at all certain she could ever wear them.

"I was hoping you'd take the trunk with you, today. I could run you back to Guildford tonight. Unless you and Nick....?"

"That should be fine. I've nothing fixed with Nick. We

usually have a meal at a cafe and sometimes see a film, but as I said, we've no set arrangement. He won't mind, I'm sure."

Angie could see Sylvie's expression relax.

"It may seem a bit hurried. You see, we're not staying here. We're leaving very soon for America. We'd have gone in the summer but we wanted Lynn to go to Lochend, and neither of us would leave the country while she was there. It was arranged ages ago that Gideon would take over responsibility for the American branch after the war. That's where I was born and my mother lives there. She wasn't well enough to travel to the funeral."

"It's my dream to go to New Zealand and other places. My dad and I agreed we'd go after the war. When he died the dream shattered, but in my mind, I've put the bits back together and I'm going to do all the things we planned, just as soon as I can."

"You stick to those dreams, Angela." Sylvia picked up a note book and pencil. "I'd like us to keep in touch. Is there an address perhaps? You said you had a guardian, a lawyer?"

"Dillard Thrift, Oakley Avenue, Hampstead. Number forty-nine."

Sylvie noted the address.

"I might not write often Angela, but I'll not forget you. Especially at this time of year."

Sylvie gave Angela a kiss.

"You're so different, Sylvie, from what I thought at first. Even Lynn used to say..." She bit her lip.

"It's okay. I was a selfish mother at times. Lynn wasn't always an easy child and our lives were so busy. I loved her without reservation. We were closer in the end. Things were working between us."

"I could see that. Lynn was happy, she'd stopped her moaning."

Sylvie glanced at the clock, "We'd better go through for lunch."

Olga's cooking couldn't be faulted and Angie ate well on

golden omelettes and crisp chips. Sylvie and she chatted about the farm and the dogs - what Angie would do in the future.

"Take time in deciding what you'll do with yourself, Angela." Dolinda and Morton will advise you, I'm sure. Something will turn up, soon." Sylvie said as she waved goodbye at the door.

Angie refused the offer of a lift to Albany Place. It was her territory; her's and Nick's. She arranged to phone Sylvie to tell her where to pick her up later for the drive to Guildford.

"It's daft meeting here," Nick said when Angie joined him in Albany Place. "It's not the same, is it?"

The three storey flats that were being erected on the site opposite certainly didn't represent the past, Angie agreed.

"And it's not the most convenient spot to get to. Sorry I'm late. I was with Sylvie Arnold."

"How was the funeral? I wondered about going, but I'd have felt a bit of an intruder."

"Nice thought. I was with Lynn's uncle and aunt and I doubt if I'd have seen you. My eyes were blurred most of the time."

Nick gave Angie a hug. "It's over now. And the war, and our past. There's a golden future ahead. Wait and see. But not tonight, I've got to work. I'm sorry, but it's eat food and leave."

"That fits in beautifully," Angie explained about Lynn's trunk and her arrangement with Sylvie."

"You'll look a million dollars, Angie. You'll have to add a fraction to your curves, I guess. Your uncle could alter things for you if need be."

Uncle! Angie realised she hadn't been in touch with Cyril; not one word since she left. She would write from Dolinda's.

"Where are you going when you leave Guildford?"

"I'm not sure. Things are buzzing in my head."

"Bees in your bonnet," Nick quipped.

"I'm thinking of going to Glasgow to see Henry."

"Thought she was in Ayr?"

"They took her to Glasgow by ambulance on Wednesday. She's in a hospital for tests. The invite from her grandmother's open."

"Makes sense," said Nick. "You'll need somewhere to stay when you come back. A job. You can't live on thin air."

"I've my allowance. I get it all now I'm not staying with Uncle Cyril. Cash is all right for the moment. I'll work something out."

Nick, grabbed Angie's arm, "It's freezing. Let's go to the arcade in Edward Road. It's just re-opened and I'm feeling lucky. He was, too. Spinning three X's and a row of golden bells, he turned his sixpence into ten shillings.

"I'll pay for the tea," he promised.

Nick was standing beside the cash register paying the bill for pie and chips when Sylvie arrived.

"Can I give you a lift to Chartres?" Sylvie offered. "Angie tells me you're working."

"Thanks very much." Nick sat in the rear of the Sunbeam Talbot, admiring its leather upholstery. "She's a nice car."

"I'm selling her if you're interested?"

"Me? I'd love it. It would be convenient when I'm on late. I got my license in the army. But, no. I couldn't afford this."

"To you a bargain for a quick sale. Did Angie tell you we're selling up?"

"Yes, she did. How much?"

"Say £75. Would that be too much?"

"That would be giving it away."

"That's my price. I don't need the money and it is my car. I can do what I like with it."

"I'll think about it. Can I let you know in a day or two?"

"Nick you couldn't," Angie was surprised he even considered it. "You'd have to pay for petrol and the maintenance."

"I don't see why not. I've a steady job and a fair bank balance. You can go places with a car. I could taxi folk about and make enough to pay most the petrol. It's certainly worth thinking about, Mrs Arnold."

"She's not that new, of course. I had her well before the

war. But she's been looked after and you can see the mileage is low."

Nick saw. It was, very.

"Don't let her go to anyone else while I check things out. As I said, I'd thought of buying a banger."

"She's no banger, that's for sure. I'll hold until I hear from you."

"Thanks."

They came to a halt at Leicester Square. Nick jumped out. "I'll let you know by the end of next week. Bye."

Sylvie left the city streets and drove south. "What a nice lad your Nick is."

"I think so," Angie said, then, seeing Sylvie's smile added, "He's just a friend. No romance."

"Shame. You make a handsome pair. I nearly offered to give Nick the car but I thought he'd rather pay for it. It's going to be of no use to me. It would have been Lynn's. I was going to let her have it once she could drive well enough."

The road ahead was skimmed with ice and the journey to Guildford had to be a slow one. Sylvie had telephoned Morton to tell him they were coming by car and could she stay overnight and he was watching for them from the window. He lifted the trunk into the house and Lorne and Kevin helped drag it up to Angie's room. Angie wondered not for the first time what she would do with it. With no settled base, her suitcase was as much as she could manage.

Sylvie was up at six, Angie was told, and away by seven. She, herself, had slept till after eight.

"There's a note for you on the table," Dolinda said.

Angie found it and read,

'Tell Nick I've had a rethink. He can have the car at the end of the month. I don't want anything for it. Just a promise he'll keep an eye on you. He can sell it if he feels it's going to cost him too much. Good luck, and thanks for all your support."
Sylvie.'

Angie showed the note to Dolinda.

"She can't mean it. Lynn's death's affected her brain," she said.

"She's sane enough. She's really a very nice person. I used to find her a bit aloof. We had a long talk over breakfast and she's determined to give most of her things away before she leaves for America next month. She's offered me some of her furniture, says I've to choose what I'd like."

"They must be very rich to give so much away." Angie said.

"They are. Very rich. Have you looked inside the trunk?"

"No. I don't think I want to, yet."

Angie did open the trunk, days later. Lynn's dresses packed in tissue, two suits, impractical shoes which would have to remain impractical as far as Angie was concerned. They were at least a half size too small. There was some jewellery, too. Mostly paste, Angie surmised. Nestling at the bottom was the white rabbit fur. Angie pressed her face into its softness and it smelt of Sylvie's expensive perfume.

"I thought you said Sylvie was a cold fish," Nick said when Angie sought him out at Chartres after a day in the city and showed him the note.

"That's the way it was. She thawed a lot when Lynn went to Lochend. Now she's gone right over the top."

"The question is dare I take the car for nothing? And the truth is, I don't think I can."

"She really wants you to have it."

"Then I'll give her twenty quid to ease my conscience."

"Tell her to give the money to a charity. Then she might take it."

"In that case, I'll make it twenty-five. Oh, it's so daft. Me, owning a Sunbeam Talbot. I never even had a bike. Never enough cash in the Crossart coffers, but I can drive."

"Stop the sob stuff. Your mum held the best children's parties in the Place and you weren't running about bare-foot, either."

"No, but I will be if I don't get back to work. Are you returning to Guildford?"

"Yes. I'll stay another two weeks. I love it there even when the boys go a bit wild. I take Taurus for walks."

"And who is Taurus. The local bull?"

"Stop being facetious. It's Lynn's dog, he's attached himself to me. I think he senses she's not coming back."

"I doubt it. He probably associates you with her."

Luigi called from the kitchen.

"I'll have to go. Can't afford to upset the boss if I'm to run a car, can I?"

Dolinda was out when Angie got back but she managed to rouse Morton from the fire to open the door.

"I'd have met you at the station if you'd let me know the time of the train."

"It's okay. I got a bus within minutes."

"Good day?"

"I looked at the shops and went to see Mr Thrift. He thinks visiting Henry's a good idea."

"And are you going?"

"Yes, when I leave here a week on Friday. I've still to finalise arrangements with the Countess. Do you think Dolinda would keep the trunk for me till I come home?"

"I'm quite sure she will. You can hardly cart the thing around with you. Dolinda left some food on the cooker in case you wanted it. Just needs warming up."

"I had fish and chips on the way home."

Morton ran his tongue across his lips, "Salt, vinegar, piping hot, wrapped in the News of the World. I haven't had a chippie supper for ages. Bad for me, Dolinda says. I expect she's right."

Angie nodded. "I saw Nick, too. Told him about the car."

"He's a lucky young man."

"He wants to make a small payment, to charity or something."

"The mood Sylvie's in she'll like that idea."

"We were talking about the change in her. I think it's her way of coping."

"You might well be right. We all have to grieve in our own way. Work through it. It must have been hard for you when you lost your parents."

"Mm. I've hardly ever spoken about it. Lynn knew, and Nick. I was away from home. Evacuated to Sussex. When mum was killed, I think I pretended things were the same. That nothing had happened. Then dad was lost at sea and that was different. We'd made so many plans to travel and I'm still going to."

"I'm sure you will."

"Scotland's the start, like taking the first step. I was very upset when they died, of course, but it didn't hit me fully till the war was over and I realised I'd only got Uncle Cyril."

"You don't like him, do you?"

"No I don't. I think he looks like a pig. He's got small eyes that peer through round spectacle frames and he sort of snuffles through his nose and when he's excited his voice gets very high pitched and he splutters. He's fat and blubbery and his skin is slimy."

"Hold on. That's a pretty damning description. He can't help what he looks like. Except the fat, perhaps. Hand me my pouch, there's a girl."

"His manners are pig-like as well and he's mean."

"He gave you a home."

"He wanted my money."

"You're very cynical. I'm surprised."

"It's only Cyril makes me feel that way."

"I understood your problems were with the housekeeper?"

"You're right. I could put up with Uncle Cyril. Edwina was different. She's a... a lesbian."

"That's a big word for a young woman. Well, perhaps they deserve each other. But I'm sad to see you so bitter. It's not like you. Not the Angela I know. Bitterness sours a person and you're too sweet to be sour."

"I'm not bitter. I feel sorry for my uncle in a way, and Edwina's quite kind really. It's just that she can't keep her hands to herself."

"You'll have to learn tolerance in this world."

"I'm learning lots of things fast. Six months ago, I was at school. I had Lynn. Now I'm on my own again and to be truthful, I'm glad. Not at losing Lynn or my parents. Glad I'm standing on my own feet, making decisions. If I hadn't come here, I'd have managed. Don't get me wrong. It's great being with you, having and giving support, but I've got to be responsible for myself."

"You've an old head on young shoulders as they say. So you're going to Scotland?"

"I fixed it up today. Mr Thrift was arranging a refund for the Christmas trip and I went in and asked for an exchange instead. I'm travelling overnight in a sleeper. Henriette's grandmother is happy with the arrangements."

A bustle in the hall and Dolinda called out, "Hallo, I'm back." She came into the lounge still wrapped in her winter coat and rubbing her hands together to warm them.

"Brr. It's cold out there. I forgot my gloves. The wind's blowing up. Did you fix the trellis, Morton?" Morton looked guilty. "I knew you'd forget. You'll be busy tomorrow if it falls down. I tell you, Angela, he's getting worse. Senility they call it. Never marry a man twelve years your senior."

"Shall I tell her about the cake you made the other day? She nearly used salt instead of sugar."

"He's right. He's dragging me with him." Dolinda gave Morton an affectionate kiss. "What have you two been chatting about? You looked very cosy when I came in."

"Deep conversations, Dolly, about life and death and people and tolerance and Angela's leaving a week on Friday to go to Scotland"

"So you've definitely decided?"

"Yes. It's all settled. I asked Morton if you could keep the trunk meantime."

"No problem it can stay in the spare room. If anyone comes, I'll cover it in a lace cloth and put a bowl of flowers on top of it." Dolinda took her coat off and placed it over the back of a chair.

"I could ask Cyril ....."

"No need for that. Have you spoken to your uncle?"

"I'm writing to him tonight to tell him my plans. We'll keep in touch through Mr Thrift."

Taurus trotted into the room followed by Muppet.

"That's the dogs wanting out and I've just taken off my coat....Morton?"

Angie jumped up. "I'll walk them round the yard."

Angie looked up into the sky. "I know you're there somewhere, Lynn, Mum, Dad. I need you to help me. Guide me to make the right decisions." A single star twinkled back at her. It's still holding my dreams, she thought.

CHAPTER 12

The visit to Glasgow had been arranged without any hitches. Nick and Morton saw Angie off at 10 pm from a quiet Kings Cross Station.

"Don't forget to send a post card," they chorused.

Angie settled in her seat by the window. She shared the carriage with an elderly lady and gentleman, who spoke in whispers, and a middle aged man, who immediately took reams of papers from his brief case and started to work. She began to wish she'd let Mr Thrift book her a sleeper this time.

Angie opened the novel she had just bought at the station stall and began to read. Agatha Christie kept her engrossed until the murder was solved well before the express reached Glasgow.

Angie tried to gaze through the grubby windows but outside it was nothing but blackness. The journey was long and boring. She slept a little from time to time, as did the other passengers. She'd eaten the sandwiches she'd brought with her and emptied a flask of tea. Angie wondered what she would find when she arrived. Wondered what the Countess would be like. How she herself would feel at seeing Henriette without Lynn being there.

She felt an uneasy excitement as she watched the dawn break and the landscape change. The first time she'd ever been outside England. I'm on my way, Dad. It's not how I'd have wanted it, but this is the start - next month, next year, who knows where I'll be. And one day I'll fly like the seagull. It was possible, everything was possible if you wanted it enough.

The train flashed through villages, past fields, until signs of the city appeared and it pulled up in Central Station. Once through the ticket barriers, she realised she had no idea where to go. The Countess had said a car would be sent. But what car? Who would be driving it? She scanned the people around her seeking a likely face. As soon as she spotted the figure in a grey uniform, she knew she had found her man. He, too, was searching the faces as passengers left the gate. He approached her.

"Miss Angela Bolton?"

"Yes, that's me."

"I'm Hugh, the Countess's chauffeur. She sent me to pick you up."

Angie listened to Hugh carefully. She was relieved she could understand what he was saying. An elderly woman with a Scot's accent had spoken to her briefly on the train and she'd had tremendous difficulty making her out. Thinking it prudent, she had nodded and the woman had shaken her head in what Angie took to be bewilderment.

The car was a large, black saloon. Like Sylvie's car, it looked new, yet Angie suspected it was an old model. The dust covers had done their job. Hugh was perhaps in his mid-sixties. His eyes bulged, his nose tapered from a broad base to a sharp tip and his lower lip sucked under the upper one when he spoke. His top teeth were large, the bottom ones almost non-existent.

Angie couldn't see any hair beneath the peak cap and she had a feeling he was completely bald. When he grinned he resembled a mischievous gnome. So much for the braw Scots.

Hugh made a good guide, taking Angie through the main streets and past the Art Galleries. They travelled for some twenty minutes. Angie had expected Henry's grandmother to live in a mansion surrounded by trees.

Woodend turned out to be a row of elegant terrace houses not unlike Park Way in London. From the front, Angie could see no trees, but there was an abundance of rhododendron bushes. Hugh drove round the back to a mews and stopped in a courtyard, beyond which a gate led to a narrow garden, and on into a wooded area.

They entered number fourteen via a rear door and Hugh

handed her over to a plump maid, whose apron flounced over a black dress. Her dark hair was skimmed back by a stiff bow, reminiscent, Angie thought of the last century.

"Welcome. I am Estelle." The girl curtsied as if to royalty. The words she had spoken were delivered parrot fashion as if rehearsed over and over again. Angie assumed her to be French and this was confirmed when Estelle and Hugh exchanged conversation. Angie could only understand the odd word. Hugh spoke French like a native.

She was led up two flights of stairs. At the top Angie saw a corridor to the right extending past several doors, but they turned sharply left. Beside a mirrored wall was a single door. Estelle opened it and Angie was ushered into a circular room part of which was built over the well of the stairs.

It was stunningly beautiful. In contrast to the dark panelling of the stairway, there were cream walls, pink drapes, soft chairs. A rich satin overlay covered the high bed. Curtains concealed a dressing area and beyond a white marble floored bathroom.

"Henriette slept here. Now her room is below," Estelle explained pointing down the stairs just as Hugh arrived with the suitcase. She indicated a bell on the wall near the bed, and added in the same stilted tones she had used previously, "Ring if you need anything. The Countess will see you when you are ready. She is in the lounge." With a final curtsey Estelle left the room, followed by Hugh.

Angie found herself laughing. Was this real? It was as if she'd turned a page in history - 'Henriette slept here', indeed. She unpacked her case. She had added two blouses from the trunk for day wear and a ruby crepe dress to alternate with her blue one.

It had been easier than she thought to step into Lynn's clothes. The materials were of such quality, the styles so chic. Angie felt different wearing them. As if some of Lynn's vibrancy remained in them and transferred itself to her.

She decided to take a bath and wallowed in the steaming water, feeling more relaxed than she had for weeks. Her worries for the time being at least were left in London. But Glasgow had cares of its own Angie discovered, as, refreshed, she went down the stairs.

Music was coming from a room on the first floor. Angie was drawn towards it. A young girl sat playing the piano. A young girl with dark bobbed hair. It couldn't be ..

"Henriette," she cried and stepped forward. The figure turned and Angie realised she was mistaken. Yet this girl was so like Henriette she had to come from the same pod.

"No, Angela. Not Henriette. This is Celeste."

The voice came from the direction of the window. Angie saw a tall elderly woman, simply dressed in grey wool. Angie took her extended hand. She noticed there were rings on all her fingers. Angie looked into the crinkled face, and brown eyes twinkled back at her. Around her mouth the old woman's skin puckered as she smiled and the hollow of her neck deepened above a three tier pearl choker. She's so fragile; like an old porcelain vase, Angie thought, watching the Countess resume her seat.

Celeste greeted Angela with a handshake and moved away from the piano. Angie was surprised that neither Henry, nor Lynn, had ever mentioned her sister.

Henriette's grandmother beckoned her to a chair. "Come and sit here, Angela. Did you have a good journey?"

"Very good." There was silence for a second or two, then Angie asked. "How's Henriette?"

"In herself, much better. The bruising to her face and body is fading at last. But alas, the spinal injury would appear to be permanent. Tests show she may never walk again."

"They're not always right. It's early days. She's got lots of spirit."

"Let's hope for the best. I've a surprise for you. Henriette's home for the weekend. She'll have to go back to the hospital on Monday. At this moment she's resting. We'll lunch soon and you can see her after that."

They moved shortly, down brass railed stairs, to where the

dining room tabled wafer thin toast and a dish of cheeses and grapes. Estelle brought in bowls of onion soup. The dark brown liquid scalded Angie's mouth as she spooned it and she bit into a roll to sooth its passage. They ate without speaking. The tick of the wall clock emphasised their silence.

Celeste was first to break it. "It's good of you to come. We heard heaps about Henriette's visit to London."

Even her voice was like Henry's. Celeste, Angie estimated, must be about two years the younger, near Angie's own age.

"Do Estelle and Hugh usually speak in French?" Angie asked.

"A mixture of both, like the rest of us. When Daddy was alive we always used French. Of course, Grandmother and mummy were born in Scotland." She smiled at the Countess, who nodded.

"Well, I'm glad I don't have to struggle with my French to be understood. Could you tell me more about Henriette? What should I expect?" Angie said,

The Countess answered.

"She's lost weight and it shows. There's some bruising still around her left eye and it remains blood shot but we've been assured her sight hasn't been affected. Her legs? Well, they're useless. She is in fact paralysed from below the waist and, once she's stronger, will use a wheelchair." The Countess got up, moved to the fire and prodded it with a poker, sending a shower of sparks into the grate. "Who, I ask myself, is going to care for her when I'm gone?"

Celeste put down her fork and went over to her grandmother. "You know I will."

"You've your own life to lead. There're your studies to consider."

"They can wait I don't have to go to St Andrews."

"If you don't my heart will be broken for the second time."

Celeste burst into French, speaking too fast for Angie to understand. She looked on embarrassed.

"Celeste, that's enough." The Countess stepped back to the

table and sat down again. "We are spoiling Angela's meal. Ask Estelle to bring coffee, please."

Angie had watched the scene unfurl and thought it too dramatic for words. She put it down to their foreign ways. Henriette's grandmother may have been born in Scotland, but she acted and sounded like a Parisienne.

Coffee arrived thick and black in a tall silver jug with cream an optional extra. Estelle poured it into minute cups. That will never be enough for me, Angie thought, but she changed her mind as she tasted the rich liquid. Delicious, the flavour so strong that no one could take much of it.

Angie was relieved when lunch was over and she was free to visit Henriette. She opened her door. The room was a mist of scent coming from flowers vased on every ledge.

Henriette lay flat on a white covered bed. Her usually lustrous hair was limp, her olive skin waxen. Above her eye, purple bruising yellowed at the edges. She smiled and Angie saw that several of her teeth were cracked. Angie pulled a chair closer to the bed and sat down.

"How do you feel?"

"That's the trouble, I don't. My legs are completely dead and even the pain of the bruising is numbed by the drugs they feed me. Don't look so worried. I'll mend."

"I guess you will," Angie said softly. There were tears in her eyes and Henry turned her head away.

"I'm so sorry, Angie. So sorry Lynn died. Can I tell you about it, I can't speak to La Grandmere? And Celeste is hopeless. I think she's scared of me."

"How do you mean, scared?"

"Probably worried she'll have to look after an invalid for the rest of her life. I suppose it's my fault."

"It was an accident. A terrible accident. I'm sure you weren't to blame. Lynn told me you were a good driver." Lynn had never said that. She had said Henry drove too fast, but Angie wanted to reassure.

Henry looked surprised. "You don't know? You think I was

driving? It was Lynn. Lynn who caused the accident. If only she hadn't been so stubborn."

"Lynn driving? But she couldn't. She didn't have a licence. She was just learning."

"I'm telling you. Lynn took my car keys when I left them on the table in the cafe. It was a joke at first. She begged me to let her have a shot at driving. Just to the corner. I said no, of course, but she insisted. She went on and on. In the end I said okay. Lynn drove perfectly to the corner of the road but she wouldn't stop. She turned and began driving down the hill. Far too fast. I couldn't do a thing about it."

"You don't have to explain further. Not if it upsets you."

"I'm all right. She lost control as we neared the bottom. I remember the tree and the front of the car buckling up towards us, the terrible smell of burnt rubber and the crunch of metal and crack of glass. We were thrown out on to the road. Well, I was on the verge."

So Lynn had been responsible for her own death. Somehow learning that made Angie feel better. She could relax with Henry now. Poor Henry. Angie could picture Lynn running off with the keys. See her laughing as she sat behind the wheel. Why did you do it, Lynn? Why did you do it?

"I'm glad I've told you. I felt very bitter at first. I wished I'd died. I hate the thought of using a wheelchair. But I'm getting accustomed to the idea. Perhaps I'll be able to do something useful."

Angie fought back tears again, "Maybe the doctors are just being cautious. Maybe you will walk again."

Henry shrugged her shoulders as if resigned. "They sent for the priest. I could hear it all. He read the last rites. I wanted to shout, "Don't be so stupid. I'm alive. I'm not going to die. I couldn't see Lynn, never dreamt the priest might be for her." Tears came into Henry's eyes and spilled on to her cheeks. "She wasn't even a Roman Catholic. I never thought for one moment..."

Angie knew her own emotions were near to bubbling over.

"At least you weren't both killed and you know what they say, where there's life there's hope. I'm going to go now. I promised your grandmother I'd only stay a few minutes. The nurse is coming." She kissed Henriette. "I'll be back later, probably about four. Would you like a game of cards?"

"Why not? Do you like my bedroom? La Grandmere was going to put you in the blue room. I insisted you had mine."

"I love it. It's so pretty. See you about four."

Angie closed Henriette's door and ran up the two flights of stairs, brushing away the tears stinging her eyes. Celeste was standing on the landing.

"What did you think of her?"

"She looks so much thinner, but she's bright considering," Angie cleared her nose.

"She is brave, isn't she? It's going to be hard for her."

Angie studied the worried expression on Celeste's face.

"Your grandmother's right. You should stick to your plans. Go to university. Perhaps your grandmother could find someone to take care of Henry."

"Henry and I don't get on, you know."

Angie sensed Celeste needed to talk. Funny how she felt like everyone's agony aunt. Celeste followed Angie into the room and they sat side by side on the bed.

"It started when we were quite young. We were always arguing."

"I don't have any sisters or brothers, but isn't that the norm in families?"

"Maybe, but we were dreadful. We reached the stage when we were only speaking to each other if we absolutely had to. I was pleased when Henriette went to Lochend. Yet, when I heard about the crash, I felt awful. As if part of me had been injured. I was so scared she'd die. I still feel wretched. I want to make it up to her."

"That's good. So now you can be friends?"

"Henriette won't let me get close. I've sat with her and tried to talk, tried to make her laugh. It just doesn't work. I thought if

129

she knew I was willing to give up university for her, she might come round. When Grandmother told her she got all upset and shouted that she didn't care if she never saw me. I'd got legs and could walk right out. She thinks I feel sorry for her, and she's right. But for me it's far more than that. I'm her sister. Sisters should help each other."

"She'll be feeling pretty mixed up. Give her time."

"That's what Grandmother said. Anyway you'll understand why I can't go to university."

"No, not really. Giving up your career isn't going to make things better between you. You'll have to prove your feelings in other ways. I'm sure your grandmother will fix something up."

"There's another thing. Henriette says she doesn't want people to gawk at her. I'm not people. You'll tell her, won't you? Tell her how I feel. Make her understand she's got to see me, let me help."

"I think you have to find a way of convincing her yourself."

"Well, I don't see why you can't do it. You owe me something. If it weren't for that friend of yours, Henriette wouldn't be where she is."

"And you would still be arguing with her. Not caring a toss."

"You English. You always twist things. You're too clever. Lynn thought she was clever. Thought she could drive and look where it got her."

"Celeste, be quiet before you say too much. Lynn was my best friend. I'm not going to listen to you speaking like that. No wonder Henry argues with you."

Celeste stamped to the door and flung it open. "I shall tell my grandmother you have insulted me. You are our guest."

The door slammed as Celeste stormed out.

"Good God, where have I landed now," Angie said flopping on to the bed.

She decided to go for a walk. Down the narrow garden, through a latched gate, to the woods, she strolled among the tall pines, still angry with Celeste. A scuffle on the path behind her made Angie turn round to see the Countess coming towards her. Angie feared fireworks.

"You like walking among the trees, Angela? So do I. You can't hear the traffic. It's a good place to gather one's thoughts."

"Did Celeste tell you about the disagreement we had?" Angie determined to be direct.

"She said you were rude. I find that hard to believe. Celeste is a funny girl. Sometimes I think she is only happy when she is arguing."

"It was about Henriette not wanting her around."

"Sisters! Those two have never been close. I think Celeste is jealous. Henriette was the popular one. Always gregarious. Now, I guess, she is getting all the attention. Celeste has brains, but she is impatient, impulsive and incapable of loving anyone but herself."

"She said she wanted to help."

"These feelings she says she has for her sister may be sincere, but she is the last person to help Henriette. If she sacrificed university, we would never hear the end of it. You must help me persuade her to continue her studies."

Here we go again, Angie thought. Why have I got to do anything?

"I'm sure things will sort themselves out," she said, evenly.

"I will ask Celeste to apologise to you."

"It doesn't matter. I get over rows quickly."

They had covered the path through the wood and retraced their steps back to the latched gate.

"I'm going to see Henry again in a little while. We're playing cards."

"You are already good for her, Angela. She hasn't wanted to do anything up to now."

Henry was sitting up against a bed rest waiting for Angela.

"You're late", she complained lightly, "it's two minutes past."

Henry seemed in good spirits. Angie decided to speak to her about Celeste.

"Why won't you see Celeste? It's upsetting her," she asked, as she shuffled the cards between games.

"Celeste is a pain in the neck."

"She's your sister."

"Worse luck."

"I'd love to have a sister."

"You deserve one. Celeste doesn't really care. She's just trying to salve her conscience in case I die or something. You don't know her."

"I've already had one row with her. I guess she is difficult."

"Impossible, you mean."

"She's offered to stay at home and look after you instead of going to university."

"Probably wants to poison my food."

Angie ignored Henry's last remark. "Until you get over this your grandmother will need some help."

"I realise that, but not Celeste. Couldn't you stay, Angie? Or is Cyril's shop more inviting?"

"I don't work in the shop any more."

Angie told Henriette about Edwina and why she left her uncle's place.

"You'll have to find a job, won't you?"

Angie nodded.

"What's wrong with being my companion?"

"Nothing, I suppose. But I can't live here, in Scotland."

"Why not?"

"Mr Thrift would do his nut."

"Grandmother could fix it. She's got influence." Henriette reached over and pressed the wall bell. "I'll ask her."

"Don't be silly you can't."

"Why not?" Henriette repeated. "It would be fun."

"I've got to go back."

"Why, why, why ?"

"Because......"

Estelle came to the door. "Mademoiselle?"

"Ma Grandmere, ou est-elle?

132

"Elle dorme."

"C'est bien. Merci Estelle." Henry turned to Angela, "I'll speak to her tonight. Then we can discuss things."

"You're rushing me, Henry. I need a chance to consider it."

"You will think about it, though. Thanks, Angie. It would be great having you around. I might even survive the wheelchair."

"I've told you. I'm promising nothing. It's all a bit complicated."

"Right. Let's get on with the game. Spades are trumps"

Dinner found a still sullen looking Celeste being formerly polite, the Countess effusively bright, and Angie preoccupied.

Afterwards upstairs in her room, Angie relaxed. She soaked in another bath, before sitting up in bed, her dressing gown round her shoulders.

Could it work? Could she really come to live here as companion to Henry? Angie took a pen and paper and began to write.

REASONS FOR ACCEPTING HENRIETTE'S OFFER

(1)   I need somewhere to live.

(2)   I need a job.

(3)   I like Henry and would like to help her.

(4)   I like the Countess (I think).

(5)   I want to travel and learn about other countries.

(6)   I like what I've seen of Glasgow. I could begin here.

(7)   I'd be independent.

(8)   I'd not bump into Seb.

REASONS   AGAINST   ACCEPTING   HENRIETTE'S OFFER

(1)   I know so little about the Countess and her family.

(2)   I know no-one out with their household.

(3)   I like living in London.

(4)   The job would be a commitment - there could be no half measures.

(5)   Celeste seems hostile and how do I know the Countess will
          want me?

(6)   My French isn't very good. They could all natter away and I almost
          certainly wouldn't have a clue what they were saying.

(7)   I could get used to the luxury life - might even grow soft.

(8)   I'd miss seeing Nick.

Angie was surprised at her last reason in each section. She had tried not to think of Seb since the funeral, yet, now his name kept coming into her mind. She was still angry. As for Nick - he was part of her life and she knew it were true. She would miss him, but there were no strings attached to their friendship.

"So there I have it. Eight 'for', eight 'against'. I could toss a coin."

Playfully, she took a halfpenny from a pile of loose cash she had placed on the bedside table. "Heads I stay. Tails I go." She threw the coin into the air and it landed on the bed, rolled off and across the carpet.

"I'll sleep on it," she said, and she turned back the satin quilt and nestled under the warm blankets.

Angie woke again at seven. The room was still in darkness and there was no point in getting up yet. She might as well take advantage of a long lie. A rap on her door at eight o'clock brought Estelle with steaming coffee.

"Mademoiselle Henriette sent me. You like coffee?"

"I love it." Especially, she thought, at breakfast time, served the French way in a huge round mug more like a soup bowl. Angie sat up, "Brr it's cold."

"Cold, oui. Il neige." Estelle drew open the curtains before leaving. Snow was falling thickly.

Angie got out of bed and looked out of the window. There was she decided nothing more beautiful than untrodden snow, except perhaps where it feathered the pines. She wondered if London had snow, and pictured the streets covered in brown slush. Would the children be sledging down Brayne Hill?

Her foot struck something as cold as an icicle. Angie bent down to pick up the halfpenny she had tossed the night before.

"Heads I stay," she whispered. "Maybe I will, but on my terms."

Angie didn't rush going downstairs for breakfast. She met Celeste in the hall.

"I've finished, but Grandmother's still eating. She says I've to apologise for the way I spoke yesterday."

"I've already forgotten."

It was an evasive apology, Angie thought. "Grandmother says." Not "I'm very sorry". She guessed it was the best Celeste could manage.

The Countess sat at the table, a stone coffee pot in her hand.

"Estelle tells me you had early coffee. This is fresh. Help yourself to toast and honey, or there are muffins, if you prefer."

Angie took the toast and spread it sparingly with butter.

"Please use more. We have plenty."

"I'm so used to the rations, I'm well trained. It's like not taking sugar."

"I'm careful, too. Good for the figure," the Countess laughed, patting her tiny waist.

Ninety, and she still cares what she looks like. I hope I'm as good if I live that long. Odd how some people die so young and others... I suppose it balances out. Aloud Angie said, "Have you seen Henriette this morning?"

"I see her every morning before breakfasting. She likes your being here."

"Did she say anything more?"

"What do you mean, anything more?"

"About me? She wants me to stay as her companion - to help look after her."

"No, she didn't."

"She asked me yesterday."

Pamela Duncan

"And do you want to?"

"I don't know. Would you like me to?"

The Countess paused, "It sounds a nice idea, but surely you have commitments. A job? You live with your uncle I understand?"

"I did, but not any more. And I no longer work for him. I've an allowance from my parents. They're dead. I expect you know that. I'll have to find another job and somewhere to live."

"So this position could be a solution for you?"

"I've been thinking about it."

"You're very young, Angela."

"I'll be seventeen in the summer."

"I find it difficult to conceive that a girl of your age must fend for herself. Surely your uncle will be concerned about you?"

"I don't know. He might be, but I would doubt it. I've got to stand on my own feet. There is Mr Thrift."

"Who is he?"

"Dillard Thrift. My parents' lawyer. He's sort of my guardian. Looks after my money."

"Should you stay, I would require his permission, Angela. As I say, you are so young." The Countess left her chair and paced up and down the room very slowly. "I suggest if you've made up your mind, I contact Mr Thrift and hear how he feels about it. Would you like me to do that?"

"Yes, I think so. I tossed a coin and it came down 'heads I stay'."

"So your future is based on the toss of a coin. I suppose it's as good a way as any. Luck plays its part in life, like being in the right, or wrong, place at a given time."

"I'm a bit worried about staying for ever. Could I agree say to one year and see what happens?"

"I shall offer you a year's contract with the option of leaving after three months if you change your mind. How is that? And, of course, it's subject to Mr Thrift's approval. Shall we say I pay you three pounds a week, plus your keep, of course. It's above the rate Estelle receives."

"That, Angie said, "sounds very fair."

"You will need time off and holidays. We will work it out. Henriette will be back in hospital in a day or two. I understand there's no real benefit in her remaining there. She's receiving no treatment other than therapy, which we can arrange to have carried out here."

"What about Celeste? How will she feel?"

"Celeste will go to university at the end of the month, I promise you. Now, you had better speak with Henriette. Perhaps she has had second thoughts."

Henry was reading. "I thought it was Dr Gillon. He'll be here soon. I think I'm to be allowed up. I'll have to learn to drive that contraption." She pointed to a wheelchair folded against the bedroom wall. "We've checked the passages and doors are wide enough. I'll have to use the front entrance because of the rear stairs. La Grandmere is looking into the possibility of a lift. It's a bit complicated. Meanwhile I'll stay at ground level."

"That's brilliant."

Henriette looked directly at Angie. "Tell me, have you thought about staying on?"

"Yes, I have. Do you still want me to?"

"Of course I do."

"Then, yes, conditionally."

"What conditions?"

"That you behave yourself."

"Stop teasing. Are you really going to stay? We'll have to put it to La Grandmere. I was bursting to tell her earlier but wanted to see you again first."

"She knows. We laid down the ground rules at breakfast. She wants Mr Thrift, my lawyer's, agreement."

"Oh Angie, that's great. I'm so excited. I feel happier than for weeks. I reckon Lynn would approve. It'll seem funny you looking after me. You're so young."

"That's what your grandmother said. You're not so very old

yourself."

"Nineteen."

"That old? How awful."

Angie and Henriette sat making plans until a rap on the door announced Dr Gillon.

"I want to have a look round Glasgow this morning. See you later," Angie said as she left the room.

She ran up the stairs and put on her new wool coat. Thank goodness she'd bought it. She hadn't thought about Wellington boots and her shoes looked inadequate for the snowy pavements, but they'd have to do. She spoke to the Countess on the way out.

"I'm going out to have a look round. I'll have to arrange for my trunk to be sent here, so if I go home in a day or two I could settle everything and come back when you want me."

"That would be sensible. You can return any time, of course. Now, go out and enjoy yourself. Lunch is optional. I'll expect you when I see you."

Glasgow in winter. The snow stopped falling and sun turned the pavements into London slush, through which Angie's shoes slithered. Despite the weather, there was a sparkle to Glasgow as if it were awakening. She walked to a main road and took a bus to the city centre.

The bus dropped her in Sauchiehall Street and she strolled along looking into shop windows. Skimped skirts flared, hemlines dropped and waistlines belted. If this were to be the new fashion, she liked it. She turned into a cobbled side street. The Scot's reputation for drinking was apparent. Every other building was a public house. Away from the main shopping area, the brickwork was dirty grey or dirty red.

Lace half curtains told her people were living behind the grime smeared windows. The contrast between these home and that of the Countess upset Angie. They were all human beings. Why should some have so much and others so little? She remembered Nick saying, "There speaks the new thinker". You didn't have to be a communist to see injustice in this city, or any city.

Angie came to another main road. Large offices and banks reminded her that Glasgow was a commercial place. She felt an urge to see the River Clyde. Like the Thames in London, she thought it would be the heart of Glasgow.

She jumped on a tram marked Clydebank, which took her through streets lined with small shops, busy with housewives doing the shopping. The journey took her past the shipyards and she vaguely remembered reading about the bombing of the Clyde, but when she came upon whole areas flattened it was a shock. This was Glasgow's blitz.

She got off the tram and walked beside heavy vehicles engaged in knocking down and rebuilding. At the end of one street a black board advertising home baking tempted Angie into a corner cafe. It was nearly full of workmen. She noted their big, dirty hands and smelt the sweat of worn jumpers. The cafe itself, apart from the floor, was clean and freshly painted. Around the walls were framed prints of paintings of the city.

There was one other woman, probably in her mid twenties. She curled up in a seat by the wall and sniffled into a handkerchief. Angie considered sitting beside her, but accepting she couldn't cope with the tears, chose a table opposite. Her eyes were drawn frequently towards the woman.

One of the men got up to leave. He patted the woman on the back and said something. He shrugged his shoulders as he passed Angela.

"They buried her man this morning. He'd his legs blown off in the bombing. Miracle is he lasted this length." he said.

War - pieces could be picked up but the scars would remain deep in the minds. The same as in London, Angie thought. She ordered tea and a scone but didn't enjoy it.

She stepped out into the street again as the sun faded in a frosty haze and the snow returned. Exploring the River Clyde would wait for another day. Angie retraced her route by tram and bus back to Woodend Terrace. She shook her coat in the hallway and made a mental note to bring Wellingtons from

London. The dining room was empty. Estelle heard her come in and, although it was late, Angie was grateful for the offer of soup and crusty bread. Feeling much warmer having eaten, Angie met the Countess as she was going to her room.

Henriette's grandmother, despite her age, was no laggard. She had reached Dillard Thrift and he had expressed surprise, but if Angela was sure, then he would be delighted. The Countess failed to mention his long discourse on how unsettled Angela had been and how relieved he would be to see her in a secure home.

Angie spent the time before dinner writing letters. At 7pm promptly she walked into the dining room to the smell of fish. Buttered plaice, broccoli and boiled potatoes, round as marbles, Peach Melba topped by a fan wafer, and each mouthful punctuated by chatter.

"We are taking coffee in the lounge. There's a surprise for you."

Angie saw the wheelchair as soon as the door swung open. Henriette looked a shadow of her former self couched in its depths. The coffee cup shook in her hand as she drew it to her lips.

"Henry, you're up."

"First time."

"How do you feel?"

"What would you like to hear? To be honest, dreadful. My neck can barely support my head. And see my arms are so thin, so weak."

"It will take time," her Grandmother said.

"I took her for a walk. Down the garden and back three times, once the snow ceased. You were out." Celeste sounded triumphant.

"I was sauntering through the Glasgow streets, savouring the atmosphere. I must learn my way around if I'm staying."

"Staying?"

I was going to tell you tonight," La Grandmere explained. "Angela is to be Henriette's companion."

"She's what?"

"You'll be free to go to university."

"But I wanted..."

Henriette interrupted. "It's for the best, Celeste. You'd have resented it if you'd given up your studies. You know you would. Thanks for wanting to help. I appreciate that."

Celeste looked sullen but she didn't protest further. Angie thought she detected a hint of relief in her eyes. Celeste's voice was cold and level when she spoke.

"It's good of you to take on the job."

Angie smiled at Henry, "I think I'll enjoy it."

CHAPTER 13

London was shrouded in fog as Angie searched out the lights of the station. It was a real pea-souper that had been bad all the way down to Euston, but here at Victoria it was worse. The cold air chilled her and her clothes hung damply. She located the platform to Guildford.

"Running about forty-five minutes late," a porter informed her. "Better go to the waiting room. It won't leave without you knowing. There's a crowd in there already."

Around twenty people huddled in great coats in the bleak waiting area. Glad she had only a light case, Angie stood until some men shuffled to make a half space for her to sit on at the edge of a planked bench.

"Foul night," she commented to no one in particular and nobody replied. Tired city workers depressed at the thought of an oven dried dinner. The forty-five minutes dragged to an hour, the hour to an hour-and-a-half. She felt her legs stiffen and cramp with the cold.

"Train's in," the porter shouted and everyone trooped out in a funereal procession. Angie was concerned that Morton was meant to be meeting her at the other end. She hoped he'd phoned to check the arrival times of the train and that the fog wouldn't make driving too hazardous. To her relief the skies cleared a few miles out with the city. Morton greeted her with a peck on the cheek.

"Well, that was a quick visit. You spent almost as long getting from Victoria Station as you did in Scotland," he quipped.

"Hope you weren't hanging around for me?"

"No. I heard of the fog and checked. And what's this rumour about going to live up there? Your Mr Thrift was in touch."

Dolinda's soup chased the chill from her bones and the steak pie satisfied her hunger.

"You've made up your mind, then? It's a big decision for a young girl. I suppose Henriette's grandmother will look after you," Dolinda said, when they drew their seats close to a blazing log fire.

"Hardly. She's ninety two. Not that you'd know it."

"Goodness. It sounds as if you'll have more than one invalid to take care of soon. Oh Angela, do you really think you should?"

"It seems to me life and death's a bit of a lottery. And remember I have no home at the moment. No home and no job. I quite fancied Glasgow, even in the winter with the snow falling. It has atmosphere."

"Well, from what I recall it's got dogs fouling the streets, and you have to be careful. It's like all cities - a bit wicked. You know what they say about the Scots? They're fond of a drink, and Glasgow's got a bad reputation. Knife fights and so on. You'll need to watch out for yourself."

"Don't worry. I promise."

Morton tapped his pipe out into an ashtray. "Dolinda's right. You're far too young to be on your own."

"I know. But that's the way it is."

Dolinda's and Morton's views were reiterated by Nick when Angie met him at Chartres a few days later.

"Angie. It's great to see you. I thought you were to be away a couple of weeks. How was Henriette?"

"Getting better. That is, she can get out of bed now - in a wheelchair. She can't walk. Possibly not ever."

"So why are you back so soon?"

"To sort things out. I'm going up there to live for a while at least. Maybe as long as a year. I've been offered a job as companion to Henry. A job and a home, just like that."

"In Glasgow? You can't be serious. You're not old enough."

"Et tu Brute? That's what everyone tells me, but I've to stand in my own size 7's remember."

Nick looked thoughtful. "I'll miss you."

"Me too."

"You'll write?"

"You bet."

"And watch those kilties."

"I've been through that bit with Dolinda."

"I mean it, Angie."

"I know you do," she kissed his cheek. "I love it when you get serious. Your nose wrinkles."

"Is that so. I've been promoted to second head, by the way. A few extra quid in my pocket and two freshers to lord over. That's promotion. Reckon the car did it. One glance at it and Luigi melted. There's a chance Chartres is starting a taxi-service. You know the sort of thing. Book a meal and we'll ferry you and your party to the club for a half-penny. I might get involved when I'm not serving the tables."

"Sounds interesting."

"Look, Angie. Luigi's on the prowl. We're dead busy. Any chance I can see you later? I'm off around ten."

"Sorry, I've to get back to Guildford. I leave with the trunk in the morning. I'm still cramming my lifetime in it. I'm on the move again. I feel like a tramp in a way, only my knapsack's bigger."

Nick kissed her. On the lips this time, warm with just a hint of something more. Angie looked at him quizzically. "I'll send you a bulletin," she promised.

The wind howled the following morning. Through the windows of the Glasgow express, Angie could see litter flying and trees bowing. The train was exceptionally busy. A smell of sickness caught at her throat. A passenger had brought up her breakfast just inside the carriage and an attendant was trying to mop it up, using a strong disinfectant. When he'd finished,

Angie went out into the corridor for some fresh air. She stood by an open window, letting the wind tousle her hair.

"Not much of a day for a long ride."

Angie's heart jumped. She recognised the voice instantly.

"Seb, what the hell are you doing here?"

"Exercising my legs. Seeking some fresh air, like you, I guess."

"You know what I mean. How come you're on a Glasgow train? It doesn't go to Manchester."

"Someone has to keep an eye on you. Seriously, I've been invited to a party and I couldn't resist the call of red suspenders and black stockings."

"I can believe that. You used me." Angie turned away and began to move down the corridor. She swayed as the train reeled and Seb caught her arm to steady her.

"You wanted it as much as I did."

"I thought you cared."

"I did. You were, are, so sweet."

"I'd never been with a man before. I was flattered, infatuated."

"And now, Angel? I'm the same person. Do you want me now?" Seb put his arm round her waist and pulled her close. For a second she relaxed as his lips touched hers. The magic was still there. She would have to fight harder. She wriggled free.

"You disgust me. What would your fiancee say if she could see you. If she knew about..."

"We have an understanding, Christine and I. We've known each other for two years. She accepts my weaknesses."

"She's a damned fool, then"

"Come on, Angie. We could have some fun. Seriously, I've to be in Glasgow for a month on a course. I know you're with Henry. The family grape vine broadcasts all the news. Celeste and I are friends. Mind you, I didn't think you'd be travelling today. I understood you travelled last week. When can I see you?"

"You can't. I never want to see you again."

"You're a silly little bitch."

His words cut. Angie stormed towards her carriage. The nausea there was more inviting than that produced by Seb Arnold.

She wedged herself between the window and a fat man, who belched continually through a box of sandwiches and apples. Opposite her a young man chain smoked, and his companion, who Angie assumed was his mother, slept. The woman's head jerked with each movement of the train and she moaned quietly. The girl who'd been sick had disappeared.

Angie managed to avoid Seb for the rest of the journey as she buried her nose in a magazine. In a way, she was glad he'd turned up. It had given her the chance to dismiss him. Seb was a cad, a cheating, despicable cad. She vowed she would never waste her thoughts on him again. Compared with Nick, he was scum. But her heart still raced as she remembered his touch.

Angie watched the trunk being unloaded and ensured its safe transfer to the van that would deliver it to Woodend the next day.

She caught sight of Seb leaving the station and made certain to keep well behind him as she searched for the distinctive nose and toothy grin of Hugh.

They arrived at Woodend and Estelle fussed and the Countess emerged from the lounge to offer a meal and a warm drink, both of which Angie refused.

"We have wonderful news. Henriette is leaving the hospital tomorrow. Celeste and Hugh are going to fetch her in the afternoon. You could go, too, if you wish?"

"I'll leave it to them. I'm tired. Tomorrow, I think I'll have a lie in, and spend the day getting my things sorted out and writing letters. It's great about Henriette. My trunk, by the way, will be arriving in the morning."

Angie slipped between the cool sheets, pulled the blankets round her chin, and slept.

When she woke she was aware she'd been dreaming.

146

Someone had been holding her closely in their arms. There was the unmistakeable smell of Brylcream. Not Seb, she realised, but Nick. She had been dreaming of Nick.

Henry held out her arms to Angie as she entered the dining room for the evening meal next day. "I was scared you'd change your mind. It's so exciting, isn't it?"

In contrast, Celeste gave nothing away, being neither warm nor cold in her greeting. La Grandmere, Celeste imparted, had a headache and would eat in her room. Angela was to consider herself free until after the weekend and if it suited she could start earning her keep on Monday. She, herself, would be leaving that day for St. Andrews University.

The door closed on Celeste early on Monday morning. Angie felt a sense of relief. She could get on with her job knowing Henriette's sister would not tinge their relationship. A routine was drawn out. Apart from the hour a day when a physio-nurse would call, Angie would attend to Henry's needs from toilette to amusement.

By the end of the first week, Angie knew it wasn't going to be all honey. Henry's moods pendulumed from near elation to near despair. She tired quickly, her mind flitting from one thing to another as boredom crucified concentration. Angie became adept at recognising Henry's mood changes and compiled methods to deal with them.

The clock she found was her friend. Washing and dressing absorbed the hour from 8 am to 9 am, when breakfast was taken, a leisurely affair that, with the opening of mail, accounted for a further hour.

A walk between 10.20 am and 11.20 am usually involved some local shopping. Games of cards alternated with Monopoly or Chess. Angie had never moved a pawn before. Henry became irritated as she explained the rules yet again.

"Sorry, I'm so dumb," Angie admitted.

"Not dumb, just thick," Henry said, shouting "check" for the umpteenth time. The Monopoly game belonged to Angie. She had brought it with her in the trunk. The familiar London streets, snapped up with toy money, flourished as hotels developed beside houses, stations changed hands. Chance won lotteries, paid taxes and condemned to jail.

Staying at Woodend was luxury. Assisted by an agency help, Estelle ensured that the household ran smoothly from the kitchens on the ground floor to the attic where, Angie learned, the Countess exhibited to private viewers a collection of her own paintings in oil and water colour. Angie had been allowed a studied look at them the weekend she'd arrived and had been struck by their vigour. On enquiry, she discovered the Countess hadn't employed her talent for some years. Art, Angie decided, could be a rewarding therapy for Henry and she broached the subject at dinner.

"I've never tried anything serious. Lynn was the artist at school. I suppose I could have a go. What do you think, Grandmere?"

"It's a wonderful idea. I'll ask Hugh to look out my drawing boards. One's bound to fit on to the chair somehow. You can use the utility room. I'm sure I have plenty of paint and paper."

Most afternoons were spent in the utility, or, as they renamed it, the studio. Henry was no Constable, but she could produce a fair impression of a country garden.

Angie was two weeks into her new job when Seb called. She had known his visit was a possibility but hoped he'd have the sense to stay away. She realised she'd have to be civil and Henry, at least, was pleased to see him.

"Heard you were getting married," she said.

"News travels. The big day was to have been in June but it's postponed till September because of the finals. Too much pressure. Meantime, I'm going to paint the town a vivid shade of scarlet, and you can help."

"Mm didn't know you'd heard about my artistic prowess, or lack of it."

"You're being modest, Henry. You've some of your grandmother's talent. You should see her picture of the rear courtyard." Angie intervened.

"No doubt I will. But the kind of painting I have in mind, requires less effort. So stop pretending you don't know what I mean."

"Well, stop talking rot. Wheelchairs don't fit easily into the Glasgow night scene."

"Nonsense. I've already fixed dinner for four at The Black Cat. It's a new club. Only been open a few months, apparently. I'm bringing a friend from college. We can make it for five if your Grandmother wants to join us."

"But the chair. I can't go anywhere without it."

"There's no problem. The entrance is on the street level. A wide lift takes us to the dining room on the first floor. There's even a toilet for the disabled and they're willing to supply an adjustable tray if you can't reach the table. I've sussed everything out. What more does she want, eh Angie?"

Angie didn't answer, but she could see Henry mulling it over in her mind.

"We couldn't. Do you really think? It's absurd. I've not been out at night since the accident."

"It's overdue then. All we've got to do is convince your grandmother."

Seb was at his most persuasive when he confronted the Countess in the lounge.

"I think, perhaps, you are right. It is time Henriette faced people again and I'm sure you'd like a night out, Angela. It hadn't occurred to me how cloistered our life must be here. Life is to be enjoyed."

"Would you like to come with us?" Seb asked.

"Me? No. I like my own hearth, these days. Go out and enjoy yourselves and I insist I pay the bill."

Seb's protests were dismissed.

Angie wasn't too sure about going out with Seb even in the company of Henriette. "What about transport?"

"I'd considered that. A taxi firm operates from Anderson's Garage and they say it's not a problem. They've a van with a ramp."

Seb had everything organised. Grandmother applauded.

In the afternoon, Henriette went to bed to rest and La Grandmere retired to her room. Angie found herself alone with Seb.

"It's very good of you to work all this out," she said, trying to sound appreciative.

"It means I'll see you," he placed an arm round Angie's waist. She tried to free herself.

"I'm going to please Henriette, and if you let her down I'll..."

Seb's grip tightened, "Don't fool yourself, Angel."

Angie felt trapped. If she cried out she would upset the household. Again she tried to wriggle out of his grasp.

"It's as I said, Angie, we can have fun." He kissed her first lightly, then with passion. Angie felt her knees weaken. Why, oh why does he have this effect on me?

"Christine...."

".....is miles away. Saturday night she'll be clubbing it. No doubt with me away, she'll flirt."

"And that doesn't bother you?"

"I told you, we have an understanding."

"Well I don't understand."

"You don't need to Angel." Seb was kissing her again, she tried to resist but instead her lips sought his, her body yielded. Damn Seb. Damn, damn, damn.

CHAPTER 14

Angie flicked through the clothes she'd hung in the wardrobe. She fingered the sequins on the bodice of a black off the shoulder gown and placed it on the bed. She laid a long straight dress in palest gold beside it. Both had been Lynn's. She took out her own blue crepe. Spoiled for choice, she tried them on one after the other, seeking assurance from the freestanding mirror. Lynn's gowns fitted quite well, but it was too soon. She would wear her own blue and would miss Sylvie's sapphires.

Dressing Henry was less of a problem. She had made up her mind to wear a long black skirt and ruby satin top.

"I can be a femme fatale even in a wheel chair," she quipped. She had spent a long time brushing her hair and applying her make-up and her skin appeared to regain its previous radiance. Only the hollows of her cheeks hinted at the weeks in hospital.

The Countess's face beamed as she inspected them in the hall.

A hoot from outside signalled Seb's arrival. He dashed into the house.

"Ready?" he asked. He took over from Angie and wheeled Henry to the rear of the van in the courtyard. "Hold tight."

Seb ran with the chair up the ramp and Angie climbed into the van to sit beside Henry. A blonde haired man was already seated, knees hunched to make room for the wheel-chair.

"Tom, meet the loveliest girls in town. Angie and Henriette."

Greetings exchanged they were driven through the Glasgow streets to The Black Cat, within a very neat St Bartholomews Square. Fairy lights at the entrance to the night club brightened, then dimmed, as they proceeded through the foyer to the dining room. Pictures of black cats purred from stark white walls and were repeated on table cloths, napkins and the handles of cutlery.

The Black Cat was in vogue with young Scotland. The dining room was alive with talk. In one corner, the dance floor sprung to the tap of stiletto heels, the beat of patent leather. It was, Angie thought, almost too lively. Ringing false, as if everyone was trying hard to be witty and entertaining. The menu, however, was genuine, with food that tempted and wine that glowed, as the chatter teased. Henriette managed to draw her chair near enough to the set place to eat without the clip on tray. Coffee was served at low round tables beside chaise-longues, which lined the walls. Behind mock pillars, couples clinched.

"Romantic enough?" Seb asked, holding Angie close in a slow waltz. He lowered his head until their cheeks touched. Angie nodded. It was just one night. That was all. Tomorrow she would forget him again. Angie felt intoxicated by the atmosphere as her head swirled and her heart pounded.

"Better get back to Henry," she said as the music stopped.

"Henry's fine. Tom's obviously intrigued by her. And you, Angie are utterly irresistible. You look radiant."

Seb drew her into an alcove and she felt his body pressed against her own. In another setting they would have made love. Here it was impossible. Even Seb wasn't that brazen. But he was dangerous. She would have to keep in control of her emotions. Not let him sense what she felt. This wasn't love. She could never love Seb. Yet he made her weak and he wasn't free. He belonged to Christine.

Angie pushed him away. "That's enough. Let's join the others." Her voice was cool. "I don't want to get involved with you, understand?"

"Just as you say, sweet Angel, but you are already."

He led Angie back to the table where Henry and Tom were discussing the pros and cons of living in Glasgow and doing some reminiscing.

"As a little girl, I remember crossing the River Seine and thinking it the most beautiful place in the world. Because of the war, we came here, and I found another river, the Clyde. Full of industry, yet in its own way equally beautiful. Shipyards with huge cranes silhouetted against the night sky, and the people, such characters. Warm and down to earth. But many have forgotten how to laugh since the war."

"Doesn't seem that way to me," Tom said, looking around.

"This is fantasy land. Letting your hair down territory."

"She's right," Angie butted in. "The real world's out there. When it's not grieving for lost lives, it's pining for steaks, and its women are painting seams up the back of their legs because they can't buy fine stockings. We're the privileged."

"You privileged? Henry privileged?" Seb retorted.

"Yes. Even Henry. Materially she wants for nothing. I don't know about Tom, but how often have you gone without, Seb?"

"Every night, Angie. Every night."

"Stop being an idiot. This is a serious conversation for once."

"You need another drink." Seb waved the empty champagne bottle in the air. "Another bottle, waiter."

"You've had enough."

"I can never have enough. Let's dance."

He pulled Angie to her feet.

"Seb, people are staring."

He turned and blew a raspberry at the group at the next table. They laughed, and thus encouraged, Seb continued to ape around.

Angie resumed her seat.

"If you won't dance, Henry will." He grabbed the wheel chair and pushed it towards the dance floor.

Henry responded, "I thought you'd never ask."

Dancers cleared a path as he twirled the chair on to the polished parquet and guided Henry into a slow fox trot. Tom and Angie joined the watching crowd. Henriette's dark hair gleamed in the dim light as round and round they whirled. Her face glowing with excitement. The dancers began to applaud.

"For once, I felt almost normal," Henry confessed as they settled again at their table.

"And I thought you were just a drunken idiot." Angie let Seb kiss her forehead.

"My turn now." Tom lifted his glass. "Give me a second to down this."

"Too late," Henry said. "Like Cinderella it's time to quit the ball. The taxi's due back at twelve-thirty, remember. We're already five minutes past time. I don't fancy a pumpkin."

Angie was reminded of Chartres. She had likened leaving there to the Cinderella fairy tale.

Seb grabbed the champagne bottle from the ice-bucket. "There's too much in here to leave."

Back at Woodend, the champagne cooled as Angie settled Henry in bed. Seb and Tom had conjured an invitation to stay the night and their room was next to Angie's.

"We'll finish the bottle. No point in wasting it. You pour," Seb said to Tom.

He sat on his bed with his arms round Angie. The drink had its effect. When it was finished, Seb pulled Angie to her feet.

"Tom doesn't mind sleeping on his own. Do you?"

"Neither do I." Angie slipped out of their room and into her own, snibbing the door behind her.

Seb stood outside, "If you don't open up I'll shout all over the house. Wake up La Grandmere and Estelle if I haven't already."

Angie opened the door. Seb stepped inside and locked it behind him. He lifted Angie in his arms and carried her to the bed. "Angie Bolton, you're the sexiest girl in Scotland."

Angie woke first and bathed.

"You'd better get dressed," she told Seb.

He yawned, stretched his arms and got out of bed.

"Guess so." He kissed Angie on the cheek. "You're a hot little kitten."

"Not at this time in the morning. I've to go to help Henry." She opened the door and Seb sauntered out and into the next room. Angie could hear Tom moving about.

It was odd the way she felt about Seb. She didn't even like him and yet sexually the attraction was magnetic. Angie hoped Christine wouldn't find out and vowed it would never happen again. It was so easy. Opportunity, drink, need.

"I wish he'd go away and stay away. He's so disturbing. I'm not ready for all this. Damn it, I'm barely seventeen."

Angie found Henry wide awake and still sparkling.

"Your Seb was wonderful, wasn't he? And Tom, he was special, too. Attentive, fun."

"Seb's no more than a charming cad, and he's not mine. Remember he's engaged to Christine."

"He's the one who should remember that. Maybe he'll improve after the wedding."

"I doubt it."

Seb and Tom left after breakfast, thanking the Countess for her courtesy.

"You must come again. You're welcome anytime. Henriette looks so much better today."

Tom took La Grandmere at her word and called the next day and the next. He joined in the card games, took Henriette for walks and Angie found herself making excuses to leave them alone. Seb was noticeable by his absence.

He called briefly the day he and Tom were returning to Manchester.

"Any messages?" he asked Angie.

"You could post this letter to Nick. He might get it a bit quicker that way."

"Ah. The waiter at Chartres?"

"Yes."

"Pining for you no doubt."

"I shouldn't think so."

"Then you're blind, Angel. He adores you and it shows."

"Nick? You're joking. Anyway, you hardly know him."

Nick was a friend. Next to Lynn he'd been her closest confidante - but that was all. Surely that was all.

She wished it had been Nick who'd come to Glasgow. She missed him. Those intense caring eyes. Nick, she knew she liked. He was the velvet cushioned chair in her mother's kitchen. Warm, comfortable, reliable.

Henry was in a mood when Tom left.

"Life's so boring without him," she moaned.

"Watch yourself or I'll think you're in love."

"Maybe I am, a bit."

Tom, it appeared, was entranced. He telephoned Henry most days, ordered flowers to be sent and bombarded her with letters. In June he returned to Glasgow and again Angie felt she needed to give them space so she arranged to spend a week in London. Estelle, happy to earn more money, agreed to take care of Henry's personal needs.

Nick met Angie at Euston.

"Sylvie's over there," he said pointing to a row of parked cars. "Okay, smile, but I had to call her that. She runs like a dream."

On their way through London, Angie and Nick chatted.

"Where am I taking you?"

"I haven't a clue. A hotel, I guess."

"You can come home with me if you like."

"The new flat?"

"It's not exactly a flat. A couple of rooms with a shared loo and kitchen. Thirty bob a week. The building's quite old, but it's sound. Clean and everything. You're welcome to stay. Won't be like the Countess's place, I'm afraid."

"Maybe I will, just for tonight, then. Save me hunting for somewhere else, thanks."

"How's Henry?" Nick asked.

"Much better. She's having therapy. May even walk again, and what's more, she's in love."

Angie told Nick of Seb's visit, skipping details of her own relationship with him, and elaborating on the dinner in the

Black Cat.

"Let's wish them well."

"You look as if you're flourishing, Nick. New clothes, a new flat, and you're obviously managing to run Sylvie."

"Things have been looking up. Remember I suggested running a taxi service to and from Chartres? Well, I've started it and it's doing nicely. Luigi thought it a great idea. We run three cars now. I only do a bit of the driving in my spare time. Not much else on anyway. Luigi pays me a cut of the profits as it was my idea."

So Sylvie was proving her worth. The real Sylvie would be delighted if she knew. The journey through London was smooth, swift, and without incident.

"Have you heard from Dryden Terrace?" Nick asked as they rounded a corner into a road of tall grey houses.

"I'll go and see them. I've sent Cyril a couple of post cards and a letter but he's never replied."

Being with Nick seemed so natural, Angie thought as she followed him up a flight of stone steps to the second floor apartment. She was safe with Nick.

It was chilly for June and Nick, Angie observed, had lit a fire. It was almost out when they entered the flat and he tonged coals on to the glowing embers.

"Won't take long to blaze again. We've caught it just in time. Didn't expect to use much coal at this time of year. Call this summer"

Angie looked round the sitting room. Red linoleum surrounded a red carpet, a single arm chair elbowed the couch against one wall and a mahogany cabinet, doubling as a bookcase, argued with a gate-leg table for another. Two kitchen chairs with basket seats completed the furniture.

"It's very cosy," Angie said.

"Small, you mean. You can have the bedroom. I changed the sheets in case you came. I'll doss here on the couch."

"I can't turf you from your bed. I'll sleep here."

"No way. This room's warmer."

157

Angie conceded.

The shared kitchen was busy when they went to make something to eat and the bathroom was occupied. The cafe round the corner solved the problem.

"I've to go to work in a while. We're short staffed and I promised to do a three hour stint before you said you were coming down. It's double pay. I couldn't resist it, not even for you, Angie. Come with me if you like. You could prop up the bar."

"I'd rather stay here, if that's okay. I'm needing an early night. I'll take a bath when the vacancy sign shows. How many do you share with?"

"Only three. Two men and a girl. It's not usually a problem. There's an extra loo down the garden if you're desperate."

Angie went for her bath, with a towel draped over her shoulders. She'd armed herself with cleaning materials from the kitchen, but the bathroom was spotless. Undisturbed, she relaxed in warm suds for twenty minutes before returning to the sitting room and making tea on the single gas stove. Angie curled up in the hollow of Nick's bed and slept soundly.

Nick woke her at nine with bacon, scrambled eggs, toast and tea. He ate his breakfast perched on the end of the bed while she propped against the pillows.

"You're a useful type," Angie said.

""Been on my own a long time, remember. Sleep well?"

"Great. And you?"

"I was too tired to do otherwise. We were packed last night."

"I'll find a place to stay this morning."

"Why bother?"

"I can't stay on here."

"Don't see why not. I'll make use of you if it makes you feel better. Give you the dusters."

"It's a deal."

It took barely forty minutes to clean the flat, wipe the cooker and ledges in the kitchen and mop the floor. It was Nick's turn.

"What's your programme for today? I'm off till eight but on until two, if you get what I mean."

"Have you been to Albany Place?"

"Not as often as I used to go, but yes, about three weeks ago. The land's all clear and they've…"

"Don't tell me. I'd like to go there and see for myself."

"Fine. When?"

"Now?"

"Done. I'll go and warm Sylvie up."

The weather remained cool and unsettled. Angie and Nick drove to the bottom of the hill and, parking the car, chose to climb the uneven pavement towards the Place. Rain began to fall heavily and they ran the last few yards and sheltered under the railway bridge.

"Only a shower," Nick indicated blue sky among the clouds. He was right. As a watery sun appeared, they made their way to the bench outside the Rose and Thorn. Across the road work resumed after the rain. Yellow bricks were cemented to form walls. High on scaffolding workers ran along planks.

"Five storeys," Angie said. "Think of all the families who'll live here. Mum would like that." She stood up. "I'll not come again. I've seen it brought back to life. It belongs to others now."

"That's more or less how I felt as I saw it developing. Albany Place isn't on the street map now. See? They've changed the sign. It's Albany Court. The Place can't haunt me anymore. Come on."

Angie and Nick retraced their steps back to the car.

"It's a bit odd - losing your roots. Almost as if they hadn't existed." Angie said. "I'm free to go my own way. Do as I please. I like that feeling."

"Roots will grow. Not here, but somewhere, you'll form them."

"Who needs them? I'm getting used to a nomadic life."

"Have case, will travel, eh? But you need a base, Angie. Everyone has to establish a base, some day. You'll want to marry and have children."

"Sometimes I'm not so sure about that. What's the point if someone can take it all from you?"

"Regeneration. Life's for the living."

Angie stood very still. "That's what Lynn said when she buried a dead bird."

The evening should have been quiet with Nick at work, but from above a constant tapping, followed by the scrape of furniture on uncarpeted floors, annoyed. Angie drowned the sounds with the radio until requested to turn it down by the man in the next flat. Middle-aged, portly, and probably suffering from hypertension, he strutted outside Nick's rooms.

"Tone it down a bit, ducks. Bad enough all that din upstairs. Chap's just moved in. I'm early shift. You don't live here, anyway, do you?"

"No, I'm visiting"

"Some guys have all the luck."

The tapping eased at ten thirty. Angie took a book to bed. Sherlock Holmes wasn't the best choice.

CHAPTER 15

A "FOR SALE" sign towered over the front of Cyril Bolton, Tailor's. Angie had no idea the shop was for sale. She could see and smell new paint on the doors and window frames. Although she had retained her key, she rang the bell. Edwina answered.

"Angela!" She drew back and for a moment Angie thought the housekeeper was about to shut the door in her face. She took a pace forward and Edwina stood aside.

"Sorry," Angie said. "I should have let you know I was coming." She stepped into the hall. "I saw the sign. What's happening?"

Edwina led Angie into the room behind the shop.

"Your uncle's retiring. He's been ill for weeks. A flare up of kidney trouble he had some years ago."

"Kidney trouble?"

"He doesn't talk about it. You must have noticed how puffy he is. His face, and particularly his hands."

Angie reddened. The piggish features and podgy fingers were due to illness. She felt guilty for ridiculing them.

"How is he now?"

"It's under control again. But he's had enough. He's moving to Brighton."

"And you?"

"I shan't be going with him. I'm going to stay with Alice."

"Who's looking after the shop at the moment - Jed?"

"Mr Conway left a month ago. He's with Goddard's in Monk Street, more money and security. Matt's been helping out."

"I'm sorry. I didn't know."

"Well, you're here now, I suppose. We could do with more help if your uncle will take you back. And I shouldn't depend on that."

"But I'm not staying. I've to return to Glasgow at the weekend."

Edwina's eyebrows rose, "I see."

"Is Uncle Cyril around?"

"He's in his rooms. I'll tell him you're here."

"No. I'll go up myself."

Angie climbed to the first floor and rapped on Cyril's door. He opened it. His shoulders were rounded, his cheeks and jowls bloated. He wobbled slightly when he saw Angie and remained silent for a few seconds before saying, "You're causing a draught, come in."

"I'm in London for a week. Why didn't you tell me you were ill?"

"And you'd have come running back?" he sneered. He went to his desk, shuffled some papers and pulled out a photograph which he handed to Angie. "I've taken a bungalow over looking the sea east of Brighton. A spot called Deneston."

"Who's going to look after you?"

"Edwina doesn't want to leave London but it's all arranged. A nurse cum housekeeper. I got her through an agency Dillard Thrift recommended. I'll go as soon as someone buys the shop. Thought Thrift would have told you."

"I haven't heard from him for some weeks."

Cyril lowered himself into one of the leather chairs. "Sit if you want to."

Angie chose a chair to his side. She wasn't sure she wanted to face him. "So how are you feeling?"

"Better."

"Are you happy about leaving?"

"I don't know. No use staying on. I like the sea."

"Will you keep in touch with me?"

"I suppose so. Thrift acts for me, too."

"Did you get my cards?"

"Yes."

"You didn't reply."

"Did you expect me to?"

"No not really. You're my uncle, someone should have let me know you were ill."

"Hmn."

The stilted conversation continued for a further few minutes. Edwina came in with afternoon tea for three. She fussed over Cyril as she poured from the pot. "Have you taken your tablets?" Cyril stirred and grunted. Edwina took this to be negative. "I'll fetch them. It's the orange ones, isn't it?"

Cyril nodded. Edwina appeared to enjoy her role as nurse. She's an odd mixture, Angie thought. Somehow it wasn't in keeping with Alice. She, herself, felt entirely out of place.

"I'd better be going. I'm staying with a friend until tomorrow." Something made Angie refrain from saying exactly where. "I'm hoping to see Dolinda. If you need me 'phone there." Angie scribbled the number on the pad on Cyril's desk. "I'll probably be back in Scotland on Sunday. I'll keep in touch."

In the event Angie stayed with Dolinda until Sunday, renewing a hand-licking, ankle rubbing relationship with Taurus who sniffed her out the minute she arrived and rarely left her side. The Sunday and Monday nights she spent back with Nick before catching the early train on Tuesday.

Henry hadn't had time to miss her. Tom saw to that. La Grandmere was preoccupied with workmen redecorating her bedroom and Celeste had still to arrive home for the summer recess.

As she lay on the satin quilt on her bed, Angie realised that despite being here with Henry and her family she was still very much on her own.

"Have case will travel," Nick had said. It had to be like that, she had to keep on the move, especially now Albany Place was erased from the street maps. She guessed the roots would shoot one day, but not yet.

Angie looked out of the window. A full moon rose in the darkening sky and stars glittered.

"You're there, I know it. Maybe it's not heaven but those stars contain particles of the dead. Mother, Father, Lynn, the dead bird." They were all smiling, guiding her. Especially Dad. Pointing somewhere. North, east, south, west.

She took a sheet of paper, tore it into four pieces, and wrote the letters N. E. S. W. on it. She screwed the paper into tight balls and clutching them in one hand threw them on to the bed. She picked out the one nearest her. W. When she left Glasgow. She would travel west.

Celeste came home in the morning. She looked well but seemed withdrawn as if she had something important on her mind. Angie decided the chances of finding out what it might be were remote.

She was wrong. Celeste needed a confidante and she sought, not La Grandmere or Henriette, but Angela to fill the role and she knocked on Angie's door late on the night of her homecoming.

"Hope I'm not disturbing you. I heard you moving about so knew you were still up. Can we talk?"

Angie invited Celeste in and listened.

"I've got to tell someone. I can't face Grandmother and I'm not burdening Henriette with my troubles."

"I could sense something was wrong. You've been so quiet. Is it university? Your studies?"

"No nothing like that. Look you must promise to keep what I say to yourself."

"I guess that's okay... unless..."

"I don't want anyone else to know. Not ever."

Angie promised.

"I'm pregnant. Eight weeks."

Angie squirmed awkwardly, unsure how to respond. In the end she came up with, "The father... are you in love?"

"Love? Of course not. It was just a wild fling. A one

nighter. I doubt if I'll see him again. He wasn't one of the students. Just a charmer I met at a dance. Too much to drink and we clicked. Just once. I never dreamt... it's bad luck."

"I see." Angie knew the comment was inadequate.

"Are you shocked?"

"No. Not really. It could have happened to..to..." Angie stopped herself saying me. "To anyone."

"That's what I tell myself."

"What will you do? Will you go back to university?"

"I've thought a lot. I can't keep the baby. It's not possible. I'll have to get an abortion. And remember, I'm a catholic."

"That complicates things. You've seen your doctor? You're sure?"

"Not my own. A friend at university recommended one. They're the only other people to know. Anyway this doctor says he'll do what he can but I'll have to pay."

"Have you got the money?"

"Enough, just. But how do I tell La Grandmere I've spent it? She's bound to find out. She checks that sort of thing."

Angie and Celeste sat silently contemplating for some seconds.

"You'll have to go away to have the abortion?"

"Yes to a clinic near Dundee."

"You could say you were going on an expensive holiday."

"Perhaps, but it's a bit weak. I wondered if I could say I'd lent some of it to you?"

"Me? What for?"

"We'd think of something. Your fares to London..."

"I'm just back from there, and I'm not a pauper. I've my own money. You'll have to think harder - a study course you could pretend to take that costs a fortune, or an expensive piece of jewellery you're desperate to buy."

"Maybe if I can't lend you the money, you could lend it to me, or some of it. I could pay you back gradually; Grandmother wouldn't notice that."

"My lawyer holds my money. I've about two-hundred

pounds in my bank. I'd like to help, but it's a daft idea. You'll have to speak to your grandmother. She's a right to know."

To Angie's horror, Celeste threw herself across the bed and burst into tears, "Never, never, never." It was some time before the weeping subsided. "What am I going to do? It would kill Grandmother."

Angie thought La Grandmere would withstand the shock but Celeste was upset enough. She had to placate her.

"I think we should tell Henry. Perhaps between us we can raise enough. It's too late now. I've got to get to sleep. We'll discuss it again tomorrow."

"I'm not telling Henriette. Not tomorrow. Not ever. If you can't help forget it. I wish I hadn't said anything to you."

Celeste went to her own bedroom, tears retracing their tracks down her cheeks. Angie lay awake for ages. She'd never seriously thought about babies. It was that easy. Just once was all it took if you were unlucky, or lucky, depending on the circumstances. Seb and she, they could have...it was unthinkable. And all this confidante business. At seventeen, she felt more and more like an agony aunt.

Angie didn't see Celeste until well after breakfast.

"Henry's sitting up waiting for the doctor. I've got half-an-hour. Let's go for a walk."

They went out through the rear garden into the woods.

"Are you sure you've thought this out?" Angie asked.

"Positive. I've been over it again and again. Abortion's the only way. It's what I want."

"It's like killing a baby."

"It's not a baby. It's something inside me like an obstruction that's got to be removed. I hoped you'd understand. I should have known." The tears flowed again. Tears didn't suit Celeste.

"Shut up, Celeste. Weeping isn't going to solve anything. Look I reckon I'm doing the wrong thing, but I'll lend you a hundred. Will that help?."

Celeste brightened a little. "Thanks. I'll scrape the other two hundred myself."

"Three hundred pounds! Is that what it takes?"

"That's what it takes."

Celeste put on a show of normality over dinner. Angie found it more difficult. Secrets were like wedges. You were always on your guard, biting your tongue. She hated it.

Angie was glad when, a week later, Hugh brought the car to the front of the house to take Celeste to the coach station.

"A course in the middle of your holiday, indeed. You work too hard. You've been looking strained recently." La Grandmere stood in the morning sun heading the send off party. Henriette wheeled herself to the pavement.

"Bet it's more fun than work."

Celeste looked towards Angie, "I hope so." Uncertainty reflected in her eyes. Angie took her hand and whispered, "Good luck".

Back indoors, Henriette was bored and showed it. "There has to something more exciting than sitting here," she moaned.

Angie could think of nothing to stimulate her until La Grandmere produced a pile of brochures.

"Pick a holiday. Not too far away. It's time we had some sea air. I thought perhaps next month."

"You're a marvel, Grandmother. That's what I need. A change of walls for a couple of weeks and I'll be ready for Tom when he comes back."

Estelle interrupted them at five o clock. "The telephone for Mademoiselle Angela."

Instinct made Angie take it upstairs.

"It's me, Celeste. I'm not at the clinic, I'm in Stirling - half way between Glasgow and Dundee. In a tiny hospital run by nuns."

"Why? What's happened?"

"It was awful. I didn't feel great this morning. I got dreadful pains soon after the coach left. The road was so bumpy I started bleeding and was sick. The driver took me to this hospital. I'm in bed and I've to lie dead still all the time.

167

They wanted to phone Grandmother but I begged them not to. Instead I was allowed to make this call. The nuns say there isn't much hope of saving the baby."

Celeste paused, Angie didn't know what to say.

"Are you there, Angie? Did you hear me?"

"Yes, I heard."

"Would you phone the clinic and cancel my admission." Celeste rattled off the telephone number and Angie scribbled it on a scrap of paper. "Explain what's happened. With any luck, they won't charge."

"Are you all right?"

"Silly question. At this moment I'm in agony but a miscarriage has got to be better than an abortion. Guess I'll be in here a few days. If I'm released early I'll find a hotel. By the way, if you want to call I've registered under the name Carole Martin. Both here and in Dundee. I can hear them coming. Better ring off."

"Take care."

"Will do."

Angie contacted the clinic right away. Fearful someone might come upstairs, she kept the conversation to a minimum, noting their address and offering to send further details by letter.

She felt a strange sense of relief. She wouldn't be party to an abortion after all. No church, Catholic or otherwise, could blame anyone for a miscarriage. Poor Celeste, it must be hell.

Downstairs, Henriette was still thumbing through the holiday brochures. "I fancy Blackpool. We've been there before. Loads of hotels to choose from and I could push myself along the prom, it's so flat."

The Countess pointed out that the east coast of Scotland might be more convenient for travel and Blackpool lacked a certain something.

"If I'm going on holiday I want to go somewhere lively."

It was settled. They would visit Blackpool. Henriette took charge of the arrangements and seemed to glue her chair to the telephone. She found a hotel with no steps, wide entrances and corridors and ground floor bed, dining and lounging rooms. With La Grandmere footing the bill, expense was no object. Henriette booked the best.

Angie related news of the holiday to Nick in their monthly bulletin.

"Lucky you," he replied. "I'm having a day at the races with Sylvie and Gideon. They're in London on a visit. Looking fitter than when they left. America suits them. They dined at Chartres the night before last and were asking after you. They live in Los Angeles, or rather Santa Monica, just outside the city. I guess you know that. It's on the coast too. Sounds fun. They're issuing invites all round. Well, maybe one day. Enjoy the sea."

It was odd, Angie thought, how things worked out. Not much more than a year ago she was waving goodbye to Updean. It seemed much longer. Then she was alone, well almost, in the big city. Along came Taurus, a snuffling little dog, and the world changed. Taurus led to Lynn, Lynn to Henry and luxury. Was she happy? On the surface, yes. She couldn't ask for more with everything laid on for her, accommodation, food, a job, companionship. All there without having to press a button. It wasn't real. None of this was real. She told herself that over and over again. Reality lay in the stars. I've not forgotten Dad, I'm building stepping stones. It can't be this easy. Like having babies. But that's another story.

Celeste returned ready to resume life as if nothing had happened.

"I feel as if I've woken from a nightmare. I want to forget it in a hurry. It's all over. If I weren't still sore, I'd be turning cartwheels." She handed an envelope to Angie. "Here's your hundred pounds. I didn't need it. Nature's much cheaper."

Angie took the money. Despite Celeste's breezy manner, she could tell the episode had cost Henry's sister more than money. Angie, too, had learned from it.

"Now, tell me all about this holiday to Blackpool. I can't

wait."

"Henriette's in charge of that. She'll give you the details."

Blackpool - another place, Angie thought, to add to the growing list and it was west. Well, a bit west.

It seemed to Angie when they arrived after a tense journey with Henry out of sorts and uncomfortable for the most part, that Blackpool strung for miles in one long avenue of hotels. The sun seared in a cloud free sky. Below the sea wall, the water purred as it lapped against soft sands. The town was alive. Holiday makers strolled hand in hand and children squealed as they splashed in the waves and built sand castles.

Colour was everywhere. In the flower beds and in the curtained windows of the hotels, where window boxes gave life to scarlet geraniums. Their hotel was on the outskirts of the town and, if not the biggest, justly laid claim to being the best. Henry had secured a suite of rooms on the ground floor.

Angie, it was decided, would share the largest bedroom with Henry, with the Countess and Celeste having individual rooms. A long balcony, decked with loungers, linked the apartments. It was hard to imagine that it had so short a time ago housed American troops. A memorial stood nearby behind low railings. Its fresh black granite stone listed the names of the local war dead. It was a stark reminder.

They had arrived late afternoon and there was barely time to unpack and bathe before dressing for dinner. Henriette opted to eat in their room.

"I'm tired," she complained. "Anyway, the stares will be easier to cope with in the morning. By then, hopefully, I won't have to fake a smile."

"I'll stay with you."

"No, don't. Just get me to bed now and I'll stay there till morning."

"Okay, but you'll never last that long. I'll come up once I've eaten."

The hotel had enough guests to make it interesting and Angie studied them as she dined. How similar they all were.

Well dressed, pockets obviously lined with large notes. They'd already put the war years behind them and seemed unaffected. The words "life is for the living" came into her head. Lynn would have revelled in this holiday.

Theirs was a quiet table, La Grandmere seemed engrossed in the food and Celeste looked more exhausted even than Henriette. An early night was on the cards for all.

In the event, Angie stayed up quite late. She attended to Henry and returned to wander through the gardens. At the rear of the hotel were several flood-lit tennis courts and Angie watched four young people playing a match. It had been a long time since she'd held a racquet.

"You play?" A boy of around eighteen joined her, his limbs tanned against the white of his shirt and shorts.

"Yes, a little."

"That's good. We're making up teams for a match tomorrow. Hotel club members versus the guests. Be here at four."

"Sorry, I've no racquet or tennis clothes."

"The hotel can help you out. They've got everything. Tomorrow at four, remember. Could you bring a friend?"

"Possibly, yes but...."

"No 'buts'." The boy ran through the gate and into what she took to be changing rooms. Angie smiled after him. An impulsive type. Born boss, she thought. I don't even know his name, and he certainly doesn't know mine. She watched the game finish. The boy hadn't come back out.

Angie went inside the hotel and was tempted by the noise in the cocktail bar. She ordered a soft drink and found a corner seat. Some sort of entertainment was taking place in the form of a game involving a giant sized clock and an equally huge pack of cards. Angie couldn't understand any of it. She finished her juice and went along to the suite to find Celeste in the lounge reading a magazine. La Grandmere had already retired.

"Shall I get them to bring us coffee or something?" Celeste asked.

"I suppose so. I've actually just had a drink at the bar."

"By yourself? That was daring and naughty. You're under-age."

"Not really. It's very informal and the drink wasn't alcoholic. They're playing a silly game."

"What fun. Not tonight, but tomorrow maybe."

"Talking of games. Do you play tennis?"

"I should hope so. Doesn't everyone?"

"They've got courts. A boy asked if I'd be in a guests' team tomorrow at four o'clock. They supply the gear. He said to bring a friend. Are you fit enough?"

" I'll soon find out. Better keep it from Henry."

"Why's that?"

"She used to be the local champion. It will hurt."

"She might want to watch."

"Perhaps."

"I'll ask her in the morning. Goodnight"

Angie crept into the room and without putting a light on stumbled to her bed. She heard Henry shifting in bed. "God why is it someone trying to be quiet makes more noise than when they're moving around naturally? For goodness sake settle down."

"Sorry, sleep tight."

"I'm unlikely to do that now." Henry's bedside light clicked on. "I'll have to go to the loo again."

Angie got up to help her, "No bother." She could tell the instant she reached Henriette's bed something was up. Henry's eyes, swollen not from lack of sleep but from crying, looked down at the sheets. Instinctively Angie put her arms round her. "What is it? Are you in pain?"

Henry pushed her aside with considerable strength. "Pain? What's pain? Half of me can't feel anything. I need the toilet, I tell you."

Angie helped her into the bathroom. "We brought a bed pan we'll use that next time. Save you getting up."

Henry lingered long enough to wash her face as well as her

hands. Angie transferred her from the chair back into bed.

"Why won't you tell me what the matter is?"

"You're the matter. Everyone's the matter. We shouldn't have come here."

"But you planned it. You wanted to come."

"I thought I did. What's the point? People in wheelchairs are just an encumbrance."

"Come on, Henry. This isn't like you."

"That's it. I don't know what's like me anymore."

"I thought you were so much happier. You've been coping brilliantly and you've got Tom."

"But for how long? How long will anyone stick with someone who's useless?"

"You'll never be useless, and you know it. Why, Doctor Gillon's even got you on your feet. I reckon you'll be taking some steps soon. He as good as said so."

"But do you believe it? It takes such an effort to stand I doubt I'll have the energy to move. Tom's asked me to marry him when his exams are over. Me, marry him? How could I? I care for him too much to saddle him with all this. He's young. He needs someone who can run and swim not a chronic invalid who has to be waited on."

"Why didn't you tell me - Tom and you? That would be wonderful. You're so good together. Can't you see it? Tom loves you enough to want to stay with you for the rest of his life. You should be laughing."

"I told you, I can't marry Tom."

"You'll hurt him more if you turn him down."

The tears poured again. "I already have, Angie. I've told him I couldn't marry him."

"And what did he say?"

"He said to give myself time. To use this break to decide. At home it seemed easy. I'd a feeling he was leading up to this and I planned what to say. But tonight I'd nothing else to do but think I hate myself, what I've become. Everyone thinks I'm strong, but I'm not."

"The trouble is you can't change what's happened. You have to accept it. I think you're the bravest person I've ever known. I'm so proud of you. Let's set ourselves targets. Let's aim at you walking down the aisle with me as your bridesmaid."

The tears stopped. A smile crept over Henry's face. "You really do believe I can do it?"

Angie drew the curtains back to peer out at the night sky. The stars were shining, "I'm sure of it," she said.

The next morning, aware Henry had to face up to something else, Angie told her about the tennis match.

"I don't have to play, of course," she said.

"I'll come and watch. I could coach you from the side lines."

"I'll need some of that. I haven't had a game for ages though I used to be in a club. Is Celeste any good?"

"Not bad. She was very promising before she gave it all up and started messing about with a crowd who were no good. Angie, I've never told anyone else this. Celeste has been a pain since she was about thirteen. She tried to grow up too quickly. Boys and all that. She was pregnant when she was fourteen and a half. My mother would have dealt with it differently, La Grandmere flipped. She sent her away for an abortion despite our religion. It was hushed up, but a lot of people guessed. Grandmother vowed if anything similar happened again she'd throw her out. I've never known Grandmother to be so angry. Celeste's improved lately but not a lot. Guess it's her nature to flirt. Remember you haven't heard any of this."

Angie had listened astonished. So Celeste had been through all that rigmarole before. Two babies and she's only eighteen. No wonder she'd refused to tell anyone. How stupid could she get?

"Angie, you look horrified. It does happen, you know. It's not so awful. I'd hoped to have lots of babies. Now I doubt if I've any hope. "

Angie changed the subject, "What would you like to do until the tennis."

"Go down to the shore I think. If that's possible."

The wheelchair clinked across a path to the beach. It was early for Blackpool but a few children played in the water under the guidance of parents.

"Could you push me right down to the water's edge? I want to feel the spray on my face. I'm not a great swimmer - I mean, I wasn't a great swimmer, but I love the sea."

"Me, too. My dad was a sailor."

"I'd forgotten that. What were your parents like?"

"Mum was quite small with fair curly hair and she blushed easily. Dad was the traditional tall and handsome type, in my eyes, anyway. My mum was very practical. Good at being a housewife and surprisingly firm when she needed to be. Dad was a dreamer. He was always telling stories that made me laugh."

"My father was a bit aloof. Children should stay in the nursery type. He did love us though. They both did. Mum was very adventurous. That's how they died - with the resistance. I've never heard the whole story. We were with Nat most of the time - at Grandmother's. Natalie was our nanny. She stayed until four years ago when she got married. I think she was glad to leave in the end. She found Celeste a handful and I was no angel."

They walked about half a mile along the shore. It wasn't easy pushing the chair across the damp sand. They climbed a ramp to the pavement.

"Hope the weather stays like this all the time," Angie said loosening the button at the neck of her blouse. "Shall we sit by the pool this afternoon? You can dangle your toes in."

"That won't do me any good. I'd rather sprawl on a lounger if you can manoeuvre me on to one. I've started reading Cronin's The Citadel."

As they entered the grounds, Celeste appeared with a group of three boys in attendance. She looked stunning in a blue and white swimsuit and knew it.

"I've met up with some of the tennis players. This is Peter,

175

no sorry, this is Peter, that's John and the one at the back is
Eric." Peter was Angela's acquaintance of the day before. The
girls identified themselves. Eric took over the chair and
wheeled Henry into a buffet lunch. La Grandmere was chatting
to an elderly lady who was wearing an enormous black hat and
whose legs bulged with varicose veins. The Countess smiled at
them as they entered but didn't approach.

For once Henriette appeared hungry and Angie was
delighted to see her finish a full plate of chicken salad. The
outburst of the previous night seemed forgotten already.

Celeste came in for lunch and offered to play cards with her
sister on the balcony. Henriette decided the cards could take
over from A J Cronin, but Angie declined an invitation to join
in and, relieved of her duties, she lazed the afternoon away
beside the pool, going for an occasional swim to cool off as
temperatures rose. At twenty minutes to four she went in search
of Henry and Celeste and found them engrossed in a game of
whist.

"Still here?" she said. "I'd thought you'd have given up long
ago."

"We did, but we came back to it. Celeste took me up the
little path at the rear of the hotel. It leads to a miniature farm.
Rabbits and hens, three cows and half a dozen sheep. It belongs
to the manager. He let me bottle feed a lamb whose mother
died delivering it. Guess what? They've called it Cyril."

"Thank goodness it wasn't a pig. I'd better send Cyril a card,
I suppose."

Celeste laughed. "Is he really that bad."

Angie shrugged. Since she'd learned of Cyril's illness she
knew she shouldn't call him a porker, and yet, she found it hard
to feel sorry for him and had no intention of faking such
emotion.

"We'd better hurry. Tennis in seven minutes. I picked up
these on the way from the swimming pool. We've to return
them after the match. The racquets and balls are down in the
clubhouse." Angie spread two sets of tennis gear across the

chair. "Take your pick."

"You shouldn't have bothered about me. I've a skirt with me. I might wear the shirt. It's nicer than mine."

They made the court with barely a minute to spare. The boys were hovering anxiously by the clubhouse door.

"We thought you weren't coming," Peter said.

The hotel club team consisted of Peter, Eric and three girls. Beside Angie and Celeste, there were three boys in the guests' side. It was agreed that Nicola, a district champion would play against one of the boy guests. Danny, overweight and suffering from hay fever drew the short straw.

He and Nicola played on the first court, Peter and Sandy, a good looking boy with ginger hair, took over the second and Celeste and one of the club girls were on court three. Angie had to wait for her chance. She sat alongside Henriette well behind the sidelines. A number of club members acted as line judges and umpires. Peter appeared to be in charge. He came over to Henriette.

"Do you think you could be a line judge on Court One?"

Henriette's face lit up with pleasure.

"I'd love to."

She wheeled herself over to the court and took up her position behind the baseline.

Angie stayed on Court Three to support Celeste. Henriette was right about her sister's tennis, for although at times she was erratic, overall, her strokes were impressive. She won easily in straight sets - six two, six one.

"Phew! Glad that's over. I'm definitely out of condition."

The guests lost the other two matches.

The second group of games began. Angie was drawn against Sally, a girl who looked about fourteen but assured Angie she was twenty-two. Angie started badly losing the first four games on the trot. Celeste encouraged her to try the forehand to her opponent's backhand.

"We can't afford to lose this one" she urged.

Angie fought back to lose the first set four-six. By now her

177

game was beginning to work. The rhythm had returned to her serve and the urge to achieve sent her opponent skeltering all over the court. Angie took the set six-three.

"Keep it up. You can win this." Celeste encouraged. Angie held on to her opponent for five games. But it was not to be. Lack of recent practice and a sudden surge of energy in Sally and the match was lost.

Celeste commiserated. "You played well. It wouldn't have made any difference, anyway. Amanda lost. We had only one winner - me."

"Ah well, we tried," Angie said as they trooped into the clubhouse for drinks. "Where's Henry?"

"Over by the window."

Henriette sat in her wheelchair amidst a crowd of boys and girls conversing freely. Her face was alive. Apart from when she was with Tom, Angela hadn't seen her look so happy since the night at "The Black Cat," when she'd been twirled on to the dance floor. The doubts of the night before were quelled. This holiday was going to work after all.

Angie chatted to Sally, explaining that, although she came from London, she actually lived in Glasgow now. Sally revealed that she'd be going through London en route to see her older sister, Maeve, who worked as a nurse in a hospital in Brighton.

"My uncle lives near Brighton. Oddly enough, he's not long out of hospital."

"You must tell me his name. Perhaps Maeve will have met him."

"Not very likely. It's a big town. He's called Cyril Bolton."

"Maeve usually phones tonight. I'll ask her."

In their bedroom, Henriette was enthusing about the tennis.

"Thanks for getting me involved. I've found something else I can do. Maybe I'm not so useless."

"What did I tell you."

The world, Angie realised the next day, was indeed the proverbial small place. Maeve, it seemed had nursed Uncle

Cyril during his last stay in hospital.

"He's a very sick man." Sally told Angie. "Maeve thinks he won't live long."

"He's been ill on and off for some time, but he's not that bad," Angie said. "Someone would have told me."

She bought and posted a card to Cyril wishing him well, and having done what she considered to be the right thing, she pushed him to one side and concentrated on enjoying the rest of the break. This holiday was working. Henriette was having fun, she was having fun and Celeste was behaving herself. Their remaining days in Blackpool raced by.

CHAPTER 16

Back in Glasgow again, the sun extended their holiday. It was no weather for work. Henriette's mood jumped from one of elation to one of complete despair which Angie found disconcerting. She was glad when Tom wrote to say he was free for a few days and would visit.

"What will I tell him?" Henry wailed.

"Stop being so theatrical. I know what I'd say."

Two letters arrived for Angie on the same day. One included invitations for everyone to attend Seb's wedding in London, on September 20th. The other was from Mr Thrift.

"Your uncle has been readmitted to hospital for further tests. He should be home again at the bungalow in a few days. I must warn you, however, he is very poorly."

Angie wondered if he had received her post card. Cyril would hate hospital. He always hated any hint of ill-health. She phoned the bungalow and the telephone was answered by a woman. "Yes, it was Mr Cyril Bolton's home, but she was sorry he wasn't available."

Angie explained that Cyril was her uncle. "How is he? Is he still in hospital?"

The voice whined at the other end of the 'phone. "He'll be home this afternoon. He's not the easiest of patients, you know. I'm uncertain how long I'll stay here. I know you have to make allowances for his illness, but his manner is so curt and he can be so difficult."

"I'm sorry," Angie sympathised. "I found him impossible when I stayed with him. That was one of my reasons for leaving. Is there no possibility Edwina, his former housekeeper, could be persuaded to return to him?"

The nurse said she had met Edwina on a few occasions but

understood she had no intention of going back to work for Cyril.

"Well, keep in touch, please, and give him my regards when he comes home."

Angie thought a lot about Cyril over the next few weeks. Both Cyril and Seb. She had decided not to go to the wedding although Henry and Celeste would be present and Tom was to be best man.

"Why don't you come? Weddings are always fun." Henry tried to make her change her mind, but Angie was adamant.

"I might go down south to see my uncle while your there, but I am not going to Seb's wedding."

Henriette was obviously puzzled by Angie's decision. "I guess Celeste will help out then because Tom will be pretty occupied with his duties."

Angie remained unmoved. This was one occasion she would be happy to miss.

A letter from Dolinda altered all their plans.

"Such a dreadful pity," she wrote. *"The wedding's cancelled. No reason given. And at this late stage. Seb came to tell us himself. He said it was "just one of those things" So casual like. I was looking forward to seeing everyone. Seb passed his exams, you know, 2nd Class honours. The graduation's the day before the wedding. That is the day before what would have been the wedding. I feel so confused Seb was asking after you and told me to send his fondest love. He has a soft spot for you, Angie, I'm sure of it.*

Taurus keeps jumping up at me as I write. Do you think he guesses this is a letter to you?

Morton has a cold. The boys are going back to school in two weeks. My, how the summer's flown. Come and visit us again before long, and take care."

Dear Dolinda. Seb had a soft spot all right, but not the way Dolinda thought.

Henriette was upset about the cancellation of the wedding which Seb confirmed the following day, but she seemed more settled once she'd spoken to Tom.

On their own plans she told him, "Give it a few more months Tom and if you still want me then, unless *I've* changed my mind, count yourself hooked. "Till Christmas, then. I fancy starting the New Year as a fiancé. A Christmas engagement and a spring wedding."

"Don't rush me. If it goes ahead, I've resolved to walk down the aisle."

"Get practising. I won't wait too long."

Angie delighted in Henry's happiness. Celeste on the other hand was more pessimistic.

"Tom's such an active man. He'll need all his patience to cope with Henriette. What do you really think, Angie?."

"I reckon they'll be fine. It won't be easy, of course, but there's a lot of love in their relationship and they're comfortable together. There's no pretence. So many marriages flounder on pretence."

"How do you know?"

"Observation. The happiest people are those who can be themselves. Like Morton and Dolinda."

"I don't know them so feel I can't judge. And what about Seb? Would it have worked for him and Christine?"

"I doubt it. Seb is incapable of being with one person. Christine's well rid of him."

"Mm. Maybe your right. He tried it on me once, but he's not my type."

Just as well, Angie thought, Celeste had enough troubles without coping with someone like Seb. Her examination results involved a re-sit and she planned to go back to University early to get in some study before the term started.

Another letter arrived from Mr Thrift towards the end of October. Cyril it seemed had been in and out of hospital a number of times in the last few weeks. He was concerned that Angie should be informed, and suggested that when the chance arose she should go down to see Cyril and he, himself, had a number of things he would like to discuss with her.

Angie spoke to the Countess.

"Of course, Angela you must go. Your uncle will be pleased to see you. Henriette will be well cared for. Estelle can take over your duties and Tom plans to be here the next two weekends."

Henriette moaned at losing Angie.

"It's never the same when you're away," she said, but she understood. Angie was unsure of her own feelings. Visiting Cyril was not something she looked forward to, but Mr Thrift was another matter. She would like to see him, and there was Nick. He had written faithfully every second week since she left London. Angie would love to see Nick again.

* * *

There was a chill in the air as Angie arrived in London to be met with a hug and a kiss from Nick.

"God, it's good to see you. You look more like a million dollars every time. Give us a twirl."

"Little shop round the corner. You don't look so bad, yourself," she fingered the lapels of his navy blazer.

"Pure Marks and Spencer," he quipped.

"Do you still like it at Chartres?"

"Yes, better than ever. I've been promoted again. I'm head waiter three nights a week and in charge of the taxi service the other three. Mondays are mine."

"So what do you do Mondays?"

"That would be telling. Well, if you must know, I do the ironing, the cleaning, the mending and ..."

"That bad?"

"I'm afraid so. No females around. No time for them, to be honest." He gave Angie another hug. "Until now that is? Will you be staying at my place."

"Tonight and tomorrow, if that's okay? I'll be seeing Dillard Thrift Monday morning and we're both going down to Cyril's in the afternoon."

"Any news on how he is?"

"Nothing more as yet. I'll 'phone from your place."

"The street below you mean. I'm not getting a phone installed. Too expensive. I get to use Chartre's when I'm there for free."

Nick might not have got himself a telephone, but the flat looked ten times better than Angie imagined. New furniture in the sitting room and new curtains and bed covers in the bedroom.

"It's a put-u-up, now. You can have a choice of beds this time. I'd still advise you to let me sleep here," Nick said pointing to the bed settee. "The hours I keep aren't compatible to visitors getting a good night's rest. By the way you're coming with me tonight. I've reserved a table for you, and I've a surprise laid on. I gambled on you staying here tonight at least. Don't look so alarmed. I'll get a special discount when I pick up the bill, and you'll get the best service in the house."

Unlike Nick's flat, Chartres hadn't changed; the same intimate atmosphere, the same dance floor; the music full of memories. Angie pictured Lynn in her lemon dress and Henriette, legs gliding across the floor. It seemed a lifetime away. A little over a year ago. If only the clock could turn back.

Angie was ushered to a table set for three, and had been seated for barely a minute when Morton appeared. She jumped up to greet him.

"So you're my surprise. Nick couldn't have thought of anything nicer. Is Dolinda here? And is your cold better?"

"In the cloakroom. Putting on a dash of lipstick, I expect. Got to look her best and, yes, the cold's improving."

Dolinda came to the table beaming.

"Well, isn't this a great idea. I haven't been so spoiled for ages."

They didn't order the wine. It appeared in a bucket on a little trolley at the side of their table.

A smiling Nick took their order.

"I can recommend the whole menu," he said. "Take your choice."

In between the courses, Dolinda and Angie chatted continuously, whilst Morton sat back unable to get in more than the odd word.

"Like a couple of school kids," he said to Nick who hovered near their table all evening.

The dance floor was busy but both Dolinda and Angie decided this wasn't a night for fox-trotting.

"We're staying at The George, less than five minutes away by taxi. If we'd brought the car we couldn't have enjoyed the wine so much. We've to get back first thing so doubt if we'll see you again this visit. It's been a wonderful evening. Now, Nick, I insist we pay our share."

"There's nothing to pay. It's all taken care of. Luigi let me invite you for next to nothing, I promise."

"We can't thank you enough. Angie can we offer you a lift anywhere in our cab?"

Angie looked at Nick.

"I'm free at one tonight, if you want to wait till then we can go home together."

"Guess I'll wait for Nick," Angie said embracing Morton and Dolinda.

She checked her watch - an hour and five minutes to wait. She ordered more coffee. A man of about forty sat at the table adjacent. He, too, had bid farewell to his friends and now sat alone. He looked up and his eyes met Angie's. She turned away and sensed him come towards her.

"May I join you for coffee?"

"If you want to. I'm waiting for someone."

"Aren't we all," he smiled and he patted Angie's knee under the table. Angie moved her chair back and sat at an angle, her legs crossed.

"That's much better," the man said. "I can see them now. You've a very shapely ankle." He extended his arm fully until his hand could just touch Angie's calf. Angie looked round for

Nick but he was nowhere to be seen.

"Would you please leave my table."

The man, completely ignoring her demand, continued to stroke her leg. Angie pushed the chair right back this time and stood up.

"Leave or I'll scream so loudly even you will be embarrassed."

The man rose, "No need to twist your knickers. Give me a kiss and I'll go." He lunged towards Angie and in her haste to get out of reach her chair toppled to the floor sending a plant flying. The crash of breaking china had not only Nick but half the staff running to see what was happening. Angie attempted to explain amid interruptions from the man.

"She asked for it. Nothing more than a tart. Sitting their eying up the men. She ought to be banned."

For one moment Angie thought Nick was going to deliver a punch on the man's projecting jaw, only the intervention of Luigi who had arrived to see what the commotion was stopped him. He listened to both sides of the incident.

"This young lady's a special guest of the Club. I would be pleased if you'd leave now, unless Angela you want to press charges for molesting."

"No, let him go."

Nick could remain quiet no longer. "If I ever see you in here again there'll be trouble, all right? I won't have my fiancee treated like that."

Nick took the man by the arm and showed him out.

"What's this about your fiancee, Nick.? Have I missed something?" Luigi asked.

Angie's face was crimson. Nick looked sheepish.

"Nothing. Sorry, Angie. It sounded better than saying my friend."

Luigi put his finger to his nose, "No smoke without fire, eh? You might as well clear up and go home, Nick. We aren't too busy," and he smiled his way back to the door, pausing en route to apologise to other diners for the disturbance.

"Ah well, at least we got an extra half hour out of it."

Nick said as they entered the flat.

"It was one of the most embarrassing times of my life. He was a jerk. An absolute jerk. And you didn't help calling me your fiancée. You've given Luigi something to gossip about."

"I've said sorry. It just came out. I was so angry. Anyhow, I suppose it was wishful thinking." Nick took Angie into his arms. "I'd give anything for it to be true. I've thought about you so much, Angie. I love you. It's as simple as that. I know you regard me as a friend, but is there any hope? Would you consider marrying me one day, Angie?"

Angie cuddled into Nick. "You're more than a friend, Nick much more, but don't spoil things. I trust you. I can stay here with you and know you won't force yourself on me. I'm not ready for marriage, not yet. I'm too young. But I'd like to be close to you, and, yes, there is hope. There's no-one I'd rather be with than you."

Angie couldn't believe her own words. But she knew them to be true. She looked up into Nick's face. He stroked her hair back from her cheeks and kissed her lips. A slow lingering kiss. Angie experienced, not the sharp tortuous sparks she had felt when Seb kissed her, but a deep warm glow as rich as velvet, as warm as a summer day. She knew from then on her relationship with Nick could never be the same and was glad.

Angie slept soundly despite the eventful evening. Nick brought her tea and toast at eight and by nine-thirty she was entering the offices of Dillard Thrift. His secretary, a girl with a bored expression and a voice that matched it, ushered her straight in to Dillard's room.

"Lovely to see you Angie - and how well you look. A shade thinner perhaps but so - what's the word for it? - chic." He took her hand and held it as he looked her up and down. "Your parents would be proud of you."

"Thank you. You look good, too. Is there more news of Uncle Cyril?"

"Nothing else, I'm afraid. He's at the bungalow but I

understand he goes back into the General in a day or two. It's just a matter of time I believe. He might have as long as a year but it's more likely to be a few months. I'm sorry not to have better news."

"Are we going there today?"

"I thought we should drive through and arrive for about half-past-two. Mrs Wilkes, the nurse, is expecting us. She's an irritable woman and not the sort to be kept waiting. I don't know if you've any plans for the rest of the morning, but I suggest we meet here for lunch - we can go to Kate's Kitchen round the corner, it's very good. Shall we say twelve, then?"

Angie stepped out into the street. She had two hours to fill. She wandered up the road and found herself heading towards The National Gallery. It was as good a place as any to while away the time.

Angie liked art. Liked to study the way the artist used his brush strokes for effect. Bold, thick oils, delicate water colours, clear lines, blurred images. Matisse was her favourite. His work was not too cleanly defined. Unusual colours used side by side, yet all blending. She looked through a file of prints for sale and stopped at a still life Matisse had painted - 'The Pink Table Cloth,' fruit and flowers, light and sustenance. If she were to buy any of the prints it would be this. The Gallery had a 3' by 3' of the Matisse and several miniatures. She toyed with the idea of buying the large copy. Where would she put it? She'd have to find a frame. In the end she settled for a miniature that could sit on her bedside table like a photograph and decided to buy two more miniatures, both Degas, one for Cyril, the other for Henriette.

Angie sat in the square for a while watching the pigeons.

"Always 'ungry aren't they? Little blighters. Precious few crumbs to spare, that's for sure. See - I've me weekly bit o' beef. Wouldn't feed an ant. Time this government got it right. "

Angie nodded at the old lady. Although the weather was warm for late autumn, the woman was wearing a heavy tweed coat buttoned high at the neck and her hair was tucked behind a floral headscarf. Big black boots sloshed as she shuffled along. She grinned and revealed two yellow teeth. Mumbling as she went, the old woman trundled on. London was full of characters.

Angie was punctual for lunch but Dillard was already waiting for her outside his office.

"Left a few minutes early so that I wouldn't get held up with a last minute call or something," he explained. Kate's Kitchen was small. Neat square tables were clothed in white cotton and each boasted a vase containing a single carnation. Kate it seemed cooked, served, cleared up and worked the till with the help of one girl straight out of school and still counting on her fingers.

There was nothing light about the snack size steak pie and chips. It would have fed Angie for dinner and the cherry pie oozed fruit and was liberally doused in custard. The flavour was delicious.

"Couldn't eat another morsel," Dillard said when Katie checked that they'd had sufficient. He turned to Angela. "A quick cup of tea and we'll be on our way, okay?"

Dillard Thrift quizzed Angie about life in Glasgow as they motored the London to Brighton Road. Traffic was quiet and Angie settled back to admire the colours of the trees. Shades of red mingled with yellow and brown as leaves fluttered to the pavements in the light breeze.

Dillard had also noticed the leaves. "Not be long till the winter's fully here again. Sad time winter."

Angie said nothing. She was thinking of last October when she and Lynn had such fun together. Angie wished Christmas could come and go without being noticed.

* * *

Uncle Cyril's bungalow was outside Brighton on the coast road beyond Rottingdean. It was set on chalk cliffs high above the shore and was one of a group of houses, all identical externally, from their brass knobbed doors to their neat square of garden. A boy was working on Cyril's lawn when they arrived. "She's down the road at the chemist," he said. "You're earlier than we expected. I'm Fred. Her son."

"You're doing a good job there, lad," Dillard praised.

"He can't bear to see it a mess and he's not able himself. I'm a butcher's boy really. It's me half day and the bit he pays me takes me and my girl, Joan, to the flicks tonight. Frankenstein. Like a good horror." Fred put the shears down. "Hold on and I'll let you in. Better wait in the lounge till me mum's back, I reckon."

Fred wiped his boots religiously on the doormat and showed Angie and Mr Thrift into a comfortable room. Angie recognised some of the smaller pieces of furniture from Dryden Terrace. With Fred resuming his work in the garden, the house was deathly quiet. The large mantle clock ticked loudly and a puff of smoke billowed from the black coals in the grate. In a few minutes the fire would burst into flame.

"Shall we sit?" Dillard said in hushed tones. Angie found herself whispering in reply.

The front door opened and a thin wiry woman of around forty-five swept in.

"You're early. I'd to collect some new medication. I'll go up and see if he's ready for you."

They could hear her talking to Cyril. "I can't force you, of course. It's what the doctor ordered this morning. If you don't want to get better that's your look out. That Lawyer and your niece are here. I'll send them up." The nurse's feet clattered on the stairs.

"Obstinate old man," she grumbled. "Thinks he knows better than the doctor. You've to go up. It's second right, next to the bathroom."

It was a dull room with light green walls, cream paint and fawn curtains and carpet. Not the place to cheer up an invalid, Angie thought. Uncle Cyril sat up in bed his back cushioned by several pillows. The puffiness of his face and hands was more apparent and his skin was a yellow white. He cut a pathetic figure. Angie felt a surge of pity as she moved towards the bed but could not bring herself to kiss or touch him. Instead she smoothed the crumpled top sheet.

"I understand you've been having a bad time. I'm sorry. I've brought you a present. She took the Degas from its bag and handed it to him."

Cyril, wiped his spectacles and looked into Angie's face. His expression was of surprise. "A present? For me?" He studied the print for some moments. "This I like. Thank-you, Angela. It was very thoughtful." He turned his attention to Mr Thrift. "Glad you could come. I've a few amendments to the will. Did you bring it?"

"It's here." The lawyer, brought a file of papers from his briefcase.

"It's that damn nurse. She's not worth her wages and I'm not going to give her the two hundred. I want Fred to have it."

Dillard Thrift glanced at Angie, then turned back to Cyril. "Is it in order to discuss the terms when Angela is here?"

"Don't see why not. She's my closest relative, whatever she feels about me. I don't approve of some of the things you've done, Angela, but you do seem to be making something of yourself. I owe it to your father. He was a straight man. With the exception of a few minor bequests to my friends, and a thousand pounds to Edwina, everything I have is yours when I go - and I doubt if I'll keep you waiting long."

Angie felt embarrassed. She knew her cheeks were turning scarlet. "You mustn't talk like that. You could live for years."

"I hope not. I've no wish to hang on. Life becomes incredibly difficult when you feel ill all the time. Anyway as I said it's yours. Don't do anything foolish with it. Never know what's ahead."

"Thank-you. I don't deserve it."

"That's as may be. It's a fair sum and there're no strings attached. They just lead to misery. Right, now move over and let Thrift in."

Angie stepped back and Dillard handed over the papers for Cyril to sign. She noticed how awkwardly he held the pen

191

between his podgy fingers.

"Done," he said. "Now leave me in peace and tell that nurse to bring the new medicine. Stupid woman's only doing her job, I suppose. Wish I had a younger nurse. She might be more tolerant."

Downstairs, Mrs Wilkes was still sulking. "He can wait till it suits me. Nobody should talk the way he does. I do my best and what happens? I get shouted out. Don't be surprised if I decide to move on. There's plenty of people about wanting someone with my experience." She stalked into the kitchen closing the door behind her and leaving Angela and Dillard to see themselves out of the front door.

"She'll get over it," Fred said to them as they got into the car.

"We'll stop for afternoon tea in the town. Where are you going from here Angela?"

"I'd intended staying in Brighton for a day or too. I'd expected to see Cyril again but he was a bit dismissive. I gather he doesn't like visitors."

"He doesn't find it easy to deal with them, that's certain. I'd go back again in a day or so. You could 'phone first. Your next trip won't be for a while, I suppose?"

"Probably not. You will let me know how things go?"

"Of course, I've just remembered - ' The Breadbin'." Mr Thrift turned off the shore road at Rottingdean and made for the main street. The 'Breadbin' was in the middle of the narrow thoroughfare. A tiny but crowded tea room that smelled of home baking. The counter was stacked with freshly made bread but it was not this that had tempted Dillard Thrift. He pointed to the griddle and ordered buttered crumpets. They were brought to their table piping hot and dripping butter and jam. Angela helped the lawyer clean the plate and they washed the crumpets down with equally hot tea."

"Glad I remembered this place."

It was getting dark when Dillard dropped Angela off at the Clock Tower in the centre of Brighton. She had no idea where to stay but there was an abundance of hotels. She walked down West Street and along the brightly lit sea front. The hotel she chose 'The Shire' was one at the end of a terrace directly off the promenade; convenient for public transport yet quiet enough to allow for a good night's sleep. The dance halls Angie had passed held no attraction for her and though tempted by Cary Grant at the Odeon Cinema, she felt too tired to go out. Angie ate lightly and slept soundly.

Waking before seven the next morning she took a stroll on the promenade before breakfast. She sat for a while on a wooden seat and watched the waves play against the shingle. The pebbled shore was, she thought, the town's biggest drawback. It was far removed from Blackpool's beautiful sandy beaches. There was a small patch of sand near the West Pier and she imagined it packed with children in the summer, all fighting for enough sand to build a castle. Brighton obviously depended on its other attractions to bring in the holiday crowds and she understood there were plenty of them.

Uncle Cyril used to talk of the antique shops. Perhaps she would go in search of them later. She was surprised he had told her about the money, but she had no doubt how she would use it. Our dreams will become reality very soon, Dad. She'd thought it would take years to fulfil them but somehow things were happening in a rush. It was all so easy. Something was bound to happen. One day she'd wake up and find everything had gone wrong.

After breakfast, Angie discovered the antique shops located in a series of cobbled lanes between the Old Steine and West Street. Through the tiny windows she could see everything from a pair of Victorian bellows to an ornate sixteenth century candelabra. There was jewellery, too. Gold and diamond rings and silver bangles. A Victorian brooch attracted her to one display in particular. So delicate, it had tiny seed pearls set in eighteen carat gold in the shape of a crescent moon. Angie stepped inside the shop to enquire the price, then stared aghast at the figure bending to lift a box from the floor. His shirt was popping from his trousers to reveal a layer of flesh. Angie recognised the rump immediately. It belonged to Grimsby.

"Cor luv a duck what are you doing 'ere? Thought you was in Scotland swanning it with the gentry," he remarked, as finally transferring the carton from the floor to a shelf, he looked up. "Been visiting yer uncle, I s'pose. Saw 'im, meself the other day. Miserable old bugger didn't seem too pleased at me coming. Gotta make excuses though, eh, 'im being so ill. And he's to put up with that old Wilk. Gawd, I said if ye 'ave to 'ave a nurse make it a nice bit ... Did 'e give you a smile or a wellie?"

Angie wasn't surprised at Grimsby's garrulity. "He was his usual self, really. But he's very ill."

"No need to tell yours truly that, ducks. Didn't I visit 'im in that General Hospital. Stinkin' of disinfectant. Never thought he'd come out walking. Promised to haunt me he did. Probably will, too. I 'ate to say it but I'll miss the cussed devil when he's popped it. He needs you, you know. You're family. Well sort of."

Angie wondered why Grimsby qualified his last remark. Of course she was family. "I came in to ask about the brooch on that display tray. Can you tell me the price?" she said, changing the conversation away from her uncle.

"Well, it's a nice piece. Belonged to a Lady someone or other. To anyone else I'd ask fifty. To you, lovie, for me old mate's sake, let's shake on thirty."

Though dubious about Grimsby's fifty, Angie knew thirty pounds was a fair price. It was still a lot of money for a whim but....

" Here take it in yer mitt. See 'ow fine it is."

Angie loved the shape and feel of the brooch. It went with the stars and after all in a month or two she might come into a small fortune.

"I'll take it," she said and counted the notes from her purse. She would need to go to the bank before paying the hotel.

Grimsby cushioned the crescent brooch in a tiny velvet box.

"Give Cyril me regards and tell 'im I'll drop in again in about a week. And tell those Scotch lairds where you bought your trinket. Just a hop step and jump and they could be on me doorstep."

What a man, Angie laughed. So this is how he lined his pockets. A light drizzle of rain dampened her hair. She decided Cary Grant would fit comfortably into her afternoon.

Angie didn't visit Cyril again till Thursday. Mrs Wilkes was in a more cheerful mood as she showed Angela up to Cyril's room.

"He's slept all morning and actually thanked me for his lunch. You've picked the right day to come."

Angie wasn't so sure of that when she saw Cyril. He was lying flat on his pillows and his skin was paler than before.

"How are you?" she asked realising how inane the question sounded.

Cyril took a few seconds to reply, "Not too well, to be honest. I've no energy. No energy at all. Haven't even read the paper."

Angie followed his glance to where the daily paper lay untouched at the bottom of the bed. "Would you like me to tell you what's in the news?"

He nodded. Angie read the headlines and moved on to the general pages. Cyril made no comments until she came to a story about a robbery in an antique shop in the Brighton Lanes.

"Not Grimsby's place, I hope?".

It wasn't. Angie recounted her visit to Grimsby's shop. "He let me have the brooch at a bargain price."

"Doesn't sound like Grimsby. You have to be careful. Bet he saw you as a soft touch."

"It's a beautiful brooch and I promise, it was worth what I paid. He said he'd come to see you shortly."

Cyril grunted closed his eyes and appeared to be falling asleep. Angie decided it was time to leave.

"I'll be returning to Glasgow in a few days. I'll keep in touch." She knew as a niece she should kiss him, but she couldn't, instead she took his hand. "Keep well."

Angela returned to London the next morning and made straight for Nick's flat. Nick opened the door in his dressing gown.

"Had a late night. Special do for Lord Blacksmith and family. His daughter's announced her engagement to some ponse. I'd to taxi them home at three and it was after four when I got back here."

"You don't need to make excuses to me, Nick," Angie said kissing him lightly. Nick asked after Cyril and she gave him the details of her trip.

"You know, I still think he looks like a slug-like pig, yet I was genuinely sorry for him. He doesn't get on with the nurse, and I'm not surprised. I didn't take to her myself. I keep thinking ... he's my only relative - I should be looking after him. Especially if he's leaving me his money. I couldn't do it though. It would never work, but I feel so guilty."

"I can think of worse crimes," Nick consoled.

CHAPTER 17

The return journey to Woodend was slow, but painless. In her absence things had moved swiftly. Henriette's mind was made up. She would marry Tom. No waiting for Christmas to announce the engagement. No waiting to be able to walk down the aisle, though that would be a bonus. A spring wedding was planned. By then, Tom would have qualified.

"We're going to have a house built to order. Not a mansion but one big enough for everyone to visit. You will stay with us, won't you Angie? I'll still need you."

"What does Tom say about that?"

"We haven't discussed it. There's been so much excitement. It would be my decision."

Angie reckoned that was unlikely to be the case. It would be Tom who would pay her wages and having your wife's friend staying with you as newly weds might not be the ideal start.

"Let's forget that for the time being. We'll sort it out when we need to. Now where are you getting married and what's your dress going to be like and how many bridesmaids are you going to have and who's to be bestman?"

"You don't really expect me to answer that lot. Look?" Henry took a small box from under her pillow. "Tom gave it to me last night. Isn't it fantastic." She held the box out to Angie to examine. Inside a ruby and diamond engagement ring glittered in the light.

Angie gave Henry a hug and a kiss. "It's absolutely perfect. I'm quite jealous." She didn't tell Henry of Nick's proposal. That was her secret and in any case she probably wouldn't marry for years. Maybe Nick would get tired of waiting and elope with some other girl. She found herself hoping that wouldn't happen. Meantime she was content to enjoy Henry's happiness.

"La Grandmere's organising a big party at Christmas to celebrate and I'm not going to wear the ring until then. Celeste will be with us, hopefully having passed her exams."

The Countess expressed her delight to have Angela back and asked after Uncle Cyril.

"You must tell me if there are further developments. We can make arrangements for you to go back to England as is necessary. Estelle coped very well."

"That's a fib, Grandmother, you know I was always moaning my bath was too cold and she has no idea how to set out my clothes. I missed you like hell, Angie. Except, of course, when I was with Tom."

The weeks which followed were busy. Plans for the wedding were made and altered daily as Henriette changed her mind about everything from the number of guests to the colour of her bouquet. Dr Gillon had arranged a course of intensive therapy at the hospital. Getting the bride on her feet, it seemed, was of prime importance and Henry was definitely making progress. With the help of a frame she could stand for several minutes and, although her attempts to walk usually ended in defeat after a couple of wobbly steps, she would try and try again.

"If determination has anything to do with it you'll be skipping into the church."

"I don't care how I get there. Someone can carry me if they like."

The 'phone call from Mr Thrift came when Angela was least expecting it. She had received a brief note from Cyril only that morning saying he'd been feeling better and had even managed to get up for part of the day. There had been no mention of any trouble with Mrs Wilkes.

Dillard Thrift came straight to the point, "Mrs Wilkes walked out today. She said she wanted to leave right away and your uncle waived the agreed notice saying he was glad to see the back of her. He's on his own, Angela, in the bungalow."

"So what's going to happen?"

"I've fixed up a daily but there appear to be no night nurses available. Edwina has agreed to stay tonight and tomorrow night after that she's going to Spain with Alice for a month. I don't suppose there's the slightest possibility of your coming down to take on the job? It would only be for the short term."

"Me? I couldn't leave now. We're so busy here. Henriette's making plans for her wedding. I'm running around everywhere."

It wasn't true, of course. Henry was insisting on organising things herself. Angie just gave the first excuse that came into head. She couldn't go back to live with Cyril. "Surely there's somewhere else you could try?"

"All the agencies are fully booked. Put bluntly, no-one's available till someone dies. I do realise this puts you in a spot but ..."

"Give me time to think. I'll phone you back."

Angie replaced the receiver. She felt tears hot against her cheeks and ran into her room. I'm not doing it, not for all his money. There had to be someone, somewhere. Why couldn't he go into a nursing home? Her intelligence told her Cyril would never agree to that. Angie remembered Sally and the tennis match. Her sister worked in Brighton. Sally had written down her phone number in case she could look her up when in Brighton. Perhaps she could help. Angie searched and found the number.

"Hullo, Maeve? I'm Angela Bolton. I met your sister Sally in Blackpool and she gave me your number. I was wondering if you might be able to help me."

Angie explained about Cyril and hoped Maeve didn't mind her calling. Maeve said she'd be glad to help if she could. She, herself, was tied up but she offered to call some of the girls and said she'd ring back.

"Be sure to reverse the charges," Angie said.

She spent the next hour tidying her room and jumped to answer the phone when it rung on schedule. Several girls might welcome the work in exchange for board. Being night's it wouldn't interfere with studies. Would Angie send details?

"It would be better if you contacted Mr Thrift, my lawyer. He's in London and he's dealing with my uncle's affairs." Angie gave Sally the Dillard's telephone number and address. "If you can fix something up I'd be over the moon. Tell Mr Thrift to let me know what's happening either way. Hope we can meet some day."

Feeling a lot happier, Angie went down stairs to see Henriette and found her in the lounge.

"Where have you been? I thought you must have gone out." Henry chided.

Angie related Mr Thrift's phone call and told Henry about the arrangements she was trying to make.

"Look, Angie, wouldn't it be more sensible if you went back for a while," she turned to her Grandmother who had just come into the lounge, "Angie might have to go to Brighton to look after her uncle. We'll manage, won't we?"

"I'm sure Angela knows she can go anytime. I've told her before."

"But I'm not going. I guess it sounds awful but I couldn't stand it. Even though he's so ill. I couldn't nurse Cyril." Angie shuddered visibly at the thought and the Countess looked surprised. "You don't know him. I can feel pity for him but I can't love him like I should an uncle. I don't want his money. He can give it to whom he likes but no-one can make me look after him." Angie ran out of the room and back to her bedroom. She didn't come down again that evening but she did telephone Dillard Thrift to tell him about Maeve.

"I'm disappointed you haven't changed your mind, Angela. Let's hope your friend's sister comes up with someone suitable."

Maeve did indeed put Dillard Thrift in touch with three student nurses all eager to augment their training allowances. Dillard called on Edwina to help select one, and the favour fell on Miss Elizabeth King, a robust girl with a bright sense of humour and apparently unending patience.

Elizabeth took over from Edwina immediately and seemed unperturbed by Cyril's manner. To be truthful Cyril was quite pleasant to her, the lawyer told Angela when he phoned. "She's a thoroughly nice girl and I get the impression Cyril likes her." Angela found it difficult to believe Cyril could like anyone. She was glad, however, that things were settling down in Brighton. Now she could concentrate again on her work with Henry without feeling guilty. Arrangements for the engagement party at Christmas had to be finalised.

Glasgow was the most difficult place in the world to find Christmas presents Angie decided after several consecutive days spent shopping with Henry and only a handful of gifts settled. Angie related her problem when she sat with the Countess in the lounge listening to Henriette struggling with Chopin on the piano.

"Celeste may not surpass Henriette in many things, but playing the piano is one," La Grandmere commented turning her chair to face the window. "I do believe this will be a mild winter. The berries are late on the holly. Now, tell me Angela how did you and Henriette enjoy your shopping trips?"

"I'm not having much success finding presents. Most things are too expensive and I've no intention of spending a fortune. I'm saving up for my travels remember. It's the thought that counts, as the saying goes."

"You're quite right. You must come along to the Fete at the church near the university. I try to go every year. There are bargains to be had including all sorts of crafts and paintings, of course. I guarantee you will get all you need. It would be difficult to take Henriette but you and I will go on Friday."

The Countess had not exaggerated. Stalls laden with everything from serviettes to door stops, gilded vases to potted plants; all competitively priced. Angie finished her shopping and, at the suggestion of the Countess, they went for tea at a cafe off Bear Road frequented by art students.

A man dressed in black from his high necked jumper to his baggy trousers, approached their table. Angie remained silent as the Countess spoke to him in French. "Guy is an artist from the Pyrenees. I met him here some time ago when I was showing some paintings. He wants to do a quick charcoal sketch of us sitting here for a magazine. We make, he says, an interesting subject. He cannot afford to pay us but would do a copy for us. I told him to do a portrait of you instead as payment. All we have to do is sit and chat and drink our tea. It will take only half an hour. What do you think? Shall we let him?"

"I don't mind."

"And neither do I. Though what is interesting about an old lady's wrinkles I don't know."

They spoke of Henriette's party and the wedding, of Cyril and his ill-health. "It can be hard as you get older, Angela. The mind remains young and vital in most of us. The body itself wears out. Your uncle is comparatively young. His illness must be very distressing."

"I guess it is. I'm so relieved they've fixed a nurse for him, and one he seems to like. I couldn't bear to leave Glasgow at the moment. I like it here. I feel secure and yet I am my own person. London never gave me that feeling. I felt displaced even though I was born there. Ever since I went back after the war." Except, she said to herself, when I'm with Nick. She had tried not to think too much of Nick and what he had said.

"War," the Countess was saying, "is a great destroyer. It will take a long time for many people to pick up the threads of normality. Believe me, I have lived through both great wars."

So intent were they on their conversation they had forgotten the artist until he returned to the table with his finished pictures.

"I will pay you first", he smiled. He held up a portrait of Angie. "It is of course merely an impression. I have tried to capture the mood. Quite serious but very beautiful."

Angie was impressed.

"It's brilliant. You were so quick. And you flatter me." She knew the minute she saw it she would send it to Nick for his Christmas.

Guy gave the Countess the other picture to look at. It was a vigorous sketch. Less flattering, more truthful and depicting the cafe background with simple accuracy.

"I like it," La Grandmere said. "You should do well. Go to Paris. It is full of talent and there are facilities for the artist to succeed. Bon chance."

Guy rolled Angie's picture and tied it with a thin ribbon. "Thank you, you were good sitters. I shall go home and work on this." He took his drawing and left the cafe.

The Countess stood up, "Time we were on our way too, Angela. Henriette will be waiting for us."

Back in her room Angie carefully flattened her portrait and placed it, protected by a layer of card, it in a large envelope. On the back of the drawing she'd written. "To Nick, Portrait of Angela, Christmas 1946.

* * *

Parties suited the Woodend household. Sixty guests spread in the spacious rooms of their home to celebrate Henriette's engagement to Tom. Rooms upstairs and down were equally open and all but the bedrooms held reception tables filled with sparkling wines and spirits.

Tom's mother, father, three brothers and little sister arrived from Suffolk. They were pleasant, down to earth, people a little over-awed at the opulence displayed. To her credit La Grandmere fussed about them as if they were royalty.

"I'm so proud of Tom," she told them. "It needs a person with special qualities to take on Henriette. I'm confident Tom has that ability. He's wonderful with her."

"He has talked of little else since he met her," Tom's mother beamed. "I'm sure he will make her happy and if he gains his degree, he should go far."

"Of that I've no doubt. You only have to look at them together. I've never seen Henriette so radiantly happy."

Henry was as usual encircled by friends. Angie felt slightly out of it, realising she knew no one other than the immediate family. Celeste joined Angie in the hall where she stood looking on.

"You haven't got any champers, Angie." Celeste dragged her into the dining room and thrust a glass into her hand.

"I've had three already," Angie protested.

"Well, you've a way to go to catch me up. This is fun isn't it. Come and meet Tom's brothers."

They were handsome boys. Tall, fair and obviously enjoying the party. Celeste flirted outrageously with George, the eldest, sitting on his knee and placing her arms round his neck. No wonder, Angie thought, she gets into trouble. George, however, seemed able to cope. He pushed her away, playfully smacking her bottom. Celeste grabbed the other two brothers, one on each arm, and took them off to the upper lounge. "Come on I'll play the piano and everyone can sing."

Angie watched her leave. "She's incorrigible," she laughed to George. "Don't take her seriously."

"She's a lovely girl, like her sister, but she should take care. Some men would take advantage of her."

They already have, Angie said to herself. She smiled at George, "I hope your brothers are trustworthy."

"Here, they're on their best behaviour, elsewhere that might be another story."

They moved out into the hall and George sat on the bottom stair and beckoned Angie to join him. "Do you like working in Glasgow?"

"Of course, I do."

"Don't you miss your family?"

"I've no-one close. They were killed in the war."

"What will you do when Henriette and Tom are married and move to Edinburgh?"

"Move to Edinburgh?"

"Didn't you know? They're having a house built near where Tom's going to work. It's being made to measure to accommodate the wheel chair. Henriette's Grandmother's giving it to them as their wedding present."

"No. I didn't know."

Angie was surprised Henriette hadn't said anything. She thought they'd be staying in Glasgow?"

"Sorry," George said. "I've upset you."

"No, not you. I wish she'd told me that's all."

"I expect she was going to."

"Probably."

"Come on let's join the others." George took Angie by the hand and helped her upstairs. He put an arm round her waist and guided her into the lounge. Celeste was playing and singing a series of popular tunes and a group of guests crowded round the piano to accompany her. She stopped when Angie and George came in.

"So what have you two been up to? Seems you're the one with the winning ways, Angie. Now what would Nick say?"

"Stop being an ass, Celeste." Angie wriggled free from George's arm, "We've just been chatting."

"Who," George asked Angie as they found a seat at the perimeter of the singers, "Is Nick?"

"NIck's in London. He's a special friend."

"So that means I haven't a hope," George said putting on a sad face. "And just as I was thinking what a nice girl you were."

"I haven't changed because of knowing Nick."

"Can I have a kiss, then?"

"Don't see why not."

George's lips were warm and soft as he kissed her. Nick wouldn't mind. Not a kiss. She guessed he'd kissed other girls. Suddenly, she felt angry. Cross that she was here in Glasgow and Nick was in London.

"Excuse me," she said and left the lounge. She ran up stairs and lifted the phone in the corridor outside her room and rung Chartres. "Nick, I hoped you'd be at work?"

"Angie what's happened?

"Nothing. I wanted to speak to you."

"At one-thirty in the morning?"

"I'm at Henriette's engagement party."

205

"Oh, yes. I forgot. But why are you phoning?"

"I don't know. I miss you. Wish you were here."

"Glad of that. I was about to go home."

"Could you come here now, for Christmas?"

"You must be joking. Chartres is fully booked. We'll be run off our feet."

"That's it then. Night."

She put down the telephone. No Nick, might as well enjoy herself, anyway. Angie went back to the party to find George chatting up a girl in a black sleeveless dress, his arm draped across her shoulder. Angie picked up another glass of champagne and made her way up to her bedroom. At least she could dream.

The night was cold and frosty and the stars hung bright in the dark sky. "I'm okay, Dad and Mum. Honest, I am. Just a bit too much to drink. I can't wait to go to New Zealand, Dad. There's nothing here for me. Not now. Hold me tight. We'll go together."

She finished the drink and fell into bed. Volcanic mountains and spitting geysers and Nick running about in his dress suit with trays of cherries floating in champagne.

"Where did you get to last night?" Henriette asked. "Estelle had to see me to bed."

"Oh dear. Too much wine. I went to my room and fell asleep. I'm sorry."

"You're forgiven. That is if you spend the morning with me. I've so much to tell you. What a party. I think I was the only one left sober and I can't stand at any time. Actually that's not true. See?" Henriette eased herself from the wheelchair and walked three faltering steps holding on to the dressing table. "I'm getting there, Angie. I can sense the strength returning little by little. I can stand still for about three minutes without toppling. I wonder if this is what it was like as a toddler? Your legs weak and unsteady but there's this tremendous desire to move forward."

"I can see a difference," Angie felt as excited as Henry.

"You're much steadier. Steadier than I was last night, that's for sure."

"Did you enjoy it? It was fun, wasn't it?"

"Great," Angie agreed and, despite Nick's absence, she wasn't lying. She was still puzzled why Henry hadn't mentioned the house being in Edinburgh but decided to leave it till another time.

"Tom's family are going back this morning. They have kennels. It's difficult to leave the animals for long. He's away, too. Until Christmas Eve. It's a whole year Angie. Tomorrow. A whole year since the accident. I still miss Lynn, don't you?"

"Every day, when I'm going to bed, I talk to her, and my mum and dad. You don't need to remind me. I wrote to Dolinda last week enclosing money for flowers. She's going to place them beside Lynn's memorial stone."

"Wish I'd thought of that."

"Your name's on the card. They're from us both."

"If only it hadn't happened."

"Life's full of if only's".

CHAPTER 18

Christmas and New Year were quiet. After Henriette and Tom's engagement party it was as if everyone had expelled their energy. The tree was splendid, the food excessive but it was definitely a period of sitting around recuperating. A time for family gatherings. And I've got no family, Angie thought. No real family.

Henriette needed Angie first thing in the morning and last thing at night. In between Tom was getting lessons on how to cope. Even Celeste seemed at a loose end towards the end of the break.

"I'm beginning to wish I was back at college tomorrow instead of Friday. Rarely a dull moment there."

"Wish I'd had your chances," Angie said. "I could have stayed on at school but there seemed no point. I'd already done an extra year, anyway. Learning to stand on my own feet was more important than having more qualifications. Still is, I suppose. All my ambitions hinge around travelling."

"You should try talcum powder."

"What do you mean, talcum powder?"

"For your itchy feet."

"Idiot." Angie tossed a cushion at Celeste, who caught it and clutched it to her knees.

"I've another two years of study, then I'll have to decide where I'm going. I don't mean travel, though that could come into it. What I'm going to do with my life."

"You'll marry and have a dozen kids."

"Could be fun, with the right man. I always catch the wrong ones."

"You frighten the good ones away by being so extrovert.

Cool down and see what happens."

"Didn't know you were an expert."

"I'm not. You're okay Celeste, but a bit over-bearing. Men like subtlety. Charm them with your brains, not your bust."

"That," Celeste said, "Sounds good advice. There's this chap at Uni'. He's really clever and he's got the looks of a Cassius - lean and hungry. I'm trying to catch his eye. Maybe I should flutter my Shakespeare instead of my lashes."

"Let's go for a walk."

"It's freezing."

"We could wrap up."

"No. I think I'll curl up at the fire and play Patience. Unless you want to join me in a game of Whist?"

Whist it was and the Countess joined in. Angie heard sleet pelting against the lounge windows.

"Glad we didn't go out. Look at the weather now."

The telephone interrupted their game. Celeste answered it. "For you, Angie. London. Mr Thrift."

Angie knew what had happened before she spoke to Dillard. It was over. Cyril was dead. She shivered as she came back to the warmth of the fire but there were no tears.

"Bad news, I'm afraid. My uncle died at lunch time."

The Countess took her hand. "I'm so sorry."

Celeste offered her own condolences.

"We'll have afternoon tea now. It's a little early but a cup of tea settles one."

"I'm fine. It's a blessing really. He suffered quite a bit in the end. It feels odd being here when I guess I should have gone down to help him. At least he had Christmas and New Year."

Estelle brought the tea and Angie felt the tightness in her head ease. Death was becoming too familiar to her.

"Mr Thrift said his friend Grimsby was with him, so he had someone there. I thought when Uncle Cyril died I'd feel nothing, but that awful lost feeling is there. I can't pretend I liked him but he did take me in when I'd no-one. I wasn't very

209

nice to him."

The Countess fidgeted in her chair and Celeste cleared away the cards.

"You will have to go to Brighton for the funeral. Would you like Celeste to go with you? She could arrange a few more days from university."

"It's no problem," Celeste confirmed.

"I'll be all right on my own. Dillard told me not to rush down. The funeral won't be for several days, but I think I'd like to go tomorrow. I could help arrange things. I'll phone Mr Thrift this evening."

* * *

"I wish I'd been here," Angie said as Dillard Thrift drove her to the bungalow.

"No good dwelling on that now, Angela. Young Elizabeth did very well and you did get her for him. He seemed much more content when I saw him a few days ago."

The earliest the lawyer had been able to fix the funeral was for the following Thursday.

"It was his wish to be buried in London. It will be a small funeral. I've been in touch with his old friends and they want to be present, and Edwina and Alice and one or two of his customers. You'll be the only family, of course."

"I'll leave you to settle everything, Mr Thrift. I haven't a clue where to begin."

"You can start by helping me go through his papers."

Cyril's room had the chill of death about it. The electric wall fire was off and the bed stripped. All the documents Cyril had were in his bedside drawer, together with photographs. Angie waded through the latter.

"There're some of my dad and a few with him and Mum, and my grandparents. Most of the people I don't recognise."

Dillard Thrift seemed intent on reading something. He read the same sheets over and over again before speaking to Angela.

"Let's go down and see if Elizabeth can find us a drink. Or would you prefer something hot, like tea?"

"Hot would be nice."

"I wasn't sure what to do," Elizabeth said as they settled on hot chocolate. "I've nowhere else to go at the moment. Someone's moved into my previous digs. Can I stay another week until I get fixed up somewhere?"

The lawyer turned to Angie, "That should be all right, shouldn't it?"

"Of course. I expect we owe you some money. Your wages and the phone calls you had to make. Let us know."

"Thanks. It's a bit awkward but I am hard up."

"We understand." Dillard Thrift took out his wallet and handed over some notes. "I hope this is sufficient."

"That's more than it should be. Would you mind if I went to my lectures now? I've missed a few today and yesterday."

Elizabeth King left Angie and Dillard to drink their chocolate.

"I've discovered something that might be very important, Angie. Heaven knows why your uncle, or your father for that matter, never mentioned it. He must have known it could complicate things." Dillard got up and poked the fire. "I think perhaps you'd better read this for yourself." He handed Angie the sheaf of papers he'd been reading upstairs.

The first document was a well creased birth certificate in the name of Ebenezer Freer, born to Grace Freer. Under the section headed father was stamped the word illegitimate. Angie moved to the next page. A certificate showing that Ebenezer Freer was adopted as a child and given the name Cyril George Bolton.

"He wasn't my real uncle then?"

"Genetically no. Legally," Mr Thrift explained, "he was. What this does mean is he wasn't the blood relation he claimed to be."

Angie felt a curious degree of pleasure. When she'd first met Cyril she'd hated the idea that such an odious man could be her uncle. She'd always puzzled how he could be her father's brother. They were so different.

"So why did he keep stressing that I was his only relative."

"I think he needed to belong. When your father went back to sea after your mother died, I know Cyril agreed to take care of you should anything happen to him. Possibly for financial gain. Your father left him some money, you know. I'd like to think it was because he genuinely regarded you as his family. His only family."

"There was Edwina. She's some sort of cousin far removed."

"Edwina's ties are with your mother's people. You'd better read the letters that follow."

Angie turned back to the papers on her lap. There were a series of letters all dated in the last six months. They came from a Martin Freer who claimed to be Cyril's brother and it was apparent that Cyril had refused to meet him and had ignored the correspondence. Why, Angie wondered, if as Dillard Thrift thought, he wanted to belong?

The last letter had arrived two days before his death and in it Martin Freer was proposing that, since Cyril had not answered any of his letters, he would call in person one day the following week.

Angie was stunned into silence as she handed the documents back to Dillard Thrift.

"I have to assume," the lawyer said placing the papers in his brief case, that this man Freer won't know of your uncle's death unless he has spotted it in the Times. I will have to contact him."

"Will this have an effect on my uncle's will?"

"I doubt if the fellow has a claim on the estate. The adoption was legal and if his story is to be believed then I assume he, too, is illegitimate."

"But if he's Cyril's real brother he has more right to everything than I have. Morally at least."

"Don't worry about a thing, child. Cyril's will is binding. Now, let's lock up here and we'll stop at the Breadbin for a snack. Unless you were planning to spend the night here."

Angie shuddered. There was no way she would do that.

They left a note for Elizabeth repeating that she was welcome to remain and that they would keep in touch."

Dillard Thrift wrote to Martin Freer as soon as he reached London. Angie had agreed to stay with the lawyer and his wife until the funeral. Nick would have been her obvious choice for a bed but as yet he didn't know she was in London. Angie telephoned him at Chartres that night.

"Nick, I'm in London - at Mr Thrift's. Uncle Cyril has died. There are things to arrange. It makes sense to be here ... No I'm fine ... No I'm not running away from you. I'll call round in the morning about lunch time. See you then." She blew Nick a kiss before replacing the receiver.

Angie wandered round town in the morning and paid a visit to Dryden Terrace, having learned from Mr Thrift that Matt had bought the business. The shop was open and Matt was working at the counter. He greeted Angie warmly and sympathised with her over Cyril's death. "Never got a chance to see the old bastard before he went."

Angie wondered if he knew the truth of his last statement and she asked, "Did Cyril ever mention a brother to you?"

"'Course he did. Your father, Tommy. Used to speak of him quite a bit."

"No, another brother, Martin."

"He'd another brother? You've got me there. No there was no-one else. He'd have said. Tommy was the only one. Surely you'd know if you'd another uncle."

Angie didn't tell Matt any more. If Martin were genuine they'd all hear about him in time.

"Will I see you at the funeral."

"Yes, I'll be there. Do you know the old devil still owed me a fiver. We'd kept it running from our last poker game."

Angie made no offer to pay Cyril's debt. She knew he'd not forgotten his cronies. No more than a dozen men and half that number of women were at St Matthew's to pay their respects. Angie spoke to several of them before the service including Edwina who, like Angie, remained dry-eyed.

"You're forgotten fast around 'ere," Grimsby said. "I thought she at least would spare a tear."

Angie was pleased to see Jed.

"How's Wendy Elizabeth?"

"She's wonderful. Walking about and chattering away. Quick for her age at everything."

"Takes after her dad, then."

"I'm not doing so bad. I'm in charge now. We're buying a house on the Croydon Road. Nice little terrace with a garden. Moving in two weeks. Couldn't let his funeral pass, no matter."

The service was simple. Cyril had not been a religious man and no-one could recall him ever attending a church.

"I'd a job persuading the vicar to conduct the service at all," Mr Thrift told Angela. "Fortunately the promise of a donation towards the new organ did the trick. It usually does. The Church is always in need of money."

The vicar, a dour man, spoke unemotionally about Cyril's skills as a tailor and praised his fortitude during his illness. He ended his talk with the words "May the Lord's will be done" - which Angie interpreted to mean Heaven or Hell for Cyril depending on what God decided. She hoped he'd earned enough points to deserve a place in the upper chamber, but wouldn't bet on it.

Angie stood at the door to shake hands with the mourners. Odd, she thought, she hadn't seen him arrive but there was no mistaking the identity of the man at the end of the queue. Though thinner, he had the same round face, small eyes and piggish expression. Martin Freer did not have to prove he was Cyril's brother. It was there for everyone to see.

"I'm glad you came. You must be Martin. Mr Thrift told me about you."

"And you will be Angela. The lucky young woman who thinks she's getting my brother's fortune."

Angie was taken aback. "It's not like that," she protested. Dillard Thrift came to her rescue.

"Now Mr Freer this is neither the time nor the place. I

intend to have a meeting with all those concerned in the estate of Cyril Bolton. You are welcome to come along."

Angie was glad when the fuss was over and those who'd stayed on for tea and sandwiches at the local hotel had departed. Dillard Thrift had arranged a meeting for the following day with beneficiaries and Martin Freer.

"Seems he's your uncle's brother, alright. I've had a word with Edwina. She'd never heard of Martin. Said she got a shock when she'd seen him enter the church just before the vicar started. Thought she was seeing a ghost."

"There's an uncanny likeness, isn't there? Even for brothers."

Dillard Thrift had asked Martin Freer to come early next day so that he could explain the legal position to him. Angie was there, too. Once Mr Thrift had verified the authenticity of Martin's claim he put the case to him clearly.

·   "As I see it Mr Freer you have no claim on your brother's estate. Being legally adopted he became a full member of the Bolton family and the will he has made is valid. However, I have spoken to Angela and she feels you should be given some consideration. I must point out I don't share that view. You have had no contact with Cyril until six months ago. Surely if you were interested in your brother you'd have made plans to see him sooner?"

Martin Freer grunted.

"Thought he was dead long ago. I tried to reach him when our mother passed on but couldn't find him."

"How did you trace him in the end?" Angie asked.

"I didn't. I was in London doing some business and this man in the street came up to me and said, "You've lost a lot of weight Cyril. I hardly recognised you." So I told him I wasn't Cyril and he said I was the image of Cyril Bolton the tailor in Dryden Road. I went round there but the place was shut. It had a sold notice on a board. I took down the Estate Agent's name and they told me he was a sick man and gave me his new address."

"I'm very surprised they didn't inform me," Dillard Thrift observed. "Well, as I say. Angela has suggested that I give you a portion of the money that is coming to her. Say a figure of £3000 pounds."

Angie was about to protest that she had intimated a much larger sum but the lawyer's face warned her to keep quiet.

"I'll not settle for less than four thousand. I reckon if I took this to court they'd give me a sight more than that."

"Look Mr Freer" Angie began. "I'd be perfectly happy with........"

Dillard Thrift interrupted, "If you took this to court my man you'd be out of pocket and you'd have to wait an age for the case to be heard. Angela seems agreeable to settling for the £4000 figure. A cheque will be forwarded to you in due course. If you would just sign this deed of settlement." He quickly drew up a paper for Freer to sign. "Thank-you, that seems to be in order. Now, the others will be arriving any minute. If you'd like to stay...."

Martin Freer left. Content at being considerably better off than when he'd arrived.

"Exactly the way I figured it. Brother or no brother, he was only interested in the money."

"And I'd have given it to him. I'm not sure I want it now I know he's not my real uncle."

"And you'd have been very foolish. Cyril wouldn't even acknowledge him. How do you think he'd have felt at you giving him his money."

"Guess you've a point."

"Ah. Here they come and right on time. People always are when there's a will to be read."

Cyril had left each of his cronies £500, £3000 to Edwina, a welcome £200 to a surprised Jed, a small sum to Fred, and an even more surprising codicil witnessed by Fred bequeathing £100 to Elizabeth King, who wasn't present. He said she had rescued him in his last days. Once Martin Freer had been paid, the remaining estate, amounting to £23,000 in cash and shares was Angie's. No trust, no conditions, just as Cyril had said.

"The will could take a few months to execute," Mr Thrift pointed out. "You will all hear from me in due course."

"So Cyril finally turned up trumps. Let's go down to the pub and drink to the old codger," Matt suggested. "That is if you don't mind being seen in a pub, Angela?"

"With all of you to look after me, why should I worry. The first drink's on me."

Mr Thrift declined to join them, "I've work to catch up with here. Will you be coming home with me later, Angela."

"I think it's time I saw Nick. I'll be returning to Scotland in a couple of days. I'll arrange to pick up my things. Thanks for everything." Angie took his hand, shook it and then on impulse gave him a kiss. "I'll keep in touch."

"You'd better. And don't spend that fortune before you've got it."

Angie rang Nick from the Golden Horn. "Any chance you could pick me up? I've had a number of cherry brandies and am sharing a bottle of vintage cider with Edwina. Don't think I could make it to your place otherwise and I'm looking for a bed for the night."

The Sunbeam Talbot drew up at the Golden Horn as the somewhat inebriated bunch were spilling through the doors and on to the street. There were kisses and hand shakes and a bottom pinch for Angie from Matt. "You haven't changed any," she laughed.

"Do any of you need a lift?" Nick offered and Edwina and Jed accepted.

Nick and Angie declined invitations from both to call in and meet first Alice and then Jed's wife and baby. Back at the flat Angie snuggled into Nick. "I've missed you since the last time. Over Christmas and all that."

"Good. Maybe if you were here all the time you'd get so used to having me around you couldn't bear to go anywhere else."

"And you might get so sick and tired of seeing me you'd

wish I'd go."

"Never." Nick kissed Angie, laughed and kissed her again till she struggled for breath.

"Steady on." She wriggled free. "Remember I come here to stay because I can trust you." She knew she had to hold back, daren't let herself get too tied and yet ...

New Zealand could be a reality in a few months time if she wanted it. If? She'd no doubts. There were no "ifs". The urge to see all those places her Dad had mentioned wouldn't die. Within a year, she vowed, I'll be there.

We'll be there, Dad, and Mum and Lynn. I'll look into a New Zealand sky and you'll be with me, watching me.

Nick was staring at her, "Penny for your thoughts."

"You couldn't buy them for a thousand pounds." She guessed from his expression he felt excluded. It's not like that, Nick. I'm not sure. Not clear yet where you fit in. To his face she heard herself saying. "Nick, where ever I go, what ever I decide to do, you'll be part of it when I'm ready, if you want to be. What that role will be I don't know. We're bound by the past and I can't envisage a future when you're not around."

"Such words of comfort, Angel."

"Don't call me that. It sounds insincere."

"What do you want me to say? Yes, Darling, I will wait for ever no matter how far away you are? I'm human Angie. I realised I loved you a long time ago. I've been patiently waiting for you to feel the same about me. Now, I'm sure you do. But you won't commit yourself."

Angie said nothing.

"Well I want to know where I stand? Angie Bolton will you marry me?"

"I'm too young. Marriage isn't my first priority. I don't have a choice. Nick if you make me answer you now, you won't like what I say. Give me time, please." Angie looked straight into his eyes. Those warm, brown eyes, so trusting.

Nick got up and moved towards the window. "Sorry, Angie, I didn't mean to pester you. I can wait. Don't make it too long, that's all." She joined him at the window. He kissed her again gently this time. They stared into the night. "It's a nice night. Lots of stars twinkling."

"Spying on us more like," Angie said putting an arm round his neck and closing the curtains with her free hand. This night was private.

"Temptress."

"Where am I sleeping?"

"My bed's on offer. I'll use the put-u-up. You can change the sheets."

I can still trust him, Angie thought, but I'm damned if I want too.

"It's okay, we won't need the put-u-up. There's plenty of room for two in the bed."

"You mean ...?"

"You know what I mean, idiot."

"But I haven't any .... ."

Angie thought of Celeste but realised she didn't care.

"Damn it for one night."

CHAPTER 19

Angie woke. Nick was still sleeping beside her. She kissed the back of his head. Dear, dear Nick, what a fool she had been to want to keep him at bay. It will all work out. She would like to go to New Zealand and when she came back Nick would be waiting. After that night, she knew there could be no-one else for either of them. Their love was written in the stars. Young as she still was, Dad would have given his blessing. One day they'd marry and have children. One day ... Nick stirred, turned round and took her in his arms.

"If you think you're going to get away from me now, think again," he whispered.

"I love you Nick. I guess I always have."

"And always will?"

Angie nodded.

"Will you marry me, Angie Bolton?"

"On one condition. That we go to the other side of the world for our honeymoon.?"

"If that's what it takes. I can't afford it yet."

"I knew it," Angie laughed. "You're only after my money."

* * *

Scotland seemed a world away from Nick. Angie busied herself helping Henriette prepare for her wedding.

"I've decided on daffodil yellow for the bridesmaids' dresses. You, Celeste and Tom's little sister, Hilda. You do like yellow?"

"Of course, it's the essence of spring as your grandmother would say. Seriously, yellow is lovely.

"And I'll have the same colour repeated in my bouquet and the cake decoration and the table settings. It will be a yellow and white wedding. Oh, Angie, I'm so excited."

"How's your house coming on?" Henry still hadn't told her about Edinburgh.

"The house? Great I believe. I haven't seen it myself. I decided to leave all the planning to Tom but I've chosen material for the curtains and furnishings. Grandmother says we can spend as much as we like, but I don't want to take advantage of her generosity. You know we've persuaded her to come with us to see if she likes Edinburgh?"

Angie shook her head, "No you hadn't said. You haven't even told me the house is in Edinburgh. George told me at your engagement party."

"Angie, I'm so sorry. I must have forgotten. It doesn't make any difference, does it? You'll still join us?"

"We'll discuss that nearer the time but ..."

"It can't be much nearer. Just two more weeks. Dr Gillon says I must take my chair to the church. The service is too long for me to stand but I can get out of it for my vows if Tom holds me tight. But you were saying ...?"

"I'd better tell you now. I won't be going to Edinburgh. I'm returning to London, to Nick. We plan to marry ourselves one day."

"You ... getting married? That's wonderful. I don't know how we'll manage without you, but it's great news. You're a sly one. Never said a word."

"I didn't want to steal your glory. Anyway, it won't be for ages."

"Nick must come to my wedding."

"He can't get the time off work. He told you when he declined the invitation."

"Couldn't he try again?"

"He's saving for our honeymoon. Working all hours."

"He shouldn't. I can't be good for him."

"He thrives on it and it keeps him out of mischief."

"Oh, Angie, isn't life exciting? If only Lynn could share it with us."

"I think in a way she does. She always said "Life's for the living." But there has to be more to life than this earth."

"You're getting far too deep for me."

"Too deep for myself. Now let's check the lists again. A hundred and thirty guests definitely coming with three possibles and fourteen definitely nots. The printers will need to make out the place cards. I understand the hymn sheets are ready."

Henriette and Angela confirmed the arrangements. The dresses were fitted, the cake baked and iced, the flowers chosen. Grateful to leave things in their hands, Henriette's grandmother hovered over them. The only thing they hadn't been able to organise was the weather. It poured. The whole of Scotland seemed to be sheltering beneath white umbrellas.

Angie had been busy all morning. Visits to the hairdressers, facials, manicures, dashing in and out of the rain. However, it couldn't dampen their spirits. Celeste was being more zany than ever and Hilda leapt up and down like a kitten. Henriette had to be taken to the toilet all morning.

"Nerves," la Grandmere declared. "It was the same even in my day."

She looks so beautiful, Angie thought, as she placed a tiara twined with yellow flowers in Henriette's dark hair. Hugh and Estelle had covered the wheel chair in white satin and tied yellow ribbons to the arms and handles. The Countess stood beside it in a long midnight blue dress. Completely plain, it set off her jewellery to perfection. Her thin face looked flushed and for once she appeared flustered.

"Are you sure you haven't forgotten anything?" Hugh had gathered staff from neighbouring homes to form an arch of umbrellas to the cars. Henriette could have chosen a male relative to give her away, but in her eyes the Countess was the only person for the job.

Celeste as Chief Bridesmaid pushed the wheelchair to where the groom was standing with his best man. The Countess walked beside the chair and Angie escorted Hilda, who in a fit of shyness kept her eyes to the ground and looked close to tears.

Angie didn't glance at Tom till they had almost reached him. She felt a sudden wave of shock as she recognised the man beside him. It was Seb. Angie didn't know he was to be best man. She wondered why she'd never thought to ask and was glad Celeste would sit beside him at dinner. Funny, she herself had helped to arrange the seating at the top table, however, those officiating were designated only by their office – Bride, Groom, parents, Best man, Chief Bridesmaid and so on. Seb turned his head and nodded to her and she acknowledged the nod with a tight smile. Seb was bad news.

Angie put him out of her mind and concentrated on the ceremony. The music, she enjoyed, but there were so many blessings, so much palaver. She could understand why Henriette was only allowed out of her chair for the exchange of vows and placing of rings. If Nick and she were to be married in church it would have to be simple.

At last it was over. Tom and Henriette were man and wife. The rain miraculously eased as they stood on the church steps for photographs. Angie was finding it difficult to keep Hilda in order. Gone was the initial shyness to be replaced by over-excitement, and the little girl couldn't stay still for a second. Angie wondered at the Countess, so upright when she herself was feeling weary.

All tiredness was forgotten when they arrived at the Central Hotel for the reception, yet in the privacy of the powder room Angie and Celeste relaxed enough to put their feet up on a couch for a few minutes

"Was it that bad?" Henriette laughed.

"Yes," they chorused.

The thought of champagne and choice food revived them and they resumed their duties at the reception. Angie successfully avoided Seb for most of the evening and attached herself to George and a group of his friends. Inevitably, Seb came over.

"I've been trying to get a chance to speak to you. I heard about Cyril. Sorry and all that."

"It was for the best. He was very ill," Angie said.

"Would you have this dance?" Angie realised she could hardly refuse. They danced closely in silence at first. Angie dreaded the old electricity would be there but, in fact, she felt nothing. Not even when she'd to lift Seb's hand when it wandered.

"What about it, Angie? We could slip away together and never be noticed. There's a little room ..."

"I wouldn't go with you again if you paid me."

"Come on. I'm not kidding. We had fun together. We could still."

Angie stopped dancing and moved towards the seats. "You think you're God's gift, don't you? Well for your information I'd rather go with…"

"One of the waiters?" Seb taunted.

Angie ran from him into the powder room. He was the most despicable man, she thought, and what was wrong with being a waiter? Why had she ever gone out with him? Ever let him get close? Oh, Nick, why couldn't you be here?

"Angie, are you all right?" Celeste poked her head round the door. " I saw you dash in here. What was Romeo saying that upset you> He's a bastard. Why Tom's friendly with him, I don't know. Come on, you're meant to be having fun. Don't let Seb win. They'll be cutting the cake in a minute. Don't allow him to spoil Henriette's day."

The cake was cut. The toast drunk. The incident forgotten. Eventually, the wedding party broke up and, whilst Tom whisked Henriette off to some unknown honeymoon destination in a shower of confetti, Angie returned with Celeste and the Countess to Woodend. Sleep was Angie's aim as she drew up the sheets, but it didn't come readily.

What was she doing here in Scotland, hob-knobbing with the very rich as if she were par with them? Beautiful clothes, lazy lifestyle – this wasn't living. At least, not the living she really wanted to do. Henriette had needed her but now she had Tom. Despite what she and the Countess said, Angie wasn't convinced she fitted into the new set up. In a month's time the Edinburgh house would be ready and the Countess would leave Woodend to the servants to keep prepared for odd visits. What a waste. By the time she fell asleep Angie had come to a decision.

In the morning, La Grandmere engaged Angie in conversation. "If you are determined not to come with us, you may stay here at Woodend for as long as you like. Celeste will be around quite a lot. In fact we'll all come through frequently. I couldn't give up Glasgow for always. I'd miss it too much."

Angie knew the Countess's offer was sincere but there was always the chance she 'd fall in love with the east and even if she hated Edinburgh and returned, she, surely, wouldn't want Angie around. Although old, La Grandmere was very independent.

It was time, Angie decided, to pack her trunk and head back to England. It was odd that only a short time ago she had said she couldn't bear to leave Glasgow. She would speak to Mr Thrift in the morning but not to Nick, not yet. Perhaps enough money could be advanced for her to buy a flat. Was that what she wanted? A permanent base? No. The more she thought about it she concluded that if she were going to travel it had to be now. That night she turned over in her bed, shut her eyes, forgot about sheep, and began counting the stars. Soon the dream she had held for so long, her dad's dream, would be fulfilled.

Next morning Angie told the Countess she would leave Glasgow in two weeks time. She telephoned Mr Thrift and asked him to try to find her somewhere to stay.

"The bungalow's been sold as you instructed but the new owners don't take it over until the end of July. You could use it for the time being."

"I don't think so, though I might find a place in Brighton. I fancy somewhere quiet, near the sea. I need time to think about my future."

"You won't find anywhere better than the bungalow.

225

Remember the view from the cliffs? It would be a great place to gather your thoughts."

"Maybe you're right. Could you sell up Cyril's furniture and refit it?"

"That would be silly if you're only staying a couple of months."

"I suppose it would. It's just that I don't … I'll try it and see how I feel. If I don't like it, I can always move out."

"Precisely, that's the sensible thing to do."

Angie wrote to Nick.

" I'm coming back. Going to stay at the bungalow for a few weeks. I'll be up to see you but not immediately. I've some things to sort out."

Nick would think the 'things' were related to Cyril's estate. Inside she felt very muddled, unsure of herself. She knew she loved Nick, yet this travel urge – New Zealand. It really belonged to her and dad. Even her mum wasn't part of it. Lynn? – well, she was on the fringe. Angie recalled the night they'd traced the map in her room above Cyril's shop. They might have travelled together if Lynn were still alive.

Thinking of Lynn, led Angie to remember Sylvie and Gideon's invitation. "Come and see us any time. California – half way house between here and there. Perhaps, just perhaps, she might go and see Silvie. Fixing up the journey wouldn't be easy but there had to be way. Nothing was impossible if you wanted it enough. Gideon was the right person to ask. Perhaps she could travel by boat, fly even. Fly like the seagull - was it such an impossible dream?"

CHAPTER 20

Leaving Scotland before Henriette returned from her honeymoon made sense. Angie packed her trunk and cases. It wasn't easy, going away. She went out for a walk along the streets and back through the woods to the house. She was turning another page and inside she felt apprehensive. This had been a safe haven and she couldn't deny she'd loved it most of the time.

The Countess was in the hallway with Celeste. They both kissed her. Estelle stood in the corner behind them sniffing into a handkerchief. The Countess walked with Angie to where Hugh was stacking the luggage into the car.

"Come and see us when you can - you have our new address. If you need somewhere to stay don't hesitate. You'll always be welcome. I wish you'd waited to say goodbye to Henriette. She'll be upset when she returns and you're not here but au revoir, Angela. Thank-you for everything and look after yourself."

"I'll try to. You take care, both of you. Give Tom and Henriette my love."

The journey to London was uneventful, the train to Brighton crowded and uncomfortable. Dillard and Grace Thrift were at the bungalow when Angie arrived.

"We've changed things around a bit to make it more homely for you. We guessed you'd prefer the small bedroom. I've made up the bed with fresh linen, and we've stocked the larder with essentials. I think you'll find everything you need." Grace said.

"Thanks. It's very kind of you."

"And now we're going to seem rude because we've to rush away." Dillard checked his watch. "You're a bit late arriving and we've arranged a meal out and a night at the theatre. I'll give you a day or two to settle then ring. By the way, I hope to have the estate wound up before long. Things are sorting themselves out nicely. No more word from that brother of his."

Angie was alone at last. She spent the evening unpacking a few items having decided most of her belongings could remain in the trunk. She made an omelette for a light dinner, took a brief walk along the cliff path and went to bed early to sleep well.

There was nothing to do in the morning but make her bed and have breakfast. It was odd being on her own. So quiet she felt compelled to walk noisily and clatter the pans as she washed the dishes. She listened to the radio. It made the house sound occupied. How on earth did deaf people cope?

Angie went into the garden. The roses were budding and tall purple irises grew along side the wall. She heard a bee buzz and watched a snail smear a trail across the path. She wasn't really alone with all these creatures about. Opening the shed door, she found a deckchair and after a hilarious struggle to put it up, relaxed, soaking in the warmth of the sun. Even the grind of a neighbour's lawnmower couldn't disturb her thoughts. She would have to decide. Have to let Nick know what she was thinking. She wrote a letter to Silvie and Gideon asking if it would be convenient for her to visit them shortly providing it could be arranged. There was, she said a possibility that she might want to go on to travel to New Zealand for a few months. She gave the address of the bungalow and said she could also be contacted via Morton and Dolinda.

Angie waited a full week before getting in touch with Nick. She rang him at home. "Would you like to come down here for the week-end?... I see, in that case, I'll come up to you, but just for the day. I want to go on to Morton and Dolinda's. Could we meet in the town?"

* * *

A Lyons tearoom at the corner of Lancaster Road was far removed from Parker's in Sauchiehall Street. Nick was already seated at a table and rose to greet her warmly with a kiss.

"What's all the mystery about? Tucking yourself away for a whole week. I've been dying to see you."

"I needed some time to myself. It's been so hectic lately. What with Cyril's funeral and then all the hype of the wedding."

"I was surprised you left Glasgow so quickly. I thought you'd plan to stay on a while. Nothing wrong there, I hope?"

"Not at all. I was sorry to leave, yet glad at the same time."

"You could have come to my place, you know."

"I know I could."

"So why the bungalow? Had you things to do regarding your uncle?"

"Not really. I was making plans. Decisions. Let's not talk about it now. I'll tell you in a day or two when I know more myself."

"So there really is a mystery. Are you having second thoughts about us?" "Don't be stupid." Angie put her arms round his neck. "Nick, I love you. It's that I'm not sure about something else. I told you. I'll tell you everything in a few days."

"I'll have to wait then. So what will we do?"

"Could we go over the old haunts? It's been so long."

"Funny you should say that. I had a letter offering me a flat in Albany Court, as they now call it. I turned it down. Reckon we can stand on our own feet without the council."

"I don't think I could live there. It would be like walking on my mother's grave."

"And my family's."

"Maybe it's not a good idea to go back. Do you know what I'd really like? A trip down the river in one of those touring boats."

London seen from the river was an eye-opener with so much redevelopment taking place. It was greener than Angie remembered with willows dipping their branches into the grey water.

"There are some lovely houses along the banks once you leave the industry behind. See that big one there - with the red roof. It's owned by a millionaire. Newspaper guy. Can't recall his name...Mason or something. He's got private yachts. When my dinghy comes in I'll swap it for one of them and we can sail to New Zealand."

"Nick, I couldn't care less about owning big houses or yachts. I'm back here in England to regain my sense of what life's really about. I want to earn my living again one day. I've had enough of luxury for the time being." Perhaps not quite, she said to herself. If she got to America, that would be the most glamorous thing she'd ever done.

"And to think my life depends on other people indulging themselves." Nick said. "The taxi side's doing well but the hours can be awful. It's no fun driving folk home in the middle of the night and they often expect you to hang around for ages. Brings in the loot though and that can't be bad. Now tell me about the wedding."

Angie described the ceremony in detail down to the last crumb of yellow and white icing but omitting to mention the attentions of the best man.

"We won't have to go through all that, will we? I fancy a quiet little job at the registry office."

"That's a possibility. At least we'd not upset any relatives if we did. We haven't any."

"Not true. I've an Aunt Molly and numerous cousins in Nottingham."

"Well we've plenty of time to think about it."

"Have we?"

Angie changed the subject.

* * *

Taurus ran to greet Angie when she arrived at Morton and Dolinda's farm. "He looks well," Angie said. "Where's Muppet?"

"She's at the kennels," Morton explained. "Pups. A minor

complication and I was too busy to cope. She's fine now. She'll be back here with her family in a day or two. Three dogs and a bitch. You don't want a pup?"

"I'd love one but it wouldn't fit into my nomadic lifestyle."

"So what is it you wanted to discuss? Is it about Cyril's affairs?"

"Not really. I just needed someone to talk too. Someone prepared to listen and advise. I thought of Dolinda."

"I'll leave you two to it." Morton crossed the garden to the field. Dolinda led the way into the kitchen. It smelt as usual of home baking and a huge apple pie cooled on a wire tray.

"We'll have a cup of tea. I wouldn't recommend you to eat anything. I've prepared a big dinner."

Angie brought Dolinda up to date with recent events.

"Now I've finished with Glasgow, I'm free to travel as I've always planned and thanks to Cyril I can afford it. Everything would be wonderful if it weren't for all the restrictions imposed, and Nick."

"So Nick's not in favour. I gather you and Nick mean something to each other."

"He wants us to get married."

"And you?"

"I feel the same. But Nick would like it to be tomorrow. I want to wait a while. I'm thinking of going to see Sylvie and Gideon and then - I'd be half way there any way - then go on to New Zealand if it's possible. Do you think it's just pie in the sky?"

"Anything's possible if you want it enough."

"I'd be away a couple of months at least. I haven't actually discussed my plans with Nick. That is - he knows I want to go but he doesn't know I want to go now and he would expect us to go together. I even suggested he took me for our honeymoon but now I don't think that's on."

"Sounds wonderful to me."

"The point is New Zealand was Dad's dream. Nick wasn't part of it. I'm not sure I want him to be."

"You mean you'd rather go by yourself?"

"That's it. Only I wouldn't be by myself. Dad would be with me. Not physically of course but ..."

"You don't need to explain any more. So you'd like me to judge if your thinking is sound? My advise is tell Nick in the way you've told me. If he loves and knows you, he'll understand how you feel. He might not like the idea but he should respect it. Mind you it might be hard to arrange. I'd ask Gideon, if I were you. He's in the travel line."

"I already have. The last thing I want to do is upset Nick. It's funny how you can be close to someone and not realise how deep it goes. I think I really fell for Nick the day we met at Albany Place but it's taken two years for me to realise it."

"That's often the best kind of relationship. One that's based on a firm friendship. You're a lucky girl, Angie, and Nick will be a very fortunate young man."

"And you really do think he'll understand?"

"I don't know him well enough to say for sure, but, yes, he should. Mind you, I personally think you're to young to go on your own. I know you say your Dad will be there. But in reality, he won't. You have to face that, Angie. Your Dad's dead."

"I know, but somehow I can't let him go."

"You'll have to one day. Now, I assume you'll spend the night with us. It would be a drag going back to Brighton after dinner. Unless you're staying in London?"

"I'd love to stay if that's okay."

Angie tucked into the spare room, her thoughts on when she'd shared it with Lynn and Henriette. If only the clock could turn back.

* * *

Angie returned to the bungalow to find an air mail letter. Sylvie and Gideon would be happy to have Angie visit. There'd be so much for her to see. Los Angeles was a big city. They had just moved from Santa Monica to a house overlooking the shore at Malibu. She would love it. Gideon had sent instructions to Mr

Thrift. If Angie wanted to fly there was every chance they could fix it up. Gideon was always arranging business flights.

Angie held the letter close to her, full of excitement. Now, all she had to do was tell Nick. She telephoned him immediately.

"Yes, I got back safely. How else could I be phoning ... Stop fussing, you nincompoop ... It's your turn to come here ... Thursday? That's great."

* * *

Angie sat with Nick on the couch in the lounge, music softly filling the background. The setting was perfect.

"Nick, I've something to tell you."

"A-ha. The mystery unfurls."

"I've had a letter from Sylvie and Gideon. I might be going over to see them. Gideon and Mr Thrift are looking into it for me."

Nick stubbed out the cigarette he had just lit.

"When?"

"I've not fixed an exact date. In the next month or two if things work out. After Cyril's money's settled."

"Can't wait to spend it, eh?"

"That's not fair. You know I'm not like that."

"Couldn't you hang on a bit and I'll come with you?"

"I'd rather not. I...er ... might go on to New Zealand."

"But it's miles away."

"Nearer there, than here."

"But I thought it was to be our honeymoon?"

Angie explained to Nick how she felt in the way she'd told Dolinda. She read surprise, hurt, disappointment, a hint of anger in his face as he listened.

"You're not going all that way alone."

"I've got to. I've told you I can't share it, not even with you. I'm going."

"Stubborn little bugger aren't you?"

Nick got up and walked to the window and stood with his back to Angie. Angie remained seated for a minute before joining him. She had never seen him in this mood. She put an arm round his waist.

"Tell me you understand Nick. It's so important to me. I don't want to upset you but I can't change my mind."

Nick shrugged his shoulders and kissed her gently. "Don't worry, I'll get used to the idea. Give me time. Promise one thing. Promise you'll come back."

"Can you doubt it?"

"And we'll get married?"

"You can fix the date."

The kiss this time was passionate. Nick stroked her hair. "I don't want you gallivanting all over the world. You're my girl. If your mind's made up you'll go and I won't try to talk you out of it."

"Nick, you're wonderful. I don't deserve you."

"You're pretty great yourself."

To think telling Nick had been that easy. She was marrying a saint. Next morning, she closed the door on Nick as he sped back to London and Chartres. She missed him immediately. The silence. She switched the radio on too loudly and hoped the neighbours wouldn't complain.

Now that Nick knew, Angie found making plans for the trip easier. She spread maps on the floor and traced the routes she would take. To cruise to America would cost more probably than she dared think. To fly? Even dearer, perhaps, but she had the money. If only Gideon could use his influence. Once there, she'd have to travel to Malibu via Los Angeles. She'd stay ten days or a fortnight then move on.

Perhaps she could plan how to get to New Zealand once she was in America. Maybe she'd sail to Auckland. The City of Sails her father had called it. To arrive by ship would be appropriate. Dad would have sailed into the harbour. She wondered how long a journey it would be. Angie shut her eyes. She could see the seagull on VE Day. She had vowed to fly like it. Maybe she should

* * *

Trying to arrange everything was going to be a bit complicated but most things, she'd learned, had a habit of sorting themselves out, particularly when Mr Thrift was involved. She put the maps away and concentrated on her wardrobe. Not that she needed to buy anything new. Working out what the weather was going to be like was the main concern. Fur coats or swimsuits, or both.

In the next few weeks most of Angie's questions were answered. The cases were packed well in advance of the date she set herself. September 3rd - the anniversary of the start of the war. A day to remember. Time flew in a whirl of visits to Morton and Dolinda, the Thrifts, Edwina, and Nick, of course. She considered going down to Updean but it all seemed so long ago. So much for her promises to go back often. Instead she wrote to Mrs Crofthouse and told her about her plans. At the same time she penned a note to Henry. She'd heard nothing from her since leaving Glasgow. Marriage must be keeping her very occupied.

In August Mr Thrift confirmed by letter the settlement of Cyril's legacy. Angie would be pleased to know the sum of £24,870 had been lodged in her account. He was happy to tell her that Gideon had been able to arrange for her to fly on the 3rd September on a craft transferring some of his staff. The plane would stop at Houston where she would have to board another flight to Los Angeles. There were a limited number of ordinary passengers travelling. He hoped the details would suit her plans and that she would enjoy her visit to America and would give his regards to the Arnolds.

He was not at all sure Angie should travel on to New Zealand. Had she considered it carefully? She would know no-one. Have no-one to call on in an emergency. What ever she decided she must keep in touch throughout her trip and he wished her luck. Angie whirled with delight. Good old Thrift and good old Gideon!

The week prior to her departure Angie spent with Nick. A letter arrived from Henry as she was locking up the bungalow. A reprimand for leaving so abruptly and an assurance of her continued friendship. Celeste was casting a line for George and he wasn't wriggling away. Wouldn't it be fun if something came of it? It did happen - brothers marrying sisters. Life with Tom was bliss. She could now walk the length of their garden path with a zimmer and would throw it away soon. She asked to be remembered to Lynn's parents.

Odd, Angie thought, she hadn't missed Scotland that much and though it sounded awful to admit she was quite glad she didn't have to attend to Henry. It was just another episode in her book of life.

She was high when she reached London and Nick could do nothing to calm her down. He, on the other hand, appeared quiet, secretive even. On the night before Angie was leaving they went to Chartres for dinner.

"Sounds to me as if you can't get away quick enough."

"That's true. Not from you though. I'll miss you like hell but it will be the same as when I was in Glasgow and it is only for a couple of months."

"Would you rather I was coming with you?"

"We've been through all that."

"And you haven't changed your mind about New Zealand?"

"New Zealand belongs to Dad."

"So that means America doesn't, which is just as well. It's my turn to spring a surprise. Gideon got in touch with me. He wasn't happy about you travelling on your own and suggested I might consider coming. I've thought about it a lot and Luigi has agreed to me having time off. I've secured the last seat on that plane. I'm going to Sylvie and Gideon's, too. Despite the favourable fare, it'll make a gigantic hole in my pocket but America will be ours. After all I'm part of the Sylvie-Gideon connection. Now scream at me if you dare."

Angie couldn't believe her own ears. Nick was going to America.

"You're joking. You aren't serious?"

"Never been more so in my life. Now are you going to clobber me?"

"Nick. It's wonderful. You're wonderful. Why didn't I think of it. America can be ours. Dad won't mind that."

"And do you reckon he'll mind this?" Nick handed Angie a small box he had taken from his pocket. "It should fit all right. I pinched one of your rings to get the size right. Don't worry I put it back."

Angie opened the box with trembling fingers and her eyes sparkled as brightly as the gold band, with its cluster of diamonds, that nestled inside.

"It's beautiful, perfect." She lifted it from the box and was about to place the ring on her finger when Nick took it from her.

"Got to do things properly. You can assume the kneeling bit. Angie Bolton, will you marry me?"

"Of course I will."

Nick slipped the ring on to Angie's finger, leant across the table and kissed her. "That's settled then. Drink up and we'll get moving. I've still to pack. I've not ironed my shirts yet."

Angie smoothed away the creases in Nick's clothes as he put them into his suitcase. "There you are, the last one."

"Thank God for that. I thought it'd be time to leave before we'd finished. As it is we can grab five ... no ... four-and-a-half hours sleep."

"Who wants to sleep. We can do that on the way over."

"Guess your right," Nick said lifting her in his arms and heading for the bedroom.

They did sleep, eventually. Curled together in Nick's bed. The alarm clock shrilled them into action at 8.00am. A wash, a snatch of tea and toast and the suitcases were humped down stairs to where Willie, one of the Chartres taxi crew, stood waiting. Luigi had insisted they be driven to the airport.

"We're in plenty of time. You don't leave till twelve," he said as they pulled up in front of the airport buildings. Nick put his hand in his pocket to pay. "Don't be daft man. This is on the house. Enjoy yourselves and don't do anything I wouldn't."

"That gives us plenty of scope," Nick laughed. "Thanks, Willie. I'll see you right one day."

237

Angie was surprised the reception area wasn't busier, even though there were plenty of Americans going home. The wait to board tried her patience. Why on earth one had to report so early before take off was a mystery. Nick asked question after question and avidly read a brochure about the flight.

"Do you realise we'll be on this plane for hours and hours - about eleven I'd guess?"

They were guided with other passengers to their seats. Nick's was as far away from Angie's as was possible.

"Pity we didn't get adjacents. Maybe we could switch them."

"No Nick, we can't cause a fuss. It won't be that bad."

"And there's no-one going to notice if I slip down the aisle to see you occasionally."

A few minutes after the scheduled 12noon, they were airborne. Angie was glad she hadn't eaten much for they were barely settled when lunch was served. Several hours out into the flight, Angie knew she had inherited her father's stomach for travel. Nick, on the other hand, felt decidedly queasy.

They stood together to look from the window and Nick wished he could open it for some fresh air. He was dying for a cigarette, but wasn't sure his stomach agreed.

"Forget the fags," Angie advised. "I'll get you a brandy from the hostess. It should settle you."

"I'll give it a try. Hope the bloke I'm sharing the seat with won't object if I reek of spirits."

They ordered drinks and Nick gulped his down.

"No use, Angie. I'd better take a pew."

Angie took his arm and helped him along the passage to his seat.

"Number twenty-eight," she said. "Your fortunes are untold. The plane lurched and rain beat against the windows. "I've a feeling we're in for a rough journey."

She kissed him on the forehead and left him in the hands of a middle-aged fatherly fellow, who on seeing his slightly green appearance, immediately offered him some barley sugar. Angie hadn't considered the noise of the engines and the fidgeting of the other passengers. She dozed fitfully. Her legs and back cramped in the narrow seat whilst the business man next to her sprawled one leg on to the passageway and the other across Angie's allotted space. She read an in-flight magazine from cover to cover. If nothing else, she learned how to follow the safety procedures in the event of trouble.

Angie took stock of her fellow passengers. The other seat in her row of three was occupied by a young man who sat motionless as if scared to move. Was he really afraid of flying or indulging in some deep thought that shut all around him out. He got up to use the toilet, edging past Angie and stepping gingerly over the business man's legs. Angie thought he looked foreign, Italian perhaps, but on his return he said, "Excuse me hen," and there was no mistaking his Scottish accent.

Angie decided that with Nick at the front of the plane she might as well talk to her fellow passenger.

"You're Scottish, aren't you?"

"Glasgow."

"I know it. Have you been in America before?"

"No."

"Neither have I. It's a long journey."

"Aye."

Like getting blood from a stone, Angie thought. This man's got to be the dourest person she'd come across. One more try to draw him out and she gave up and lapsed into silence. In front of her two women gossiped. To be honest one gossiped and the other listened. She could catch only snippets of their conversation - "wouldn't trust him ... in his eyes ... and that other one with the curly hair, as mad as a hatter. Married the Barnet girl, the one with the bent nose. A right bitch she turned out." Angie decided to cast them as characters in a murder story. The murderer was the man sleeping beside her and the victim was the gossip. Her Scottish companion was a reticent defence witness and the elderly couple opposite were called by the prosecution for having seen the ghastly killing from the steps leading to their basement flat in Lambeth. Nick she decided would be the super sleuth who brought the guilty to justice.

Angie let her imagine run riot and by the time Nick, feeling much better, staggered along to see her, she was getting the verdict from the jury and the judge was donning the black cap.

* * *

Angie slept. She had no idea for how long. She hadn't been aware if the plane had made a scheduled refuelling stop. Nick came to join her again and they saw Canada from the window they had stood at previously. A vast white land mass, like looking at nothing. Time passed. A whirl of smog covered Chicago and then they were closing in on Houston. Time to adjust watches. All those hours to live through again.

As they reached the customs desk the intercom informed all passengers the flight had landed one hour behind schedule. For those travelling on to Los Angeles the connection had been held for a limited time. Customs thumbed their papers and asked pertinent questions. Yes, they had the necessary documents. Yes they knew they were in the Federal States of America. No they weren't carrying any illegal substances. The official, a cold man, offered no welcome and seemed intent on holding them back although their next plane was waiting. They grabbed their cases and looked for Gate 19.

"Are you flying to Los Angeles" a ground steward asked. "You'd better hurry plane's leaving." Angie's legs were tired but she ran after Nick, who had recovered completely as soon as he'd touched terre firma, along the moving corridor. Gate 19 was at the very end. They could see a hostess standing beside it. She seemed to be arguing with a group of passengers. The gate was closed. They had missed the connection. Angie was too breathless to speak but Nick was disgusted.

"Why the hell do they hold a flight then let it go before all the passengers can be transferred?" he demanded.

"Sorry, sir we waited as long as we could. Some of you took too much time getting through customs I'm afraid."

"That was hardly our fault," Nick argued. "If it hadn't been for that ass of a ..."

Angie tugged his arm, "Come on Nick let's get back to the waiting area. No point in losing your rag."

They made their way back. Angie's case felt like lead. "Wish I'd left half this stuff at home."

"Give it here," and, despite Angie's protests, Nick lugged both cases back to reception. He made a face at the customs official as they passed the excise desks. The man's expression hadn't changed from stone as he dealt with another batch of travellers..

"You're exceptionally lucky," a ground steward informed them and the other eight passengers who had been left stranded. "For once there's room on another flight leaving at the same time tomorrow. You must remain with your luggage."

They came round with a trolley of drinks and created a fuss when Nick couldn't find enough change and presented a note.

"Not exactly getting off to a good start are we?" he said to Angie. She had to agree. What they'd seen within the confines of the airport wasn't inviting.

"Maybe we could go outside for a while," she said, but the cases presented a problem. There was nothing else for it but to bed down somewhere in the airport.

"What do you do around here, other than stuff yourself with popcorn?" Nick commented.

"We could plan another murder." She explained to Nick how she passed the time on the plane.

"You should take up writing." Nick's remark led them to browse round a bookstall.

"We'd better phone Sylvie and say we're on tomorrow's flight" Angie said when she spotted a telephones close to the book stall.

Gideon answered. The first warm voice they'd heard since touching down in the States. No problem. He'd check at the airport for arrival times and meet them outside the terminal building as previously arranged and he'd order an enquiry into their treatment.

They left drinking more coffee until the last possible minute and fed a machine with cents. The jackpot wasn't for winning but they came away with more than when they started.

"Go on like this and we'll pay for the holiday." Nick quipped as he piled the coins into his pockets.

"It'll cover the tips." Angie rejoined. "And they won't moan about us not having any change."

They found an empty bench seat and settled down to get some sleep, but it was a long and uncomfortable wait till the Los Angeles flight was called next day.

"It's not much bigger than a London double decker." Nick observed as they boarded the half full plane. Angie was too exhausted to comment. Having first asked the crew, she stretched her legs out across an empty row of seats and fell asleep again.

Nick let her snooze through the first drinks but woke her when a meal was served.

"Better eat something. God knows what the time will be when we arrive. I've lost track."

The staff on this flight smiled and were attentive. Things were looking up.

CHAPTER 21

The intercom blared into the cabin.

"We are now approaching Los Angeles airport and will land in approximately seven minutes. Fasten all seat belts."

Millions of tiny lights flickered up at Angie and Nick as they stared earthwards. Is this what it's like to be a star, Angie wondered? Looking down on Los Angeles was like looking up at the sky on a very clear night; like a huge Christmas tree with fairy lights or a spinning Catherine Wheel. Nick, who had no sickness problem on this flight, was equally as enthralled.

"Hey, from here it's some city. What a display. What the German's would have done if they'd raided this lot."

"Breathtaking," Angie agreed. "I can't find the right words to describe it. Everything's inadequate. Perhaps, heaven on earth."

"It won't be when we get down, I guess. Just another big city, full of noise and dirt, bustle and beer."

Angie held on to his hand. "Don't, Nick. Don't spoil the magic."

They bumped to earth seconds later. Dying to get a real sleep but exhilarated to have arrived safely. The airport was busy. They filed through customs again and were treated this time with smiles. Only once outside the terminal gate did they feel as if they were on American soil.

Gideon had said, "We'll be in the car driving round the building till you come out. Just stay by the exit and we'll spot you."

What he hadn't said was that dozens of other vehicles would be going round and round waiting to pick up passengers and taxis would be vying for custom.

"Drop you somewhere?" A driver flung open his cab door

and lifted one of their suitcases. Nick wrenched it from him.

"Sorry mate we've got a lift."

The driver rejoined the ring of traffic. A sleek black limousine drew up. The chauffeur stepped forward to usher them inside. Nick and Angie hesitated. "We're waiting to be collected."

"Then wait no longer." Gideon's voice called from the rear of the car. "Pickering will take the cases. In you get."

Sylvie sat beside Gideon. There was room inside for hugs, kisses and handshakes.

"No wonder you got rid of the Sunbeam Talbot," Nick said as he settled into the plush seat. "Cars like this exist only in the movies."

"Plenty around in this country. Home's about twenty miles out of the city centre. I know it's dark and you won't see much and I guess you're dying to get to sleep but we'd like to take you somewhere before we go home. Is that okay?"

"We're in your hands. Now that we've landed I've found a second lease of life, anyway. It's all so exciting." Angie said.

"Right. Pickering will take us to the top of Beverly Hills and you can look down on the city. Believe me it's a sight worth seeing."

They drove along the Wilshire Boulevard for some distance then turned off and began to climb past tree lined gardens. It's like a film set, Angie thought. Houses lit so brightly it could almost be daylight. They reached the peak of the hills and looked down on the city.

"This is a bit like the view from the plane but even more magical," Angie enthused.

"We were brought up here the night we arrived and like you I was entranced," Sylvie's eyes sparkled. "Once you're down in the city with it's grey buildings you can forget this exists. It's a queer place Los Angeles. Young hopefuls come here and expect to find Dick Whittington streets paved with gold. It may house Hollywood but it's a hard working place and it shows. You have to be tough to live in it."

"Do you like it?" Angie asked.

"Yes, I do. Not at first. Coming back to America to live was an escape from the trauma we'd been through. Now I wouldn't want to be anywhere else. I miss London's shops. The one's here are less personal and the quality can be suspect, but I've got myself a good dressmaker. We don't go clubbing like we did in England. Prefer a quieter lifestyle. Malibu offers us that. The house is built into the cliffs above the beach. The design is unique, or so the previous owners told us. You'll see for yourselves when we get there. And there's Alice's."

"Who is Alice?"

"Not who, what. It's a renowned restaurant at the entrance to the pier. Very popular with the stars. It's been featured in films, too. But enough loitering, it's high time we were on our way. I forgot to ask. Have you eaten or would you like to stop somewhere? Or I could put out a light supper when we get home?"

"We've done nothing but eat and drink since we left London. We won't need any more tonight." Nick said.

Angie was in agreement. "Just a bath and bed."

The house was ranch style. White wood against reddish brick. They drove into a garage already housing a car and capable of taking several more. Angie and Nick followed Sylvie and Gideon up a small flight of steps to the main entrance.

"We could have gone in through the garage," Gideon explained. "But it's best to see the place for the first time from this angle."

The impressively wide hall was furnished as a reception area with one wall taken over by a massive fish tank.

"Chap who lived here before used to eat what swum about in there. Like in some restaurants. Sylvie didn't fancy that idea so ours are purely decorative."

Angie watched fascinated at the antics of the brightly coloured tropical fish and would have lingered longer had Sylvie not taken her arm.

"We'll let you see your rooms and then you can decide if you'd like to look round or go straight to bed."

She led the way up the stairs. Angie's bedroom faced the front. The double bed was inviting.

"From the balcony you can look out to sea. Your room's at the back I'm afraid, Nick. We've only the four bedrooms and the staff rooms. Two front, two back. It's as much as we need. We rarely invite more than two couples at a time."

Nick's room, also a double, had a side window with a smaller balcony. Nick stepped out on to it.

"You can shout across to each other but they don't link I'm afraid." Sylvie explained.

"It's fantastic. We couldn't ask for anything nicer." Angie said.

"Except," Nick whispered to her as they went back downstairs. "I'll miss your cold toes at night."

"Shush," Angie giggled.

In the kitchen, Gideon had set a supper of sandwich rolls, cheesecake and a bottle of good wine.

"Would you like a cooked breakfast? We don't bother. We're getting very American in our habits. It's pancakes and honey and as much toast as we can eat."

Angie spoke for them both. "That'll suit us. That's what the Countess offered me in Glasgow. We can see to ourselves, you know. Don't put yourselves out for us."

"Gideon's still working and I've been taking an interest in the secretarial side and go in to the office a few hours each week. Gratis, of course. However, I'll be free to show you around if you want me to."

"Here's to your holiday." Gideon raised his glass. They joined him.

Sylvie caught hold of Angie's hand.

"Angie, I've just noticed - a ring on your wedding finger? Does it mean.... well it must, mustn't it? I gather congratulations are in order. Now when did this happen?"

"The night before last, or I think it was. All this travelling."

"I am delighted. You suit each other."

"Well done. We could do with another excuse to go back to London. The wedding will be there, I suppose? We were so disappointed when Seb cancelled his wedding."

"We haven't decided anything yet."

"This calls for champagne." Gideon went over to the cocktail bar. Nick got up to restrain him.

"Rather not tonight."

"Quite right," Sylvie interrupted. "There'll be plenty of time to celebrate. We're keeping you two out of your beds. Up you go. See you in the morning. If you need anything shout."

Angie and Nick went upstairs. They kissed goodnight outside Angie's door.

"You won't have to put up with my grunts tonight."

"Just as well. I need a good kip. Sleep tight."

Angie lay in bed, the sleep she craved not coming. She guessed she was overtired. That and the excitement, and the heat. She hadn't anticipated it would be so hot at night. She flung the light covers back, tip-toed to the window and stepped out on to the balcony. She looked down over trees and roof-tops to the sea. How it shimmered as lights played on the waves. Malibu - a place she'd thought of only in daydreams. Now it was a reality. She was there, sharing its shores with film stars. She pinched herself to prove she wasn't in a trance. Despite the humid air the sky was clear and starry. Dad was still watching. She could hear his voice, "We'll go to far away places just the two of us." Dear dad, I've let Nick share America. Forgive me. We'll have New Zealand to ourselves, as you said, just the two of us. Not long now.

Angie shut the window and went back to bed. She began to count down from a hundred. By seventy-four she was asleep.

A tap at the door woke her in the morning.

"Yes?"

"It's me."

"Just a sec." Angie pulled her dressing gown round her and answered the door. "Why didn't you come in?"

247

"Don't want to offend our hosts. They've been up for hours. Gideon's away to work but Sylvie's here. There's coffee in the kitchen and have you got something to see. This place is fantastic ... the lounge ... it's... I won't spoil it - get up and see for yourself. I've already had a bath and I've had a cuppa. It's nearly nine-thirty. There's a new world out there waiting to greet us."

"It'll have to wait. I haven't unpacked yet."

"That will keep."

"All right. I'll have a quick bath and come straight down. We can sort the rest of our stuff later."

Angie found her way to the kitchen by tracing the smell of freshly percolated coffee. It was a long galley type room with a circular breakfasting recess at the window overlooking the garden. Tiled in warm shades of pinks against mahogany units, she was pleased to find it pleasantly untidy. A place to feel comfortable in. In marked contrast to the rigid perfection of Sylvie's London home.

Angie crunched crisp buttered toast with her coffee whilst Nick piled honey thickly on to cookies.

"Let me know if you want anything else. I've to answer a few letters this morning so if you'll excuse me. Feel free to look around. The gardens are at their best now."

"You've got to come through here," Nick said when they'd finished breakfasting. "Look at this?"

Angie followed him into a massive lounge. It had been built out of the cliff face and one wall was of natural rock, cleaned and finished to a smooth marble like surface. A huge open fireplace was hung with copper fittings. Large rugs set off the rich parquet. The chairs were big and floppy and the floor scattered with giant cushions. There were none of the elaborate straight back chairs favoured at Beechwood. Instead, Sylvie had captured an easy elegance. Angie sat back in one of the chairs.

"I could live here quite happily. It's so relaxing." She gazed round the walls at several paintings; still life and English countryside beside works of modern art. Behind her a full length study of Lynn startled with its likeness. Angie examined it. The dark hair, the wide eyes, the vivacity. It was all there. Almost as if Lynn were alive and living in this room.

Sylvie came through and stood beside Angie. "Do you like it? We had it painted from a photograph."

"It's very, very beautiful."

"I like to think she's near us," Sylvie said and her eyes misted momentarily. "Now, have you seen the rest of the house?" She showed them round indoors and out. "It's not very big really by Malibu standards but we adore it. I don't bother with a maid. We have Pickering, he does the gardens too, and Eva, his wife, helps three days a week with the housework. "I do quite a lot myself, even some of the gardening. I've grown to like pottering about. We've drawn up plans for a swimming pool."

She's changed since Lynn died, Angie thought. That was apparent even in London, but more so here. She was less aware of her appearance, not as anxious to make an impression and yet just as chic. . Gideon too seemed less stressed.

"Have you made any plans for today?"

"We'll need to unpack properly at some time. What do you think, Nick? I'd like to go to the beach and generally laze about. We did enough travelling yesterday."

"I'll settle for that. Can we walk down to the shore?"

"Easily, there's a right of way down the cliff which is a lot quicker than walking through the avenues. I'll show you. Much of the beach belongs to the houses built on it, and we've a private stretch which we share with neighbours. You'll need a key to the gate. Wait till nearer lunch time and I'll come with you. We could have a bowl of chowder for lunch in Alice's."

The walk down the palm lined path led to the main road. Across it lay the beach. A row of houses, built only yards apart, stretched along the shore and from the rear were not particularly attractive. Nick expressed his disappointment and what they could see of the sands was not impressive.

"It looks so magnificent from your place up on the cliff, but down here it's so ordinary. I'd associated the name Malibu with an exotic setting. Even the sands are greyish."

"The houses do look a bit like shanties. Quite a few need a lick of paint." Angie agreed with Nick.

"You're right. Funny when you live in a place you don't notice its faults. A lot of the houses are owned by film stars - some very famous. Trouble is they only stay here for a week or two in the year. They get them spruced up for their visit and then neglect them till the next time. Seen from the beach side they look different. That's Alice's on the pier. We'd better have lunch first."

The much talked about Alice's, Angie thought, was little more than a scout hall. The pier itself was merely a wooden strip designed for tying up boats or casting a rod. Inside, Alice's had a planked floor and dull decor. It was busy and, despite its understatement, oozed atmosphere. There was a bar with high stools and a restaurant. They squeezed into a corner table.

"That's Michaels the Hollywood film director," Sylvie said, pointing to a porky man with a nail brush moustache. He shared his table with three young women.

"Are they starlets?" Angie asked.

"They're his daughters. He's got five altogether. The one nearest us is in films. The other two are students. Their sisters are just toddlers from his second marriage."

"Do you know many famous people?"

"Not really. Haven't lived here long enough. He's our next door neighbour."

The clam chowder when it came was served with French bread and was delicious. Coffee was rich. Angie had to admit Alice's had a certain something about it. A glamour of its own created mainly by its clients all of whom appeared to dress for a snack lunch as if it were a banquet. Angie had seldom seen so many fine gold necklaces, chunky bracelets and elegant dresses. She wished she had worn something other than her blue cotton.

Leaving the restaurant, they reached the access gate and walked across the sands. From the beach the houses were supported on stilts. They had wide balconies and large windows.

"Granted," Nick said, "they've a great view out to sea but I'm still disappointed. I'd rather stay where you are any day."

"That's good to know. The beach is better than you think. Shall we take a walk to the groyne over there and sit for a while?"

The shore was almost deserted. Beneath one of the beach houses they glimpsed a couple sun-bathing and another group were rowing out towards a yacht. By the groyne some people spread on the sands but they were few.

"It's not exactly crowded." Nick remarked.

"Remember the beach is private. The water here's good for swimming. Did you bring your bathing costumes?"

"We're wearing them under our clothes," Angie said. Saves changing."

"There's a row of huts beyond the groyne. Ours is number ten. We keep everything for the beach in it. "

Sylvie was right. The hut had sunshades and deckchairs, beach balls and towels.

"If you're still wet when it's time to come home you can change in here. I'll leave you the key. I'll need to be going back in half-an-hour to keep a hair appointment."

They carried a deck chair each to near the edge of the water.

"Don't worry about your things while you're in the sea. It's safe down here."

Angie and Nick stripped to their swimsuits and sat on a towel on the sands employing the chairs as clothes horses. Sylvie put up the sunshade.

"It's deceptive today. The breeze makes it feel cooler. You can burn easily in this. You'd better use the sun oil, Angie. You've a fair skin." She threw the oil towards Angie. Nick caught it and began to rub it on Angie's back and shoulders. When he'd finished Angie gave him the same treatment.

"I can see what you mean about the beach being better once you're on it. From this angle Malibu 's okay, but, apart from where you live, it's not as exotic as I'd expected."

"You've been reading too many glossy brochures," Sylvie smiled. "They never show the true picture." She stood up. "I'm off, now. You've got the keys. It's quite a climb up the cliff to the house. You can go the long way round, if you'd rather."

They said goodbye and watched Sylvie disappear through the gate.

"Well, what do you really think?" Nick asked cuddling close to Angie.

"Like you, I was a bit disappointed with the beach area at first, but it sort of grows on you. I found Alice's intriguing. And the sun's warm and the sea will no doubt be cool. Their house is special. Not just it's appearance. It feels good."

"Glad you came?"

"You bet. And you?"

"Worth blowing my bank balance on, I'd say, though the flight really has made a big dent in it despite Gideon's discounted fares. Pity Sylvie's house has four bedrooms."

"I expect you'll get round that."

CHAPTER 22

Sylvie told Angie and Nick that she would have to work the next day.

"I'll be away by 8.15am and back mid-afternoon. I'm sure you'll be able to amuse yourselves. Eva will be in to clean up around ten."

In the morning, Angie heard Sylvie go out and watched from the balcony as she drove away. Nick called across to her.

"I'll be with you in a minute."

She slid back into bed.

"You were right," Nick said as he tucked in beside her. "I got round it."

They were up, bathed and breakfasted by the time Eva Pickering walked into the kitchen, bustling and friendly.

"Sure great to meet someone from England. I'm real proud to know you. Stan was over there serving, stationed at Brighton. Has he told me some stories about that place. Do you know it?"

A lengthy conversation ensued on the merits of Angie's previous home town and on how small a world it was. By the time Angie and Nick left the house it was twelve-thirty. They took the long route to the main road and boarded a bus to Santa Monica.

Hand in hand, they sauntered along the promenade which stretched for miles. Tall palms rustled their fronds as the pair walked on the grass beneath them.

"The sea's a deeper blue here than in Malibu and the sands are more golden." Nick observed.

"I expect it's the way the sun's shining," Angie said. "Can't be that much different. It's just down the coast."

"There're more people about. Let's see what the local hotels have to offer. There's enough of them."

Big white painted hotels vied for custom. They chose one which had tables and parasols in its courtyard and music playing quietly in the background and sat down to salad and bottled drinks.

"I've never felt so lazy in all my life," Nick admitted.

They left the clean white of Santa Monica for the grey of Down Town Los Angeles. The contrast was remarkable. Cracked pavements, and grime covered buildings drew a picture of a place that looked unkempt and smelt unwashed.

"Odd to think the Beverly Hills mansions belong to the same city," Angie remarked. Everyone seemed to be in a hurry and few were smiling.

"Reckon its a tough place," Nick said. "In more ways than one."

They turned into a side street where children were playing. Some were shoeless. A small coloured boy broke away from his friends and came up to them. His face was all mouth as he grinned.

"Can you spare us a dime, sir?"

Nick searched his pocket for a coin and the other children bounded up to them. Nick handed out all his change and the youngsters darted off and huddled together to count their good luck.

"Bang goes the bus fare," he said as they made their way back to the main street.

"Softie," Angie teased.

Opulent hotels, brass plates gleaming, mingled with the neglected buildings. Was it so very different to London Angie pondered? And decided it was. Los Angeles had even bigger contrasts and faced even bigger problems. That was evident. They crossed the wide boulevard and could read the huge Hollywood sign set high in the hills. If this were a city of dreams how many, Angie wondered, were shattered? How many fulfilled?

They came to a small park beside the Sheraton Hotel and sat on a bench. Within minutes an old man came up to them begging. Nick ignored him and the tramp went on his way muttering under his breath, "Don't you believe in God, man." Seconds later a girl Angie judged to be in her early twenties ran barefoot towards them crying. "I've a child to feed and no money left." She buried her head in her hands and wept bitterly. It was Angie's turn to empty the change from her purse into the girl's cupped hands.

"Who's the softie now?" Nick asked.

"She was genuine. You couldn't turn your back on her."

"A good actress more like. Probably one of Hollywood's rejects."

"Cynic."

Nick was right to be cynical. When they left the park, the same girl was standing talking to two men. She had sandals on her feet and was laughing.

They caught a bus back to Malibu. Not the 'rapid' service they had used earlier but the town double decker. It was packed with men returning from work and Angie and Nick were forced to stand. A few stops on a seat became vacant beside a young man. His lank, greasy hair fell in strands across his forehead. His cheeks hollowed and he appeared painfully thin under a worn jacket. Angie perched on the edge of the seat. The young man turned to her and spoke in a voice that was surprisingly soft.

"Heard you talking to your friend. Like your accent. English isn't it?"

"Yes." Angie turned her head towards Nick who was still standing. He grinned, sensing she was uncomfortable.

The man spoke again, "My grandparents came from Scotland and Ireland. I hope to visit one day, when my luck's rising high."

Angie noticed his eyes. Green and soft as a new lawn. His manner, too, was attractive. How often first impressions could be wrong. Working lad he might be, but he was no hobo. The

255

conversation continued until he reached his stop and got off the bus. Observing fellow passengers was as interesting as the scenery outside. Opposite Angie across the aisle another man was sucking or blowing a small object. Nick managed to work his way down the bus to the seat beside Angie. She nudged him.

"What's that fellow doing?"

Nick studied the man for a while, "My guess is he's a musician and that thing's something to do with training his lips to pout the right way."

"Sounds a good enough guess. Better than anything I could come up with. It looks a bit odd doing it on a bus."

"Haven't you noticed, there're lots of unusual folk in this city."

As if to emphasise Nick's point the young girl who got on at the next stop sprawled herself on the step of the bus just inside the door. She placed her head on the seat and appeared to fall asleep.

"Drugs I expect," Nick said. Other passengers ignored her as if her behaviour was of no consequence. As they neared Malibu, a huge man took the seat facing the girl. He stretched himself out until his sandals were within an inch of the girl's knees. He was wearing a filthy T shirt, and dirt thickened the skin of his massive arms and hands. A tattoo of a skull and crossbones ran the length of one arm and tucked in to the waist of his trousers was a bottle of spirits.

Angie thought he looked grotesque, murderous even. She was glad Nick was with her. She wouldn't like to have coped with him by herself. She remembered the man with the lank hair and how wrong her impressions had been. This time she knew she was right. This man was a bum.

At the far end of the bus a woman whose skin was wrinkled like a dried prune, and whose age would be difficult to determine, kept playing with her hair. It was dyed a ridiculously unnatural yellow and was caught on the top of her head by some sort of red band. From this it fountained down to her shoulders and tucked in behind her right ear was a huge red carnation.

She was tiny and very thin and wore brilliant pink trousers that looked like pyjama bottoms. Despite the heat the woman had on a heavy black polo necked sweater. Another pink jumper was wrapped round her body and tied under her bust by the sleeves. Her face was grossly made up with layers of foundation, rouged cheeks, thick black pencilled eyebrows and heavily mascara-ed lashes, and scarlet lips which mooned well over their natural line. At her feet a scruffy hold-all was stuffed with old newspapers. Angie stared incredulously.

Nick found it impossible to keep a straight face.

"A fallen star if there ever was one," he laughed. "No-one can say Los Angeles doesn't put on a good show."

But this was no show they realised as a glint of metal among the newspapers convinced them the woman carried a gun. By the time they left the bus it was empty except for the girl still sprawled on the step. They edged passed her and jumped off at the pier. The air was cool and it was beginning to get dark.

"I've seen things today I'll never forget," Angie said. She snuggled close to Nick as they walked to Sylvie's house. "It makes me realise how lucky I am, especially having you here with me. Doubt if I could have faced today without you."

"Glad I'm needed. Are you sure about going to New Zealand on your own?"

"Yep."

"What if you meet guys like the bruiser on the bus? The one with the bottle."

"Don't."

"Well, what would you do?"

"Run a mile."

"What good would that do. He'd just stretch out one of his giant arms and you'd be mincemeat."

"Stop it, Nick. You're trying to scare me."

"Sorry. But you'll have to be careful. It's not good for a young girl to be alone in a strange country."

"I'll be fine. New Zealand's nothing like Los Angeles."

"What about the Maoris? They can do a great war dance."

"I'm sure they're nice people. Anyway, I won't go near any. Now shut-up. You're jealous."

They reached the front door. Lights shone a welcome and the smell of baked gammon and onions drew them hungrily into the kitchen.

Sylvie made plans for the next day.

"Say no if you want to, but I thought a trip to the Film Studios might capture your interest. I had a word with Mr Michaels and he's willing to arrange a personal tour for you."

"Sounds fantastic to me. How about you Nick?"

"Sure."

"You're becoming Americanised already."

"The accent is catching. Can't help myself. What do you want me to say - I shall be delighted?"

"That's more like it. What time were you thinking of, Sylvie?"

"I'll find out what suits and let you know."

Angie watched Sylvie as she moved down the road towards the Michaels' house.

"I do envy her poise. She must be fifty something yet she walks like a young woman. Straight back, neat ankles and no midriff bulges. Hope I can emulate her."

"Stay the way you are and you'll be okay."

"It's a tall order."

"Women they say grow like their mothers but you'd have to shrink. You've more of your dad in you."

"And you aren't like either of your parents as I remember them."

"Take after my Auntie Mollie." Nick laughed.

Sylvie came back into the lounge, "Two o'clock at the main entrance. They're filming a "B" movie this afternoon - a drama - 'Height of Revenge', or something similar."

Nick and Angie wiled the morning away on the beach. The sun still shone. Californian weather was predictably good.

Angie wondered what London was having. A mixture no doubt. How distant it seemed. She chose some postcards from the only shop on the main street and wrote them ... Dolinda and Morton, Dillard Thrift, Edwina, Henriette and the Countess.

Pickering took them to the studios. Angie had visualised something palatial but it was like a building site with large huts on it. As they drove inside the gates to meet Mr Michaels, they passed through streets with mock houses and shops and inns. Every detail a carbon copy of the real thing. They were shown into a corrugated-roofed building. Mr Michaels was talking to a group of people. He broke off as they came in.

"Ah. You're here, Sylvie. Good to see you. Meet the crew. We're about to shoot a house fire. Don't see why you can't be part of the crowd watching the rescue. Susie - take them along to make up. Easiest way to learn about things is to be involved."

The scene unfurled. It was intended to be the dramatic rescue of a young woman from a house fire but the momentum was lost in a series of takes and retakes. In the leading role was a hitherto unknown actress called Elisa Jacobs. Playing the fireman who saved her from a roasting was Daniel Dawson, already a box office favourite. Angie considered the plot, though a bit trite, might have been exciting had it been allowed to flow.

Angie took Nick's arm as she felt her legs wobbling with nerves. He appeared to remain cool and Sylvie looked bemused. They obeyed the director and stayed at the rear of the crowd, trying to see through the dozen or so heads in front of them.

"So much for glamorous starring roles," Nick commented as they rushed on to the street for the umpteenth time.

Angie found it difficult to see how there would be any continuity in the film.. By the end of the session, they had done nothing but run on to a street, stare up at a building that appeared to be blazing, and make way for the emergency services. Nick was interested in the technical details.

"Amazing isn't it? The fire looks so realistic, yet it's all done by playing gas jets against the walls of the house to give the impression the building's alight. It doesn't really burn anything at all."

"They could hardly have real flames. Someone might get hurt, you chump." Angie said.

"Well who was it that let out a yell when the place flared up the first time?"

"All I'm interested in is if it will be right when they process the film or will these people have to go through it all again tomorrow," Sylvie said. "Let's get cleaned up. "

There was time afterwards for a quick look round the rest of the studios before they rejoined Mr Michaels. He directed his gaze at Angie.

"So how did you like that, young lady? A star for the afternoon, eh?"

"Well, not exactly a star. To tell you the truth I wouldn't want to be one either. Even doing what we did was tiring."

"You're right. It takes a lot of stamina to be in films. Sylvie you must bring these young people round for drinks at my place before they leave you."

"That," Sylvie replied, "would be delightful."

"He doesn't mean it you know," Sylvie explained as they were driven back to Malibu. "He's invited Gideon and I over a dozen times or more but never follows it up. It's his way of winding up a conversation."

"Pity," Angie said. "I'd like to have seen inside a film director's home."

For once, Sylvie was wrong the invitation to pop in for a drink after dinner came on Angie's penultimate night in Malibu. Frederick Michaels greeted them at the door and showed them into a massive room amok with chairs. From one corner open stairs spiralled to an upper floor.

"Bet you thought I'd forget all about you," he said as he kissed Sylvie on the cheeks. "Been meaning to have you and Gideon, isn't it, over since you moved in. You know what it's like. Now make yourselves comfortable. Melissa's not down yet. We'd have had you round for dinner but she was at one of her charity do's."

Angie sat beside Nick on a two seater couch. There were several of them dotted at different angles in the room. Sylvie and Gideon chose individual chairs on either side of them. Frederick Michaels began to drag a large chair towards them.

"Now if I pull up my favourite armchair we'll be cosy. Let the guests choose and then you adapt I say. In a room this size you want to sit close. And here's the little lady herself."

Melissa Michaels swept down the stairway, gushing before she'd reached the last step.

"This is wonderful. What a pretty girl. And all the way from London. And a handsome fellow, too," she took Angie's hand in hers. "It's as well Freddie's daughters aren't at home or you'd be in danger of losing him." She sat on a chaise longue close to Sylvie. Her husband rose and put an arm across her shoulders affectionately.

"Now what can I get you all? Gideon you give me a hand with the drinks."

The cocktail bar, glittered against a far wall. It's a bit like being in the lounge of a pub, Angie thought, but more luxurious. She wished she could see the rest of the house. The lounge was dramatic in its decor with splashes of colour emanating from every corner like a thrown rainbow. Chandeliers hung from a cloud grey ceiling like rain drops caught in a burst of sunshine. In most homes it would look calamitous. Here, except, perhaps, for the enormous grandfather clock that pendulumed on the wall opposite the bar, it was right.

Melissa saw Angie's eyes settle on the clock.

"Guess you're wondering what that's doing in a room like this? We use this for parties and Hollywood's are notorious for going on half the night. Freddie needs his sleep so we fix it to chime loudly at twelve-thirty. It booms out the message and every one jumps. It makes it much easier to wind things up."

Angie noticed Melissa's fingernails as she waved her hands about. They resembled Witch's talons dipped in blood. But the Michaels were warm people, with a natural ability to make guests feel welcome. Talkative, but with a listener's ear, too.

The evening was a riot of fun. They left before the clock chimed and returned to the house next door with the unsteady gait that follows too many gin and limes, whiskies on the rocks. Bed was the only place to go. Tomorrow Angie would have to pack for New Zealand. The fulfilment of a dream. I'll need you with me, Dad. And she felt herself shudder. The prospect was both exciting and frightening.

CHAPTER 23

Angie woke with a slight headache and a desire to do nothing but laze once she had packed. Nick was happy to spend the day with her on the beach.

Much as Angie had wanted, it had been impossible for her to find a suitable ship to take her to Auckland. On Gideon's advice, she'd settled on a flight leaving shortly before midnight and landing in Auckland at eight o' clock in the morning. But not the Sunday morning as it would be in Los Angeles - the Monday - she would lose a whole day.

"You'll be lazing around here on a day that won't exist for me," Angie said to Nick. "I can't quite understand it. It's a queer thing time. "

"It's because you'll be crossing the International Date Line. You'll make up for it when you return. You'll have two Sundays then or Tuesdays or what ever depending on when you come back."

"Do you think they'll tell us when we cross the line?"

"I imagine you'll be fast asleep."

"Mm.. maybe. I've a feeling I might not sleep much."

Nick noticed a look of apprehension on Angie's face.

"What's up? Are you getting cold feet?"

"Not exactly."

"Sure? You can still change your mind."

"That's the last thing I'd do. It's just that I've waited for this so long. Ever since that day when Dad said we'd go after Mum died. I can't believe it's actually happening. That later tonight, I'm going to step on a plane and head for New Zealand. Going to see all the things Dad told me about. See the volcanoes and the thermal valleys, geysers spurting miles into the air and the mud pools gurgling at my feet. The glow worm caves, black as a dark night and lit as if by a million stars. Perhaps like the sky here in Los Angeles as we landed. And my dad will be with me. I know it. We'll do this journey together."

"He won't really be there, Angie. In your mind, yes, but physically there to protect you, that's not possible."

Nick saw Angie tremble and the tears began to flow.

He kissed them away.

"It's not too late, Angie. I could come with you. There's room on the flight."

"But New Zealand belongs to Dad, remember."

"He wouldn't mind Angie. I knew him. He'd want me to be there. I'm sure of it. You see, I'm part of you now. In a while we'll be married. As one, as they say. I'm begging you let me come."

"Oh Nick, I'm so confused. I want you to be with me but ... I believe it's only once I've seen these places that Dad can rest in peace and I can let him go. I'll say goodbye to him in New Zealand and I have to do that by myself."

"I'll let you Angie. You can go off on your own if that's what you want. I'll be around if I'm needed. Once you've let your Dad go, you'll have me to turn to."

"I need you now, Nick. Inside I'm scared. I didn't think I would be. I could manage the journey no bother. It's giving him up that's the trouble. Accepting that he'll never come back to me. Accepting that he's dead."

"It's the past, Angie. You have to move on and I'm the future. I won't let you down."

At lunch time Sylvie and Gideon agreed with Nick.

"You shouldn't be travelling alone, Angie, and in your heart I think you know that. I've a confession to make. Nick confided in me his wish to go with you and I took the liberty of booking him on your flight just in case he succeeding in convincing you to let him. I want to pay your fares as a thank you for making Lynn happy."

"But…" Nick began to protest.

"It's all settled. Count it as an engagement gift from us."

"I f you've already gone to that much trouble, I suppose it does make sense," Angie conceded. "Thank you so much."

Angie felt light hearted as if she'd shed a load of worries. Nick was right. She needed someone to support her. Dad was the spirit that had driven her to travel but Nick's was the arm she would lean on now. All that independence she'd strived for meant nothing. What was it Nick had said? "I am the future."

"I must say, I'm relieved," Sylvie said as she and Gideon wished them luck at the airport. "I thought you were out of your mind planning to go alone, but I guessed you had your reasons. I didn't want to interfere though Gideon thought otherwise."

"I had, but I was wrong."

"We'll see you when you return, if only for a day."

"Thank-you for a wonderful holiday. I'll remember Malibu, Santa Monica, Los Angeles for the rest of my life. The picture of Lynn in your lounge - sometimes she seemed so close, I could hear her speak."

"That's how I feel. But she's gone Angie, just like your Dad and Mum. One day ...well who knows? Enough of this. You two are going to have the time of your lives over in New Zealand and I shall be very cross if you don't keep a diary of everything you see and do."

"That's a great idea."

* * *

Nick and Angie waved from the aeroplane window. They couldn't see Sylvie and Gideon but they knew they'd be watching the flight take-off. It was nearing midnight. In a very short time it would be Monday. Sunday wouldn't exist. Angie looked up at the night sky. Dad, I've made it. New Zealand is one golden dawn away. You've led me this far. Tomorrow will be lost in time. If I say goodbye now at midnight, perhaps I can trap you in that day - a very special day. Thank you for showing me the way. Mum, Lynn, Dad, I'll never forget any of you, but, as Nick says, it's time to move on.

Angie felt Nick's arm slide round her shoulder. The past was forgotten. The future shone brightly ahead lit by volcanoes, glow-worms and stars. She'd swung on one.

****

About the Author

An established poet and former local reporter, Pamela Duncan likes to dabble in most genres of creative writing. She spent seven years studying her chosen craft at classes run by Glasgow University.

Two collections of her poetry, SOUL SEARCH and OCTOBERS SUN were published in 2002 and 2011 respectively and individual poems appear in a number of anthologies. She has also published articles and short stories and written plays and children's stories

And through affiliation with the Scottish Association of Writers, has won many awards, including trophies and the Association's Scholarship.

'On The Swing of One Star' is Pamela's first published novel but, in keeping with her claim of being a Jack of All Trades, she has two crime \novels and two children's novels in the pipeline,

Born in Sussex, Pamela came to Scotland in her teens, where she settled in the Glasgow suburb of Giffock. She served as Writing Representative for East Renfrewshire from its conception in 1993 until its disbandment in 2011. She is a founder member and past president of Eastwood Writers, Giffnock and has been associated with the running of the Words & Music, the popular South Glasgow Performance Club for writers and musicians.

Her other interests include golf, crosswords and her ever expanding family.

About Author Way Limited

Author Way provides a broad range of good quality, previously unpublished works and makes them available to the public on multiple formats.

We have a fast growing number of authors who have completed or are in the process of completing their books and preparing them for publication and these will shortly be available.

Please keep checking our website to hear about the latest developments.

Author Way Limited

www.authorway.net

Made in the USA
Charleston, SC
02 December 2013